COULD ANY MAGIC SAVE THEM NOW?

Only her dagger remained, pooled in the sludge of the demon. Sharlin jumped for it, rolled on the ground, and threw it down the gullet of the Black Dragon as its forked tongue shot out and its fangs glistened.

Nightwing screamed. . . . Pain, infinite pain, shrilled forth, and the evil dragonlord Valorek went to his knees, covering his ears in agony. The dragon rose, curling its talons around Valorek, lifting him as the beast launched itself, keening in agony.

Dar and Sharlin had won this round. But there would be others, they knew. Many, many others. Now all the powers of evil would be massed in hatred against them. . . .

⊘ SIGNET (0451)

IN THE REALM OF MAGIC . . .

☐ **THE UNICORN DANCER by R. A. V. Salsitz.** When the guardian city Sinobel falls beneath a treacherous conqueror's blade, the Lady Alorie, heiress to the High Counsellorship and the last hope of all the kingdoms, sets forth on the unicorn's trail to claim her destiny. (143930—$2.95)

☐ **WHERE DRAGONS LIE by R. A. V. Salsitz.** Slumbering in the dragon's graveyard is a power that can rule the world . . . but now primeval powers are stirring from their ageless sleep, preparing for the final confrontation between the forces of Good and the infinite evil embodied in the Black Dragon, Nightwing. (140559—$2.95)

☐ **FLIGHT TO THE SAVAGE EMPIRE by Jean Lorrah and Winston A. Howlett.** Even her strongest Reading couldn't tell Magister Astra why she was being punished and made to tend the wounded after the bloody gladiator games. Instead she must brave a web of deceit, greed, and vengeance to find the ancient magic that can free her people from eternal slavery. . . . (141695—$2.95)

☐ **SORCERERS OF THE FROZEN ISLES by Jean Lorrah.** Medura—a realm of ice and gloom. Few men journey there, fewer yet leave her shores alive. Now the blind Reader Torio impulsively demands to join Zanos on his journey home, a journey that will bring him to the heart of that forsaken land—and face to face with the evil powers there! (142683—$2.95)

Prices slightly higher in Canada

Buy them at your local bookstore or use this convenient coupon for ordering.

NEW AMERICAN LIBRARY.
P.O. Box 999, Bergenfield. New Jersey 07621

Please send me the books I have checked above. I am enclosing $_____ (please add $1.00 to this order to cover postage and handling). Send check or money order—no cash or C.O.D.'s. Prices and numbers are subject to change without notice.

Name_____

Address_____

City_____Zip Code_____
Allow 4-6 weeks for delivery.
This offer is subject to withdrawal without notice.

WHERE DRAGONS LIE

R. A. V. Salsitz

A SIGNET BOOK

NEW AMERICAN LIBRARY

NAL BOOKS ARE AVAILABLE AT QUANTITY DISCOUNTS WHEN USED TO
PROMOTE PRODUCTS OR SERVICES. FOR INFORMATION PLEASE WRITE TO
PREMIUM MARKETING DIVISION, NEW AMERICAN LIBRARY, 1633 BROADWAY,
NEW YORK, NEW YORK 10019.

 SIGNET TRADEMARK REG. U.S. PAT. OFF. AND FOREIGN COUNTRIES
REGISTERED TRADEMARK—MARCA REGISTRADA
HECHO EN CHICAGO, U.S.A.

SIGNET, SIGNET CLASSIC, MENTOR, PLUME, MERIDIAN AND NAL BOOKS
are published by New American Library,
1633 Broadway, New York, New York 10019

First Printing, December, 1985

3 4 5 6 7 8 9

PRINTED IN THE UNITED STATES OF AMERICA

With thanks
to my editor, Sheila Gilbert,
for belief and inspiration,
and to my mothers, Barbara and Ruth;
all three are incredible women.

Prologue

The young griffins stirred restlessly in the ancient stone aerie, their wings beating against one another, their velveted paws clashing out, then they subsided to quiet once more, their leather hoods keeping them blind in the night.

The oldest did not return to sleep, for it was his prescience that raced through their dreams. He kept his great wings folded about him, leonine haunches drawn tensely under, and waited in the musty straw of his own nest for the one who was coming. He was old enough to remember what it was to nest free in the mountains, before the masters had captured him, and settled him in this stony enclosure that smelled dank and musty, of fewmets and raw meat, and the close forms of other griffins. He was old enough to remember what it was to ride the wind alone, without harness and rider—and old enough that he preferred to remain huddled and still, the warmth of his feathers blanketing bones that felt the snap of the cold night air.

The aerie door creaked open. Gabriel roused then, stretching his haunches and craning his neck, turning blindly toward the scent of girl and the warm meat that she must carry in her hands. The other griffins remained asleep, his fiery thoughts long since cooled in their veins. They had been fed well before being hooded and tethered this evening, while he had only been allowed to blood his kill . . . a sure sign that he would be flying tonight, with a rider.

The leather harness settled about his body comfortably, and he bent to rub his curved beak affectionately upon the saddler's arm as she removed the hood to feed him the bloody strips of softfoot. His keen eyes quickly appraised her riding leathers to confirm what he already knew.

When he had eaten, he drew level with her face, before asking, "We fly?"

"Yes, Gabe," she answered, and stroked his neck feathers gently in the way that mistresses have. Her tone was worried and strained as she added, "Asralyn's outer walls fell to Rodeka just before sunset. The borders have been cracked open like an eggshell. Father says that even with our low strength, it will be months before Rodeka can lay siege to us here, but I can't wait. I know we may have traitors in the house, and there's no time to waste. Gabe, I want you to take me to Turiana."

The griffin ducked, wiping his beak clean along his heavy paws. He weighed the consequences of what his mistress was asking him to do against the ire of her elders, for just as he was oldest of the aerie griffins and most venerable, she was youngest of the masters, and greatly prized by them. The love he felt for his chicks was no greater than the love he felt for this rider. He sorrowed now that he had told her of the great golden dragon Turiana and of where her bones might lie, and yet his memory had left him no choice, for this flight was one that they must take, for he remembered it.

She led him from the aerie into the night, locking the structure behind her, shivering as the wind bit into her riding leathers and cloak and threatened to rip her knotted hair loose. The griffin paced solemnly beside her. They paused a moment on the plateau, facing into the dark of the valley below, her cloak rising about her as though she, not Gabriel, were the winged being.

A shadow reared from the darkness, and the moon flashed on drawn weapon. The girl screamed and the griffin lunged forward, snapping at the apparition. She drew her own curved dagger as her war mount clawed, and when the man went down, rolling and gasping, she fell, knees bent, onto his chest, and cut his throat.

Hands shaking, Sharlin cleaned her dagger and returned it to her belt, then pushed herself away from the limp form. The griffin bated the air in his fury. She led him away, told him soothing things, praised him, and smoothed his ruffled feathers, and added, "That's one less for Rodeka behind these walls!" as she turned the griffin into the wind.

She checked her equipment, then bowed her head and murmured, "Forgiveness on the House of Dhamon, and watch over my father and mother, and help me do what I have to." Sharlin lifted her chin. Once more she palmed the leather pouch tied securely to her belt. "Are you sure this is what I need to do it?" she asked yet again.

The griffin made a dry sound in his feathered throat. "You ask me of legend, little rider. I am old, but I am not old enough to know legend. Yet I remember the herbs and spices I told you, and of what must be done."

"I know—but to raise a dragon from the dead—"

"May be legend also." The griffin shook his head, rattling the bridle. "Mount quickly. We must be off."

She did as bid, securing her toes in the saddle leathers and grasping the reins tightly, welcoming the familiar creak as she did so. Gabe stretched his wings before launching into a run across the plateau, the wind snapping at both of them, threatening them, as the griffin plunged off the plateau's edge and they dropped into the night.

She had not recovered her stomach before the beast spread his wings and righted himself on the cold air currents. The reins were useless on this ride, for she had no idea of where to guide the beast; he flew after instincts of his own, taking her on a mission that was less than hopeless—but to withstand a sorceress like Rodeka, only a spell as powerful as dragonmagic would serve.

They flew for more than half the night, till the small

moon, Little Sister, hung low and pale on the horizon.
Sharlin became alert in the saddle when the black countryside below suddenly appeared dotted with orange
flame, and the stench and smoke reached her lungs high
though she was in the sky. They were approaching Asralyn.

The griffin shuddered. "I remember!" he cried frantically, desperately pulling for height. The lines of his
sinews bulged under fur and feather and his breath
guttered deep in his chest as he fought to veer away from
the site of the victory of the sorceress Rodeka.

Sharlin wrapped her gloved hands tightly into the
leathers and clung to her riding harness. The panic of her
mount seared her own thoughts, and the cords of her neck
strained as she fought to breathe and gain control. Clouds
boiled about them, heavy with mist and raindrops, splat-
tering upon her cheeks and blinding her sight. Lightning
danced close by, and thunder buffeted them.

"Gabe!" she screamed, but her voice tore from her
throat, lost to his hearing, as lightning flashed again, and
she could taste its threat.

Rodeka! Rodeka and her troops down below, camped
after their latest conquest . . . Rodeka of dark sorceries
. . . could she have sensed them?

Sharlin hauled on the reins, one elbow popping, fighting
to bring Gabe out of his death spiral. She pommeled his
flanks with her boot heels, crying, "Turn! Turn now!" as
black thoughts lashed through her mind and she grew sick
and dizzy. Rodeka was searching for her, finding her,
tearing at her. . . .

Blue-white light flashed about them, stunning her sight,
blinding her, sizzling her thoughts from her mind. She
screamed and clutched the beast about his neck, holding
on for dear life. The dark skies boomed and deafened her,
and then there was a silence broken only by the whistle of
their falling bodies.

Like a stone falling from the night sky, the furred and
feathered beast dropped from the heavens, Sharlin hanging on tightly. The clouds whistled past and the ground

roared up, illuminated only by starlight, a pond of darkness, hurtling at them. Sharlin squeezed her eyes shut and
chanted a meaningless litany. At the last possible second,
as storm clouds boiled dark about them, the griffin spread
his wings and halted their descent.

Even so, he faltered and skittered upon the wind, and
as he dropped closer to the earth of Rangard, his crimson
blood splattered a pathway below him. The girl sat up,
uncurling her hunched body, and dug her hair from her
rain-and-tear-soaked eyes. She muttered, "I can't see it—I
can't see land anywhere."

"It's all right," the griffin panted. "I can, and we're safe
now."

The girl strained forward in the harness, but her eyes
weren't the sharp eagle eyes of the beast she rode. "All
right, Gabe. I'll trust you on this one."

"You will have to," the griffin returned dryly. He
sculled and, coughing, plummeted toward the ground
once more.

His rider jumped off and ran alongside as he plowed
into the ground, tearing up roots and mosses and prickles
before he came to a halt.

The griffin sighed deeply, shook himself, and folded
wings of gold and turquoise. Sharlin stood beside him, one
arm loosely about his neck. They looked out over the
country below, having landed on a high plain. The storm
had gone as quickly as it had come, and stars blinked at
them almost as though surprised, but not as surprised as
she was, for she knew that this was not the ravaged
borderlands they had been flying over.

"Where are we?"

The griffin rubbed his sharp beak along her arm. "I
don't know," the beast said. He buckled suddenly onto
lion haunches.

She turned then, and saw that the underside of her arm
was damp, a stain darker than night. "Gabe!"

"It's all right," the griffin told her. "I brought you as far
as I could." The beast coughed.

She swept her wind-lashed hair from her face, as the

griffin panted. "You will go on alone. You will see . . . a sign. You'll have to wait until then, princess. I can't . . . I won't be going with you."

"I can't do it without you!"

"Of course you can, and you will. Trust me."

The girl gently rubbed his crest, trying to avoid the spreading patch of blood, and listened to his whistling words. She knew the griffin wasn't lying to her, but was trying to impart the last of his wisdom, his intuition, to her, so that their mission might yet succeed. "I remember," the beast had cried just before Rodeka hit them.

Sharlin looked out over the land, a strange country she didn't know. None of her daytime flights with Gabe had taken her this far. The storm and the lightning bolt summoned by the dark queen had done more than throw the two of them from the sky—it appeared to have thrown them right across the continent. She tried not to think of what it would mean to her to be abandoned this far from home. The griffin leaned heavily against her now, breast wine-stained and breathing labored. He did not speak any more, and she knew that it was because he could not make the effort. She continued to scratch his crest.

"Your nest will be proud of you, Gabe," she said. "I promise you that."

After that, there was a long silence until at last the beast whispered, "Princess . . . could you spare a blossom or two of lyrith?"

The rarest and most important of the herbs in her pouch, a sunflower of the high desert that bloomed only during the briefest of spring rains, a sprig of lyrith was almost the ransom of a king, but she knew what the griffin wanted. The girl twisted to make sure the pouch was still tied to her belt, then said, "Of course I can. Your fire will light up the heaven, and the sweet smoke of the lyrith will carry you higher and farther than any wings." She tried to swallow down the lump in her throat.

With a harsh sound, the griffin lunged forward in her arms, and his head lolled lifelessly to one side. The girl held him for a long time, but she did not hear him breathe again. Tugging at the form, she removed the leather flying harness and tossed it aside, shuddering, for the body turned cold even as she touched it.

She tucked the eagle head under one great wing, the way Gabe had liked to sleep. She folded the feline haunches under his body and wrapped the tufted tail about his form, before she backed away. Gabe looked almost as though resting. When she returned to the body, she carried armfuls of a twisted, dry shrub, one she wasn't familiar with. Its wood was slightly oily, for all that it was tinder-dry. She sprinkled on four dried buds of the lyrith, one for each point of the funeral pyre.

Her hands shook so hard that she could barely use the flint and steel, but at last the wood caught. Orange-and-blue flame roared skyward. She sat down cross-legged, her eyes dry, and watched her warmount burn on a pyre fit for a god. In the morning, her vigil would end and she would go.

Chapter 1

A chill wind rattled through the swamp, tangling bracken and tugging at hanging branches. Moss trailed across the boggy grounds, and the chestnut stallion threw up his head in alarm and, planting his hooves firmly, whuffled that he was not going to budge another step.

His rider secured a torch in the saddle leathers before leaning forward with a free hand to soothe his mount, stroking the damp neck and feeling the network of spidery veins under the chestnut's hide. His hesitation had halted the beast, and he didn't blame the horse for its uneasiness —a swamp in daylight was trouble enough, and though he carried a torch, the smoldering orange glow wasn't enough to keep them on firm ground.

The wind whipped back the stray locks of light-brown hair not covered by his half-helm, revealing a smooth and high forehead, and clear if tired brown eyes that looked out upon the dismal swamps, weighing where land and water met. His wrists crossed lightly over the saddle's pommel, revealing arms that had already grown beyond the length of his shirt, and when he sighed and wiped his forehead with the back of his wrist, a fine mist of nervous perspiration damped the cuff, revealing a desperation that no chill could cool. The horse shifted, his lean flanks heaving, and the rider moved to stroke him again. They had ridden far and fast. Aarondar had ridden horses to ground before. It was not a memory he savored or wanted to repeat, but he shuddered as though he could feel

Valorek's nails caressing the back of his neck once again, and knew he would do it, if he had to.

Witch met by moonlight, he thought. Neither the witch nor the moons were being very helpful to him, but he had little choice in the matter.

Red clay mud caked the rider up to his hips, an uncomfortable reminder that he'd twice had to lead his horse around trouble spots. He shrugged, his leather breastplate creaking over the play of muscles, and looked to the clouded sky, where the Shield played cat and mouse with him, that great silvery dish of a moon that was supposed to have shone on his pathway tonight, seconded by a much smaller moon called by common folk the Little Warrior. The Shield was left by the gods to light up the darkness of the night, and to protect the Little Warrior, who often hid behind it. Dar rubbed his cheek, trying to ease his tension.

The chestnut twitched, then lifted a hoof impatiently. His rider clucked to him, saying, "Thought you weren't going to move, Brand," in a soft, tired voice. The wind biting at both of them, the twosome edged once more into the swamplands.

Scavenged clothing did little to protect him from the cold, and the armor was worn and older than he was, and from places farther away than he had ever traveled. The half-helm had come from distant Thrassia, with the eldritch etchings of its craftsmen still carved deep into the metal, where tarnish never seemed to touch it. The scaled boots of indestructible leather were shaped from falroth hide by mountain dwarves, calf-high in the back, with a high shield in the front that protected him all the way to the top of his knees. Those had been taken off a corpse and fit, remarkably, as though they had been sculpted for him. Dar had had no qualms in taking the boots. The dead man certainly wasn't going to need them where he was going.

The breastplate had been his father's, and had hung in the milking barn until Dar took it down, oiled it, and rearranged the straps to fit his own somewhat leaner and taller form. Sword and lance were gambled for from traders, after staking his own short sword for a buy-in. Dar liked the sword. His hand fit the worn leather wrappings well, and though the metal was dark and nicked, the edge gleamed like a silver ray, sharp and telling. The lance had proved rather useless. It had good metal in it, and the guard was decorated with gems, though small ones. He was thinking of buying a jenny, a pack mule, with it, if he could get a good enough trade in the next town. Here in the borderlands, weapons brought a good price, and he had no doubt the innkeeper who'd steered him to the witch could steer him to a fence eager to buy.

He was a desperate man, driven to the Swamps of Kalmar to solve a problem that had eluded his sword, knowing that Valorek was still on his heels, like a fox after a cackle, and he had no choice left to him.

A tree rattled next to him, noisily, its branches absolutely bare of all leaf and moss, and Dar reined his horse wide around it, for it wasn't a tree at all, but a rooted creature called the bones of the wind for its many-branched structure, a creature that captured and ate whatever small creeping beasts it could—and that was not above entangling an occasional unwary large creature. Brand's nostrils flared suspiciously as he minced through the marsh grasses in response to Dar's reining. The creature's dark, barklike mouth opened and shut in smacking disappointment as it felt their body heat graze it and pass on, prey lost.

The Shield broke through the clouds suddenly, its immense round silvery form beaming into the swamp as though it were daylight instead of midnight, and in its sudden illumination, Dar spotted the broken trail leading through the dense swamp. Leaning forward, he urged Brand onto the path before they lost sight of it. Impatience rode them both.

An owl hooted and swept above them as the tangled brush opened up, revealing a huge, muddy hillock, with a wide mouth yawning at them. Though the Shield stayed above him, Dar took the torch and raised it high, calling, "Witch! Witch of Kalmar!"

A faint glimmering shone from within the mound, and Dar shivered, for the wind circled about him, curling even through the leather breastplate and chilling his damp undershirt. He stretched in the stirrups, and Brand stamped.

"Witch!"

A branch crackled, and something stirred inside. A puffer toad near the opening swelled its body and gave a series of croaks as the darkness moved in the mouth, and Dar saw a reed curtain being drawn aside.

"Late for a visit, is it not?" a soft voice answered, and Kory, the Witch of Kalmar, stepped into view, carrying a glow basket.

Dar blinked in surprise, for he had expected an old woman, sucked of her youth and vitality, but found instead a girl only slightly older than he, her dark-brown hair bound into braids but mussed from sleep. Her sack dress that would be shapeless on a shapeless body was on her given form by jutting breasts and rounded hips. Only her bare feet were unsightly, bumped and swollen by warts of all sizes and shapes.

"You set your own time," he answered the witch. "The innkeeper told me you would only prophesy by moonlight."

"True. True." She brushed the toad aside with her foot, and he shuddered involuntarily, thinking that that was how she had gotten the many warts. The Witch of Kalmar studied him a moment before beckoning him to dismount and follow her back into the mud cave.

Brand gave a lingering nicker after him when he disappeared into the depths of the hovel, the reed curtain dropping behind him. Aarondar straightened as soon as he could, in the center of the cave, looking about him and seeing little different from the hovel of any other witch or seer he had visited. Gourds and dried strands of herbs hung from the ceiling. Supplies of various sorts lined makeshift shelves about the far walls, and jars cluttered the floors. A bed was pushed aside in the shadows. The sweet smell of crushed flowers came from its vicinity, and for a flickering of a second, he wondered what it would be like to share that bed with the Witch of Kalmar.

He shook it off and glared at her, as she laughed softly and dropped her intent stare to the bowl of clear water that occupied most of a low table in the room's center. "Just wondering," she murmured before stroking her hand across the water's surface.

The water caressed her skin and fell away in a sheet of diamonds. Dar slapped two silver coins down on the rough surface of the table. "I want—"

She held her hand up and seated herself on a three-legged stool, then motioned for him to do the same. "I know what you want. You have a problem and want a solution. That much is obvious, and it would take no seer to know it! Why not ask the dragongods?"

A reluctant smile creased Dar's tired face as he eased himself down. Witching powers made him wary, but so far he had found no one of any great talent, most guessing who he was and what he wanted by his outward appearance. He had gotten chary with his words. The three-legged stool was close to the ground, and he doubled his legs under him, hand on sword guard, unable to stand up too quickly, disliking being at a physical disadvantage.

The witch passed her hand over the silver twice before she took it in hand, and she ran her fingertips over it, then frowned. "Too many hands have held this before you. Do you have newly struck coins?"

Dar shook his head. Few would, and she nodded, before dropping the coins into the bowl of water, where they shimmered and danced before settling to the bottom. "I'll read you from the bowl, then." He leaned over to look. Was it water?

"Don't touch it!" The girl spoke sharply, and he drew back, wondering. She frowned into the water, her braids swinging forward over her shoulders. She smiled slightly. "Your armor has traveled more than you have."

Dar laughed.

"What is it you wish to know?"

He paused, lips parted slightly, for to tell the witch that was to tell her his soul, and he wanted to see if she could read that, or was another charlatan like all the rest. Before he could respond, she brushed the question away.

"You carry a pouch of bone and ashes at your side, where most men carry gold." The witch looked at him, surprise in her slanted, dark eyes. They widened. "Your parents." Her chin went up in the air as her head jerked back, and he saw the flash of her eyes when they rolled back, and a meaningless sound dripped from slack lips.

His flesh crawled, and Dar hoisted himself to his feet quickly. "I've made a mistake," he started, and reached out for her hand, but the witch shuddered and clasped both hands tight to the sides of the scrying bowl.

"You will wander far before scattering those bones and ashes to their final rest," she intoned, and the man froze at the sound of her voice, for it had gone flat and hollow.

He knew it was too late to run when she said her next words.

"The dragons watch you."

The chill raising his flesh stabbed inward to his very bones. She had power, and now Dar wasn't sure if he had done the right thing seeking her out.

"Dragons watch all of us," he answered back. The dragons were the only true sorcerers on Rangard, having taken their powers from the old gods, and leaving none to humans, dwarves, and others except those who could trade for power from a dragon. Many called the dragons gods, but Dar didn't. He came from farming blood, and soldiering blood, and knew the earth had other gods, and he privately worshiped them more than the great scaled beasts. Much evil and some good had come from dragons in the past, and though their sailing bodies no longer darkened the skies as much, they were still frighteningly powerful. He feared now that she had gotten her talent from a dragon, and if so, he was done for!

She panted, her face pale and dewy. Her chin dropped and her eyes stopped rolling, and she looked across at him, but her gaze was unseeing. "You are running,

Aarondar, and you will be running, until your life's bond is severed from the past by the claw of a dragon."

"And where do I find a claw?" he threw back at her, dragon parts being notoriously difficult to separate from the rest of the beast, but the witch didn't hear him. He found himself in a defensive stance, his sword half pulled from its sheath, for she unnerved him.

"You are pursuing your destiny now," she answered flatly, "just as it is in pursuit of you." The girl shuddered, her left hand breaking away from the bowl's rim, and she coughed harshly, then her eyelids fluttered and she looked at him, ashen with fear. "You're being followed!"

Her scream rent the air as a dark thing thrust out of the bowl of water, grasping at the fingers of her right hand. She tried to pull back, but the black, scaled hand caught her two last fingers, and she screamed again, trying to wrench free.

The arm of the beast emerged from the bowl, and Dar knew suddenly that she could yank it right through. He pulled the sword free and swung, as she twisted free, the thrashing scaled arm falling into the depths of the bowl with a splash, and she staggered back, crying with pain. Dar gulped a deep breath and chopped a second time, thrusting down with all the power of his weary muscles. The blade split the scrying bowl in two, and the curious silver-blue liquid flowed over the tabletop and pooled on the cave's damp floor.

"Fool! My bowl!" The witch turned on him, her eyes blazing in anger.

Dar sheathed his sword and ran. Her cries of anger screeched after him as he tore the reed curtain down and caught up Brand's reins. The chestnut skittered aside, startled by his sudden emergence.

"You've ruined me," she screamed. Dar pulled himself into the saddle. A hot wind singed the back of his neck when he bent to sheathe his sword. The fireball sizzled past and crashed into the mudflats. The swamps around him would be set with her traps, to protect her, and she was mad enough now to loose them. The chestnut foamed at the mouth as Dar hauled around on the bit and set him at the pathway, whipping him into a dead run.

Mud splattered into Dar's face and nostrils, for he leaned low over the horse's mane. They bounded through the marsh grasses of the swamp, scattering toads and showering clay. Brand caught the smell of his master's fear, for Dar had no intention of being anywhere near the swamp if the witch decided to go back to her trance and bring the demon through!

A man valuing his life in the borderlands doesn't ride asleep, and so Dar struggled to keep his eyes open while the chestnut picked out the way over dry ground and through tangled brush. Dar yawned again and sagged down even more. He dreamed of the last of the witch's words and didn't wake until the horse plodded wearily into the tavern yard and fetched up against the stabler who hobbled out to meet them.

Dar slid down to the ground, caught himself, and pressed the reins into the boy's calloused hand. "I want him rubbed and fed a bucket of warm mash. He's had a hard day and night of it." He flipped a coin into the air then, and the boy's eyes glittered at the bronze hardness of it. He caught it before it turned a second time in the lanternlight. The ripple of that motion spread through the child's begrimed and scarred face, and he bowed and put his fist to his brow awkwardly.

"I'll bring yer change, master," he said and clucked softly to the stallion to lead him into the warm and pungent air of the stable. A few whickers and one loud neigh challenged Brand when he joined the other mounts.

A cock crowed, reminding Dar that he had spent the best part of a day and a half in the saddle, in order to reach the swamps at moonlight. He took a deep breath and shrugged into his faded wool cloak. Again, he had no choice but to rest for the day and night, for the stallion was winded and footsore, and couldn't possibly carry him out again today. Even tomorrow wouldn't be a kind use of the beast, but Dar couldn't wait past tomorrow. He took his helm off, combed his hair off his forehead with stiff fingers, and headed toward the weathered, leaning building.

No one challenged Dar as he made his way into the inn and up the rickety stairs to his room. He'd paid for a solitary cot and had been given it, and paid in advance to have the keeper leave it for him while he rode in search of the oracle. The smell of fresh-baked bread permeated the air, and his stomach rumbled. He debated the wisdom of bathing first, then eating before sleeping, but as he shrugged in indecision, the innkeeper thumped him on the shoulder. A crust of red mud wafted free and drifted to the timbered floor.

"Master! I trust you had a profitable session with the witch!" The big man grinned and scratched the side of his nose. "You wouldn't know how much business that old hag brings me . . . that, and having the only fresh-water hole this side of the border."

Wearily, Dar returned a nod, thinking that the witch of Kalmar was a sure bet to set the demon right on his heels, and that Valorek was closer than ever. With a pleased grunt, the keep waddled downstairs.

A pallan, wrapped in dark cloth, gauze mask, and veil, wrinkled his nose as he brushed past in the eerie walk of all pallans, mysterious and hidden forever from human eyes. Dar caught the fellow by his—or its—slim arm. "Fetch a tub and hot water up to my room. And a loaf of that bread."

The pallan looked at him, eyes wide through the thin dark cloth of the face mask. "But it's breakfast." With no less speed than the stabler, the childlike being caught the penny Dar flipped into the air. "Right away, sir, unless the cook catches me!" Dar watched him go with sinuous, sensual grace, thinking that no doubt the fellow had much stranger requests from guests.

Having bathed and slept, and hung his first set of clothes out the window to dry, Dar dressed and made his way down the stairs to join the raucous company in the tavern below. Roasted joints spit and sizzled in the huge fireplaces, tankards and clay jugs rattled, and he could hear the throw of dice dancing across tabletops. Men laughed and cussed, some too loudly and some in low sinister whispers.

Though the innkeeper was a stout human, with frizzled red hair and patchy beard, his clientele was like his crew, a mixture of human, dwarf, and veiled pallan. Dar scratched his chin. He disliked crowds and picked out a dark corner, less smoky than the others, after noting that it must be dark outside again. He would have to see after dinner how his horse had fared, and check the slender legs and tendons. If they had filled and grown warm, the horse would be too lame to ride for days.

He took a bread trencher and clay pitcher back to his shadowed corner, and sat with his back to the wall, where he could watch the tavern and be warmed by one of the cooking fireplaces, and left alone.

A pallan drifted by the table's edge, dressed in midnight-blue loose shirt and trousers instead of the long robes most affected, but hooded and veiled for all that. Dar blinked at the creature's graceful turn, his gaze resting on the line of the slim torso fading into the slightly rounded hip. He wrenched his thoughts away and glared into his pitcher of beer. Too much drink on an empty stomach, he decided, carving a chunk off the meat joint and chewing on it thoughtfully. It was said that a human had never looked beyond a pallan's veil—or if one had, he'd never remembered what he'd seen. On those grounds, it was better not to think of mixing.

All the same, Dar found himself watching the pallan again as it—he—she—wove among the tables, refiling pitchers and trenchers. A peddler drank heavily, his silvery hair shining in tavernlight; remarkable for a man of that age to be roaming the borderlands without escort. Dar wrinkled his nose in disgust, for the pallan stayed too long at the old man's table and bent low to exchange quiet words, and when it left, the man watched it go with greedy eyes, his expression of lust unfaded by age.

Dar wasn't the only one watching the peddler and the creature, he saw. One of the hazers a table over ceased his gambling long enough to stare as the pallan wove a path to the bar and proceeded to load a fresh tray of mugs. Hazers lived on the bounty of the harsh lands, if bounty it could be called when caravans of traders had to leave their bundles by the wayside when their lams died of thirst and stumbled to a bawling death in the cracked black dirt. Or when the hazers cut off stray gunters from the vast herds being driven to stockyards across the wastes—better to face the wastes, occasionally, than the vagaries of the ice-and-snow-bound passes to the north. Hazers such as Dar watched now even hired on as extra drivers from time to time, but the herd boss who hired a hazer such as the one he watched now had better sleep lightly at night, and with his hand on his sword.

The man clicked the dice in his hands absently. He was angular and raw-boned, thick across the shoulders, and caked with dust. His brown hair was whipped back like a rooster's comb from a high, bony forehead. He wore leathers and a furred vest, but his prominent neck was encircled tightly with a fetish on a strap, and Dar made note of the man . . . lean and dangerous, and a believer in primitive magic, the kind of bandit who made a living scrounging the badlands.

"C'mon, Nabor, it's your throw," rasped the man sitting next to him, and he shook the hazer's elbow, diverting the man's attention to Dar.

Their eyes met briefly, flickering, and then the other looked away, to release his dice with a shake of his wrists, but Dar knew he had been sized up, too. He slouched back into his corner, letting the wood-and-mortar wall warm his back.

He finished his joint and scraped out most of the trencher loaf, the stale bread having sopped up the juices. Having had his pitcher filled a second time, he was feeling mellow. Nabor's dice game had broken up, but not before the bandit chieftain had been hailed as a winner and a cheat by several of his gang and had quieted all complaints with a hammering fist over the top of the head. Brutal, but efficient.

Dar found himself nodding a little and watching the pallan again as it-he-she darted between the tables in answer to the peddler's call for more beer. Nabor scooted his bench back, pinching the being quickly between tables. It doubled over with a sigh of pain, and Nabor took a fistful of shirt, wrapping his hand in it.

Empty mugs rolled across the tray, which the pallan desperately tried to right. One hit the floor and shattered, spraying foam. Dar and the peddler started to their feet at the same time; Nabor was watching for the peddler, who sank slowly back down as the pallan stood frozen. The veil had slipped, revealing huge eyes, and its slender hands clasped the tray tightly.

"My beer's stale," growled the bandit. "Tell the keep he owes me a fresh barrel."

Dar put a booted foot up on the next bench, thinking that if he didn't champion the creature, no one would. His heart thumped at the prospect of knocking heads with the hazer, but he leaned forward to say quietly, "This is some of the best beer on the border. A fresh mug is fair trade enough."

The bandit twisted to look at him. A raised eyebrow sent a network of ripples across his leathery face, clear up into his hairline. The fetish bobbed as he cleared his throat, and Dar knew suddenly that he was disturbed by who answered his challenge. For some reason, Nabor had been trying to provoke the peddler.

Dar sent a bronze penny spinning onto the table. "Let me buy you a fresh cup, for the one the pallan spilled, and let the creature go."

Nabor grabbed up the coin, his knuckles showing whitely as his hand closed about it. With a narrowing of his dark eyes, he nodded, let the pallan free, and dropped the penny onto the wooden tray, where it spun as the creature bolted.

The hazer showed his back to Dar and buried his face in the foaming mug the pallan brought back quickly, breath still gasping. The pallan stared at him before disappearing into the shadows. Dar put his foot down and leaned back into his own corner, and found the peddler watching him steadily. They stared a moment, and then the peddler gave Dar a faint nod of recognition as though toasting a fellow human being, awash in a sea of nonhumans, both wearing a faint veneer of civilization. Dar's skin crawled. He wasn't sure if he liked the peddler's assessment of a kindred soul—he had done something, and the silver-haired man had not. The peddler settled down to cup his hands about a battered silver goblet, and Dar went back to the pursuit of his own thoughts.

The pallan kept him supplied with small but choice tidbits the rest of the evening, and wouldn't take the penny Dar pushed at it, except for the beer. Sweetmeats and even a fresh apple, which Dar dropped down the front of his tunic to save for Brand, and a hot tuber, baked in the coals and slathered with dairy butter, seemed more than fair recompense for Dar's kindness. It delivered the goods furtively, as though afraid to call further attention to itself, and sighed gratefully when Dar signaled thank you, but he'd had enough.

The peddler went to work shortly, his pack occupying the open space between his feet, its worn leather sides collapsing under the weight of the objects within. Nothing of exceptional value passed hands . . . no reason Dar could see for the intent, though hidden, watch of the hazer and his crew. Still, Dar too watched. It was good to see a human in action again—not that the innkeeper didn't pass for human, but the peddler reminded Dar a little of his village past.

His voice boomed as he clasped the hands of his clients about his goods, stroked them into place, and congratulated them. "Good bargaining, sirrah, yes, indeed, you're a tough one. Ol' Chappie has met his match tonight. Who else will deal? Right here and now!" His hair, sparse and white, gleamed in the lanternlight, but his chin remained square and firm, shaved clean, and his skin was a weathered tan, like oiled oak, finely patterned and burled with age. Lines routed deeply, tracing laughter and character as much as they did the years. Dar liked the way Chappie picked up a bauble or a carving, ran his fingertips over the object, and assessed its worth. The pallans ran back and forth, guaranteeing an endless flow of beer, and Dar realized the man wasn't paying any longer, nor should he have, for the innkeeper knew as well as Dar that the peddler was the reason for the ever increasing, spellbound crowd that now pressed into the building.

And yet, whenever the peddler's gaze flickered over the room, he took care not to meet Dar's eyes again. Ashamed? thought Dar to himself, settling back on his elbows and crossing his boots at the ankle. He was drifting contentedly in the ambience of the common room when he remembered the witch's scream that he was being followed. Or perhaps he dreamed it. At any rate, Dar snapped upright in his chair and blinked in the smoky light, realizing that the night was half gone, and the peddler had closed his pack.

Dar scrubbed his hand across his face. He heard a clear voice ring out, edged by too much ale, but loud and strong for all its blurring.

"I have seen the dragons fall," Chappie cried, in a strong, clarion voice, as his listeners gasped and shrank back, fearful the sacrilege would curl their flesh from their bones. The peddler waved his hands, urging them back into his tale. "No, it's true! I have seen the dragons fall, tumbling from the sky as they die. They spread their sails, wings like transparent rainbows, and their bodies burn, and they scream as they fall." The peddler paused and quaffed another swallow of his freshly drawn mug. Pallans stopped in the shadows of the room and watched too, in quiet judgment, their faces veiled and their thoughts as well.

Silence cloaked the taproom. Every ear that could listen did so, even those bent over their dice and throwing sticks, pretending that children's tales didn't interest them. Such a listener was Nabor, and Dar felt a chill run down his back.

Chappie raised his broad hands, imitating wingspreads against the orange-smoked light of the room. "And when they fall, they fall for leagues, and their carcasses lie armored in the wind and the sand, until finally the scales drop off their empty hulks, and their bones bleach in the sun. They carry their magic and their treasures to the grave with them . . . out of the bones and jewels slither their hatchlings . . . and the bones go down to dust . . . them that don't rise again." The mug, freshly emptied, hit the tabletop at this pause.

Dar thought he heard the hiss of a sharp breath at those words, but the back of his own neck prickled up. He listened to a madman's tale, and was being drawn into it whole. Dragons did not die and did not multiply; they were gods, and existed unless a hero aided by another god pierced their armor through and laid them to rest.

The peddler dropped his hands. "The graveyard, I tell you. I saw it myself. I stood at the edge of the valley, and I saw . . . I saw the living worms curled about their hoards, waiting until their turn to be called up to the skies . . . to breed and die, full of magic and spite. I paid dearly to find them, but I know where the dragons go to die."

The audience rocked back and shook itself, like a hound after a long nap, and then someone laughed quietly. Another voice called out, "Go on, old man. Dragongods don't go nowhere to die!"

Chappie looked along the crowded table. "Gods, are they? Then where do they go? And where do they come from? Tell me that! A hero kills one now and then . . . but what about the others? Sorcery shrouds them . . . but even the earth grows old. What happens to a dragon, aged and creaking in its joints? How many of you know where their young come from?"

"From the sea!" Shouts of agreement followed the anonymous statement, but the peddler only smiled, and the fine grain of his oaken face shifted. "A fire-breathing drake from the cold waters of the sea? And his magic? What about that? No, I tell you and I tell you true, for I have been there and seen it myself, and—" Chappie broke off suddenly. He wiped his mouth on the back of his hand, like a man who realizes he has said too much. He sat down roughly, bumping the contents of his pack. "Another mug," he called. A rough voice seconded him, "Another round for a drunken old man."

Muted shadows and grumbling forms shifted back to their own tables and concerns, and the peddler seemed to be forgotten. A loud comment of "Crazy" broke the silence, and soon the taproom emptied. Dar rocked back himself. The atmosphere had changed. He could feel it, and he didn't like it . . . it was charged, like the sky before a lightning storm.

The swordsman drank the last of his own pungent beer and swirled the foam at the bottom. The peddler's story had been taken for truth enough by some of the listeners, and now Chappie wasn't worth one of the bronze pennies Dar had been tossing around, unless he took care. He waited until the peddler stumbled upstairs before he rose and left the common room himself.

In his room, he wrapped himself in his cloak and fell asleep, not bothering even to shed his boots, and slept deeply, dreaming again of the witch and the journey, swimming through swamp mud as dark as blood.

When he dreamed again that the witch looked into her bowl of crystal-clear water—water that could never have been distilled from that swamp—Dar sat bolt upright on the cot and shook.

When he knew he was awake, he stood up and walked to the narrow window and looked down into the shadowed alleyway between the inn and the stableyard. He saw a figure standing there, bowed against the weight of his pack, leaning into his drunkenness as into a high wind. Dar rubbed his eyes clear, then grinned.

The old peddler was sneaking out on his bill like the proverbial thief in the night. And, as Dar watched, another shadow, slim and graceful, darted out to join him.

The pallan. Dar knew it had to be, and remembered the exchange that had passed between the tavern creature and Chappie. He shrugged with distaste, thinking bitterly that he had been of similar mien earlier. Leave the old man and his young flesh to their pleasure, he thought, as Chappie put his arm about the pallan and leaned heavily upon its aid to stagger down the alley.

A flash of movement caught Dar's eye. A shadow among shadows, with the gleam of a drawn blade, awaiting the unknowing pair, and before Dar even registered just what he had seen, he burst out of the room and down the stairs, grabbing a low-guttering torch. He skidded into the alleyway as a shrill whistle cut the air, then a muffled scream, a grunt, and a heavy thud.

The peddler keeled to his knees and curled over onto his side. The pallan stood over his body, dagger flashing in hand, even as the rogue who faced them made a sweeping cut with his much longer blade. The pallan dodged back and swiped in return, but the length of its weapon and arm made it no fight.

Dar cried out in defiance and jumped into the opening, his blade slicing deeply. Something hot and fiery tweaked the flesh of his eye, and he fell back, eyes watering in pain, but struck a guard, and metal clanged sharply off the blade. A cloak had snapped in his eyes, Dar thought, blinking hard and fast, and the next thing would be a sword if he didn't get up. *Crack!* Fabric whipped the air, striking his temple, and he struck, pulling it from his assailant, and plunged his sword deep into the offender's gut.

Two shadows turned and fled into the night as he stood wiping his eyes.

Dar pulled his sword free then and joined the pallan, who was tenderly wiping grime from Chappie's lined face, and he heard the creature weeping softly. He cleared his throat.

"Too late," the old man gasped. "I was a fool tonight."

"Don't talk," the pallan whispered, and made a cradle of its lap. Chappie twisted a little.

"Years," he laughed. "Years I've walked these lands and kept my tongue. I've drunk in more taverns than the sky has stars, and I kept my tongue. Tonight I threw my life to the wind. And why?" His strong hand reached up and caressed the pallan's gauzed face. "I wanted you to hear it . . . I wanted you to know I was worth something. . . ."

"I had no doubts," the pallan answered gently.

His stomach turned, and Dar looked away, not wanting to hear the tender words between these two. He took the moment to wipe his sword clean and clear his throat. As the peddler took a gargling breath, he said, "How do you want to be buried? Anyone to carry a message to?"

He was being followed—he couldn't carry out the peddler's request—but he wanted the old man to think he would be taken care of, so he waited for the answer.

Chappie met his gaze and smiled. "No one. No god but the clear sky and open road. Not even a dragon." He grasped beneath his twisted body and with many tugs and grunts brought the pack out. "My pack . . . its contents . . . I want the two of you to have it."

"I don't want a reward," Dar protested, but the peddler held up his bloodstained hand, quieting him.

"You earned it. The two of you. Most of this is trash . . . a bit here and a bit there, but this. . . ." Laboriously, he dragged out an oilskin and a jagged triangle of slate.

The pallan brushed away a thin trickle of blood from the peddler's mouth, and Dar suspicioned that the gauze stuck damply to the being's face. Tears from a heartless pallan?

But the peddler grasped his sword hand with the iron grip of the dying and dragged him close. "The map . . . I leave it to you both."

"Map?"

"To the graveyard! You thought I was spinning a yarn?" The peddler laughed then, rough and raw. He took Dar's fingers and ran them over the slate, and Dar's flesh crawled.

"A scale!" Iridescent colors swirled in the triangle as the pallan took the torch from Dar's slack left hand and held it close.

Chappie stabbed at an eye of green. "This here's an emerald . . . worked right into it. And gold flakes. My legacy to you . . . a map to where the dragons lie. . . ." And blood splattered as Chappie spit out the last of his air and twisted into death.

Dar squatted in disbelief for a long moment. Then he took the map from Chappie's slack hand and tucked it into his shirt, behind the leather breastplate. He took the old man's body from the pallan's lap and straightened out his limbs on the ground. Without a moment's hesitation, he lowered the torch, and the peddler's rags flared into a hot, searing pyre, like dry leaves.

The pallan jumped back and stood, gulping, still holding the dragon scale.

"I killed him," it said.

"Nonsense. The hazer gutted him."

"No . . . not that. I mean . . . he came out here to meet me. It was all my fault."

Dar looked at the pallan. He didn't have an answer for that one, thinking that the creature was probably right. Then he said, "You don't want to be found here."

He walked away gruffly, uncaring if the pallan followed him or not, and hiked up the back stairs to his room. Hand shaking, he lit a tallow candle stub. The pallan entered, moved to the window, and watched the flames burn and gutter down. The stench filled the air, even though the wind was blowing down the alley in the other direction.

Dar fumbled the packet as he drew it from his tunic, nearly dropped the candle, recovered it, and spread the map out on the wooden stool he was using for a table.

It was a true map. He'd seen a few, consulted during a military campaign or two, drawn by a cartographer's hand. Dragons knew what the lands looked like from the air . . . Rangard, they called the earth, and different lands were scattered about, some strung together like sausages on a string, and others mere drops in oceans of water. Dar touched the yellowed skin. Mountains and rivers and seas were drawn in colored ink, and the lettering in flowery yet spindly shapes illuminated each area. He didn't have time to read it, for the pallan snatched it back and rewound it in the oilskin.

"It belongs to both of us," the creature rebuked him. "In the morning, we can both read the signs."

Dar rocked back on his heels, memories of the witch filling his mind. *By dragon's claw, I will be freed.* . . . And a little dragon gold wouldn't go too badly either.

He looked at the pallan. It was impossible to read emotion through the eyeslits of the mask and veil. "All right," he agreed, as he pinched the candle. "I have my bed. There's a floor for you."

The pallan stood and watched him as he rolled into his cloak a second time, and a spot between his shoulder blades itched as he remembered how well the creature had used its dagger, but he folded his arms and laid his head down. The pallan had nowhere else to go, with the peddler burning down in the alley.

The wind shifted at daylight, and he woke to the nauseating choke of smoke. Worse, the crackle of flames seemed to crawl right up the side of the inn . . . and he thought of the witch again, with her infernal screaming.

The scream was repeated, from rooms downstairs. Dar bolted from his bed, snatching up his pack and stuffing his dried clothes into them. The sword he belted on, but he left the lance standing in the corner. He kicked out the shutters of his window.

He jumped, even as he realized he was alone in the room. He thudded to the ground and staggered, grunting with pain, barely able to keep his feet. Orange-and-blue flames licked about him, soot filled the air, and wood exploded. Dar drew his sword as hoofbeats thundered down the alleyway and into the smoke, bearing down on him. All the while, he told himself that burning the peddler hadn't set the inn ablaze.

One of the hazers kicked his horse out of the cloud. He bore a torch and slashed it at Dar as he whipped his horse down on him.

Dar's blade glanced off the torch and sliced into the rider's thigh. Crimson spurted, and the horse swerved and

ran into the smoke beyond, whickering in fear, its rider
clutching desperately to the saddle.

The peddler's attackers, no doubt, Dar thought. He
took a deep breath and headed for the stable just as the
double doors burst open. Horses stampeded from the
building, their eyes rolling white-eyed and heads free of
leather. His chestnut led the escapees, and a saddled gray
brought up the rear. He caught a glimpse of blue trousers
and shirt, and hooded and veiled face. The pallan leaned
low on the stallion's withers, urging him on with a whoop
past Dar.

The map!

Dar whirled and raced down the alleyway after them,
choking as billows of smoke blinded him. He stumbled
clear of the alley into the open, where the hills of the
borderlands lay behind, and the horses streamed into the
wilderness, thundering toward freedom.

Shouts and jeers made him whirl. The hazers rode out
of the smoke and paused, their horses pawing the dirt.
Gray light glinted off their ruddy blades. They were
after the pallan, and Dar was the only object that
stood in their way, blocking the mouth of the alley. He
set himself with sword to pick off as many as he could,
and maybe to gather up a riderless horse if he was
successful.

He shrugged into his pack's strap and freed his other
hand. Nabor grinned at him. The inn roared in flame,
blasting his right side with heat. The horses flinched at the
wall of heat.

A horse screamed, loud and shrill, trapped in the
blazing stables.

Nabor pointed his blade at Dar, kicked his mount, and
charged, his mates plunging after. Dar ducked Nabor
altogether, whirled and slashed the second man across the
stomach, and nicked the third's mount on the flank, and
the horse plunged desperately with a whinny of pain. The
others thundered past him, amid shouts now as the inn
emptied of its choking occupants. A dwarf brushed past
Dar with a bucket of water slopping over at the brim,

threw its contents at the building, and shrieked helplessly with fear as a timber collapsed over him.

Nabor made to rein into the hills, but his man grabbed at the reins, and even Dar heard part of the shout. "Him what stopped us . . ."

The hazer pulled his horse into a dancing halt, torn between Dar and pursuing the pallan. Then he made a motion, and the hazers whipped their horses and disappeared around the corner.

Dar's heart sank, for he realized they were circling the inn to strike at him from the alley one last time. He staggered into the open, gulping down mouthfuls of clean air, his eyes smarting as he wiped them on his sleeve. A hot stickiness ran down his brow, and he knew then the first blow had grazed him.

A high-pitched yell broke the air, and the gray stallion charged into the yard, the pallan clothed in midnight blue clinging to its mane.

It held out an arm to Dar, just as Nabor and his crew burst out of the alley, whooping and brandishing their weapons.

"Run for it!" Dar waved at the pallan. "They're after the map!"

"Don't be stupid!" The pallan glared at him as the gray stallion pivoted and fought its grip on the reins. It reached up and pulled off the hood, and the gauze face mask drifted away on the hot air, cindering in the ashes. Dar gulped as waves of golden-brown hair tumbled down and he looked into a disdainful pair of blue eyes.

Dar looked over his shoulder at the wave of thundering horsemen, swords bared, racing toward him and the girl.

"Oh, hell," he cried, and vaulted onto the back of the horse. He held on tight as she dug her heels into its flanks.

Chapter 2

Valorek was something more and something less than a man. The lesser part of him was what eventually drove him into making the pact that made him more, but not whole—never whole, which was one of the several loopholes in the bargain Valorek made with false gods.

He'd grown too fast as a youth and ended up lopsided, one slim shoulder higher than the other, one leg a little shorter than the other, giving him an odd sway to his walk, rather like a village woman swaying when she carried a jug of water on her head. When Valorek was a soldier, this resemblance had been remarked upon once, and once only, for the footman who said it was later found dead with his balls stuffed into his mouth. There was no proving Valorek did it . . . and no proving he did not.

He wore his dark hair shaved almost to a pelt length. His coarse beard he kept cut very close, but he didn't affect shaving as men of the south did—what soldier would? Who had the time or the inclination to take a blade to his own throat every day when there were legions of the enemy too eager to do it? His olive complexion sprouted hairs like a bear—if he started shaving, where would he begin? Even the cups of his ears sprouted tufts. From beneath massive dark brows, flat dark eyes stared belligerently at the world and dared the world to stare back.

Valorek began life in the ranks, and could not remember a day when he hadn't been a soldier, or a soldier's boy, valet to man and beast. But he never minded, for he had cunning, and his quick fingers twitched away many a stray bronze penny while he served, and as soon as he grew big enough, his reputation for meanness kept him safe from the cuffs and kicks of his elders. Kick Valorek, and your horse could well go lame the next day, or the day after. Cuff Valorek and your mess pot would sprout maggots for dinner.

Then Valorek learned the value of being paid not to be mean beforehand, instead of taking revenge later. Well-placed tokens became necessary to ensure that your rations didn't spoil and your horse go lame, your harness crack and tear, or your weapons grow brittle and nicked.

And it wasn't much later that Valorek learned, with natural cunning, how to become the luck of the company. He learned how to predict the outcome of warfare with absolute accuracy, and became the valued companion of commanders.

It wasn't difficult for the slant-sided youth now nearly a man to devise a scheme to make him invaluable. He offered his predictions freely, at first, in the camps before each skirmish, when beer made the uneasiness a little more bearable and he was more likely to be listened to, as one of the diversions. Word spread quickly that Valorek was never wrong. Rumor spread that Valorek had power, of a sort, and when the commanders heard, he was summoned forth, for every man knew that even the gods are capricious, and luck is hard to come by. If one of his soldiers was a seer, the commander would grab for him.

It was done easily enough. Valorek squinted his disconcerting eyes and scratched his heavy brow, then simply made the very best guess possible and told the commander what was the most probable outcome. And then, in a tiny book that he carried on a thong about his neck, he scribbled in his cramped, almost illiterate marks the opposite of what he had predicted. Then if he was wrong and called in disgrace to the commanders' tents, he could point at the scratches in his book and say, "Why, no, sir . . . you must have misunderstood me, for here it is on the page . . . retreat at Fallen Rock Pass," or whatever the occasion called for. Then he would stand humbly as the commander apologized and coaxed him back into smiling with a small pouch of silver.

And each pouch of silver bought the allegiance of a fighting man or two, until Valorek owned and led the armies himself, sweeping across the shambles of a continent unable to rule itself, fighting hold by hold until he came to a corner of the world where men recognized another master besides a warrior . . . and he was brought to his knees in awe.

He'd never seen a dragon before, though many of his troops swore at and by one. He didn't believe in a god that ravaged the living world to keep its own life, and he knew that these were not immortal beings, that they were much like himself, though most of his world trembled in fear at the very thought of being under a dragon's reign. When he marched into Ey-V-Maborek, he was greeted like a hero, and as soon as he swung out of his saddle and made camp he found out why this misbegotten corner of the world was eager to treat a sadistic warlord like a king.

For several generations, the dark wings of the black dragon Nightwing had sailed the sky, and his presence had left its mark on the lands below. Woolies were slaughtered in their fields, heads lolling on gutted, lifeless forms. Village toddlers picnicking on their blankets in the warm sun while their mothers hoed the gardens were plucked up, never to be seen again. Dwarf trade caravans disappeared in their entirety upon the roads, and when troops of dwarves came later to avenge the supposed misdeeds of the villagers, the slaughter was worse.

The dragon god of ebony hide toyed with them, to see which of the men would be smart enough to realize who had come to their land and to worship him. It was a long time coming, and waiting, the beast hollowed out a nearby mountain and made himself comfortable.

By the time the likes of Valorek discovered the fine art of conquering, Nightwing was firmly ensconced as the dragongod of the region. He curled his toes upon the crags of his mountain, craned his sinewy neck, and watched with amusement as Valorek's army approached, and he rattled his spines with pleasure, for he had not fought in a long time, and it gave him a warm feeling in the pit of his double stomachs to know that his legend would grow here—grow and explode across human and dwarf lands like molten ore and rock from the center of the world. Boulders split under the intense grasp of his claws, and even though a fine dust rained down from the mountains upon Valorek's troops, when they looked up, they saw nothing. Nightwing had power.

The pleasure built in the dragon to an intensity akin to spawning, and so he lay in the hot shadows of the entrance to his lair for days, sides heaving with dark, glistening anticipation of the dawn of the morning when the humans would blow the warhorns and challenge him; lay and felt his organs swell and grow hard, and his heart thump in his chest, and he bellowed out the gases of his first stomach and ignited them into flames with the magic of his mind, and fired the ceiling of his burrow until it gleamed like the molten onyx of his own form, then lowered his muzzle to his forelegs, heaved a sigh, and consigned himself to restless waiting.

Thus it was that Nightwing found himself surprised by a human, by a being from one of the races which were of little more importance to him than fleas to a dog, sometimes irritating, sometimes amusing, humans, dwarves, pallans, all (though Nightwing curled a lip over his fangs when thinking of pallans, for they were a different kettle of fish, and a bit more troublesome). One dawn found not a warhorn on the air, but the crunch of boots upon the stony pathway to his lair, and the bleat of woolies, and he felt/heard/smelled their heat upon the coolish air, and crawled out of the den to see what empty-headed shepherd dared intrude upon his demesne.

No shepherd approached, but an armored warrior, though his hands were empty of all but a wooden pail, as he traversed the intricate and winding path of Nightwing's burrow. The dragon opened both eyes wide in the grayed light, and his nostrils flared, for the being brought with him gifts—the woolies could be none other, for only a fool would drive his flock this high—and the liquid splashing in the wooden pail brought saliva to the dragon's forked tongue and set his throat quivering in anticipation. Cream! Ah, but Nightwing had not feasted on cream for many a year, not since he ran on the highlands, a free and silly strider, and chased the gunters down as they bawled until their tongues hung from their mouths and blood ran from their nostrils, and they dropped before him. He could suckle from their swollen udders, curl in the sun, and feast later on their bloating forms. He flexed his claws in anticipation.

The being drove the woolies to the side of the path when he looked up and saw the dragon watching him, and the silly creatures ran and huddled against the cold rock, their big brown eyes rolling in their heads with fear. The soldier held out his hands as if to show they were empty of all but the pail of cream, though Nightwing knew well he could have a blade at his back. He was no stranger to the devious ways of men.

"I am Valorek, great being, and have come bringing you gifts such as a dragonlord deserves."

Nightwing got up. His bulk filled the burrow mouth almost to capacity, his spines scraping the glass ceiling, and he bowed his neck to look down at the scrawny creature before him. His throat vibrated soundlessly a moment as he shaped air to words, then he gusted, "I need no gifts. I am free to take whatever I desire."

Then Valorek bowed low, placing the bucket on the ground, and Nightwing glanced at the warrior's back, noting that no steel shone there, either. "I beg you to forgive me, dragonlord." One fist clenched and then opened rapidly as the man spoke. The dragon sensed not fear, but anger. Why did this being not fear him?

Nightwing brushed the thought aside and bent his mind upon the pail. It trembled, then skimmed along the ground until it rested in front of him. The beast reached out, curled his claws about the bucket and raised it to his muzzle, then let the cooling liquid splash onto his tongue and run down his throat, exploding a thousand taste buds with delight as it did so. As the beast in him enjoyed the cream, so the god in him puzzled over the warrior who had brought him such a delicacy, and not out of fear. He had observed the swaying walk—almost with a dragon's sinuous grace did this man move—and he took note of the mind which thought so fast and furiously that the dragon couldn't decipher most of the images, and it struck Nightwing that here, perhaps, was an ally instead of a subject.

He dropped the bucket and crushed it, wood splinters exploding from between his talons.

The human trembled then and fell onto his knees, as Nightwing said, very softly and with cunning, "What is it you wish of me?"

Valorek forced from a throat tight and dry a single husked word. It fell in the silence of the mountain pass and crashed into hearing like a boulder, but Nightwing only chuckled at the sound of it.

"Power."

The dragon beckoned him into the burrow, his sealed body still exuding the moist heat of the lusting beast, and in the darkness the two of them spoke the ancient phrases, made pacts, and performed the rituals, and sorcerous power was granted to the warlord Valorek.

Thus it was that Valorek did more than conquer land after that—he conquered soul and spirit, and swept across the countries like a plague. Other armies came after him to burn him out and could not, for the black sail of the dragon Nightwing furled always over him like a cloak of protection. Valorek took no prisoners and left battlefields behind him awash in a sea of blood. The only enemy he could not defeat was time, and then after more darktime meetings and bloody sacrifices, Nightwing told him how to conquer even that.

Then it was that Valorek put an end to conquest, finding at last a lush and green land, and often enriching the realm with the blood of its own defenders, he built a fortress and reigned as king, periodically turning back waves of would-be usurpers. And so time passed in Valorek's unchanging realm until the day he found himself riding far from home through the outskirts of one of the more distant corners of his kingdom, a section famed for its dairy herds. Valorek reined up harshly at a mud-filled street where a pile of boys were playing a game of king of the mountain.

His eyes narrowed as his horse bucked to a halt beneath him, skewing around in the street, and his hands tightened into high-veined fists.

"Move them!"

His lieutenant blanched a little, for they were only boys, and Milik was far from a sophisticated town, but he kneed his horse through the milling escort and had raised his short whip to club aside the peasants when Valorek raised his fist abruptly, stopping him.

The boys were coarsely dressed, apple-cheeked and fair-headed, small, sturdy versions of their hardworking parents, and they shrieked and tumbled in the mud, trying to unseat one boy, who ruled supreme atop a hillock at the street's edge. He held a peeled branch of wood in front of him like a quarterstaff and knew how to use it, too, his eyes glistening with the joy of repelling his attackers again and again. His attackers used slats and sticks to poke at him as crude swords, but they were awkward and childish, while the boy at the top of the heap knew exactly what he was doing.

Valorek cleared his throat and curbed his horse to a standstill, while his keen eyes told him all that his scouts and spies had not. Here, somewhere here in this forgotten pile of mud and gunter droppings, a soldier lived and bent his back in a peasant's garb . . . lived, married, and sired a spitting image of himself in that boy.

Valorek fumbled at his pack with a brown-spotted hand, pulled out a silver flask, and tilted the liquor down his throat as his thoughts boiled around. From such droppings, rebellions were fertilized. He capped the flask and returned it before wiping thin lips with the edge of his sleeve, his teeth clenched fanglike, as the warmth of the drink erupted down his throat and rolled into his empty stomach.

It would not be enough to clear the street of the boys, cuffing them aside and riding over or through them, instilling respect of their elders in their thick, brutish skulls. Not enough. That one boy was like a canker to be burned out . . . unless . . .

Valorek's hands trembled on the reins as his eyes drank in the sight of the boy. Taller than the others . . . darker, too, his hair still barely fair in the way of children, eyes that looked as if they could be brown instead of blue. Wide through the eyes, too, a sign of real intelligence, that. Even as Valorek watched, one of the attackers broke through the boy's guard and whacked him soundly across the side of the face with the flat of his stick. The boy threw up his head in pained astonishment, recovered quickly, bent the staff down, and tripped his assailant even as the second boy scrambled to gain a place at the top of the hill, thinking his blow would have reduced any boy to tears. Any other boy but this one.

"Dar! Dar!" his friends cried, urging him on, as the boy recovered and spread his legs to plant his feet firmly.

"Had enough?" he shouted at the attackers happily, a crimson welt along his face that wouldn't fade for days, worn for now like a badge of courage.

The lieutenant sat his horse in confusion as his king watched, entranced by the peasant children who dared to block the road unheeding. "My lord Valorek!" he blurted out.

The children wheeled, and with screams, scattered and disappeared. The boy atop the hillock lowered his staff, being the only one left, and his gaze met that of the sorcerer king, dressed all in the black colors of his patron dragonlord.

The boy lowered his eyes, tugged at a wavy length of hair in respect, leaped from the hill, and raced out of sight among the buildings. Valorek's heart beat as it had not in many a moon.

There, *there*, was the future Nightwing had promised him. There was one who would be but the first of the many Faces Valorek's black soul would wear upon the earth. He pointed. "Get that boy!"

Dar glanced yet another time out of the cave, to see if they had been followed, old habits hard to break. His movement drew the girl's attention in the confines of the grotto, and she, last a pallan, looked up at him over the fire she tended.

"Take off your wet things, if you're cold."

"I'm fine," he answered shortly. He rubbed his hands together and stretched them over the tiny flames. The mist of the waterfall invaded the cave, and even this fire was a miracle. The gray stallion stood at the back, shedding water and heat, head down, sides heaving, for bearing the two of them double had nearly broken his wind, before the girl found this hiding spot and led him in behind the waterfall.

She hugged herself, obscuring the sleek form the dark-blue shirt clung to, as she sat cross-legged next to the fire. "The pallans hide here often, from the hazers and others who would hurt them."

"They showed it to you?"

She nodded. "Yes. When my . . . my escort was killed, I escaped. I was trying to cross the borderland on foot when the pallans found me. They hid me, fed and clothed me. They helped me find work at the inn. Even the innkeeper didn't know."

"But Chappie knew?"

The girl half smiled then, her blue eyes wistful. "Yes! How, I don't know. But if he knew, then soon others would begin to guess, too . . . so when he offered to take me away, said that no one would bother an old man and a pallan on the road, I decided to leave. I had nothing to lose."

Dar reflected that she wouldn't have been as safe with the old man as she thought, but said nothing. He still felt astonished as he watched her, thick dark-gold hair, large eyes, narrow waist, and . . . other attributes. He found himself smiling ruefully as she twisted about to pull candle stubs from her pack and lit them, setting them beyond the fire's reach to illuminate the cave. Sharlin, she called herself, and it was a name that told him nothing, not her house, her people, her land, or her gods. It told him only that she wasn't a pallan, and that only because she no longer wore mask, hood, and veil.

He stirred as shadows grew in the candlelight, thinking of what he had seen, or thought he had seen, in the shadows of the burning inn when Sharlin helped him vault up and they fled. A dark, scaled shape standing in the cornerstone of the flames, like a two-legged sala-mander. . . .

His thoughts snapped back to the present when Sharlin took out the map, unwrapping it from the oilskins, and smoothed it out on the dirt between the candles and bent over to read it, eyes frowning at the corners.

"Hey! That belongs to both of us," he said, crawling over.

She looked at him coldly. "You had the privilege of looking at it earlier. Now it's my turn." Her fingertip traced the inking. "This is highly detailed. We're talking about a journey of some length, across the sea to the north." She indicated the waters.

"I know what that is," Dar answered, faintly annoyed because he had but recently fled from the north. He brushed his hand across the drawing, obscuring her view. "This map was the death of the peddler."

"I know that, too . . . now," Sharlin answered. She removed his hand with chapped fingers, roughened by her time of servitude at the borderlands inn. "And it'll be ours, too, if we don't take care."

Words danced in the candlelight, inviting Dar to squint at them, and he did, wondering how it was she knew how to read.

A broken nail tapped the skin. "It says here some of the instructions are written in secret ink, and only a wizard can cipher it."

Dar nodded in agreement, though he was a sentence or two behind her in making sense out of the scrawl. He thought of Nabor and the hazers, and the predawn raid, and shadows . . . and Valorek. "We'll be trailed by the hazers all through the open country . . . no way to shake them. The gray can't carry both of us for long."

Waves of amber hair cascaded as Sharlin nodded agreement. "You're too heavy."

"Not for a man."

She looked up and their eyes met, and for a moment he could have sworn she laughed at him. "Not for a man," Sharlin repeated, and her slightly accented voice was free of mockery.

"Then you're going after the treasure?" Dar said. "I can buy the map after leaving you in a decent city, or escort you where you need to go."

"Where I need to go is somewhere here," the girl asserted and stabbed at the legend. "I'm going with you, or not at all."

"Suppose I say not at all."

The fire hissed as spray from the waterfall misted it slightly. The girl's eyes blazed. "Then I say you're a damn fool." Her dagger flashed in the firelight and sliced the map in two before he could grab it. She held up a piece dangling from her work-worn fingers. She tossed it at him. "Make no mistake about who I am or what I intend to do . . . just as I make no mistake about who and what you probably are. Work with me or forever lose your way to riches and power."

Dar blinked, then tilted his head back and laughed, laughed until he roared at this slip of a girl who bandied words with him, cut up a precious map, and then called him a fool . . . which, in a way, he supposed he was. And she was a fool, too, if she dared to travel with him without knowing the consequences. But what did it matter, since this was obviously a fool's quest?

Sharlin cocked her head as she listened to him laugh, and when he was done, rolled up her portion of the skin and tucked it away down the front of her shirt, before curling up by the fire to rest.

It would be some hours before the gray could carry them out of the borderlands. Dar waited until her eyes closed, then quietly left the shelter of the cave and perched for a few moments on the slick, rocky ledge, peering through the hairlike fall of the river. Then he spotted below on the bank what he had hoped to see— hoofprints. Some of the horses freed from the burning inn had made it this far to the pool below to drink. He chewed on his lower lip, then made his way from the ledge back onto the open hillsides, not daring to hope he might see a familiar red form grazing below on tough grass.

He sucked his breath in as he crept through the brush and weeds. A movement had caught his eye . . . and like patchwork, silken hides of other colors emerged. He parted a branch and thanked Larn, the soldiers' god, for being with him, proclaiming that a man should never walk if he could ride. Brand cropped only a few feet away from him, white teeth neatly clipping at whatever grass shoots he could find. Dried sweat flaked off the chestnut flanks, but the horse looked sound, if tired.

Dar shifted and whistled, gently. The horse flung up his head, ready to bolt, the whites of his eyes showing, and his nostrils flaring at the sound. A shiver ran through his hide.

Dar tugged away a tough fibrous vine from the bush, a parasite that grew in ropy strands, and tore it loose. The horse trotted away a few steps at the noise and stopped as Dar whistled again.

The swordsman emerged from the shrubbery and straightened confidently, vine curled in his fingers. The key to getting the stallion back in hand was not to let him know he was free in the first place. The parasitic vine would do for a rope, though to leave it around Brand's neck would be to invite rash from the irritating sap. Dar lifted his hands so that the horse could see the rope and chirped to him softly. Two ears pricked forward in response, and though the three other horses wheeled and trotted away uneasily, before stopping to watch, Brand merely planted his hooves suspiciously.

The stallion watched Dar cross the clearing and stood quietly as Dar looped the vine over his finely carved head, then snorted and rubbed his muzzle over his master's sleeve, affectionately covering Dar with cold water and horse snot.

Dar led the horse from the clearing and upstream toward the waterfall cave. The horse followed willingly up the cliff face, then stopped, lifted his head, and looked back downstream.

Dar froze in his shadow. Figures moved, some on foot and some on horseback. The hazers! Even though he couldn't see their faces, he recognized the way Nabor carried himself as he paced out tracks at the river's edge, and worse: The witch of the swamps was there too, taking Nabor's hand and sliding down from the back of a jenny. They stood close, talking.

He tugged Brand into motion and ducked him behind the sheet of water before they could be spotted, awakening the girl with the clatter of Brand's hooves. He pinched the chestnut's nostrils before he could whicker a greeting to the other stallion.

"You found a horse!"

"More than that—I also spotted our trackers, and Nabor has the witch of the swamps with him."

"Kory?"

He nodded, and Sharlin got to her feet and rubbed her face wearily.

"We've no choice then. If we're witch-tracked, my sword is of little use . . . and she has a score to settle against me."

"But why . . ." Sharlin's voice trailed off as Dar waved his roll of map under her nose.

"There's a town listed here, Murch's Flats, a trading center, just north of the borderlands. I doubt the population is any more honest, but if it's worth its salt, there'll be at least one wizard practicing there."

She nodded abruptly. "Then we go."

Chapter 3

Dar led his horse out of the cave just before dusk, after the hazers and witch moved away from the water's edge and disappeared into the badlands. Sharlin grabbed his arm.

"What are you doing? Put some distance between them and us . . . and a witch can't track over running water. It will break her power."

He pushed his hair from his forehead and tugged on his half-helm. "I don't think water will affect her much," he answered shortly, remembering the scrying bowl. He had a feeling Kory found much of her power in water. He pulled on the vine loop about Brand's neck as the chestnut rolled his eyes and ducked away from the curtain of water. "You stay here."

"I'd like to know what it is you think you're doing."

His gaze flickered to her, taking in the dusty dark-blue trousers and full-sleeved blouse, the well-made boots, the veil and hood she had tucked into her belt, the full purse looped to her belt, the fall of amber hair over her shoulders, and lastly, the indignant blue eyes that sparked even in the shadows of the cave. "You're a mouthy one for a servant girl," he said, then swung aboard Brand's frame. "I don't intend to ride for a day, let alone longer, without saddle and harness. You stay here, while I scavenge something up."

"Not back to the inn—!"

He shook his head and kicked Brand into a lope, away

from the cliff and the waterfall. Sharlin's last words were drowned in the roar of the river. She put her hands on her hips, then turned and disappeared in disgust.

The chestnut swung out in his easy, single-foot gait that ate up the ground as if it weren't there, but today, every hoofbeat was a jolt he felt from his privates clear up to his jawbone. No, there was no way he was going to ride without a saddle, and though the horse was responsive to the pressure of his knees and the slight confinement of the loop about its neck, the parasitic vine already had torn patches of hair from Brand's silken hide, leaving ugly welts behind, though Dar's gloves protected him from the sap.

Pulling Brand to a stop, Dar straightened and looked out over the landscape at the faintly shadowed brush growing purple in the dusk. A puff of dust caught his eye.

Just as he figured, the hazers had left one man behind, trailing them, but far behind, as if they were herding gunters and looking for strays. He and Sharlin were the "strays." He clucked to his horse, pulled his sword free, and went after the hazer. The hazer was about to have an accident, common in the badlands.

With a chirp and a nudge of his knees, he turned Brand into a wash that would intersect the hazer's pathway, urging the chestnut into the sandy riverbed. A smoke tree wrestled up from the dryness, its white-and-black limbs twisting high above the wash, until it reached out over the banks and higher. It was perfect for what Dar had in mind, with its springy branches, lush with grayish-green leaves that fluttered in the wind like coins.

Dar left the stallion hobbled and muzzled in a copse just short of the smoke tree, then shinnied up the trunk with the vine rope in hand. One branch hung right over the trail. He pulled it back taut with the rope, and then sat, sword in hand, waiting for the hazer to ride by.

Nabor's man never knew what hit him. He twisted in the saddle, overlooking the wash and the surroundings, his ferret eyes squinting, and his mouth opening in a little round O as the thunk of Dar's sword hit home, chopping the vine in two, releasing the tied-back limb. The branch whistled through the air, knocking the man clean out of the saddle and over the horse's crop before he could blink. He hit the ground hard and lay still, wind and consciousness knocked out of him. Dar jumped from the tree branch and brought the hazer's mount to a plunging halt. He stripped the beast quickly, cleaning the foam-covered bit on his sleeve for Brand's sake, and clucked when he saw saddle sores on the horse's flank. He had little patience for a man who ill used a beast; he spat on the still form as he passed him, heading for where Brand waited in the brush.

Dar braced himself at the wash's edges, shrugged to ease his load of saddle and harness, then bent his knees and let the collapsing sand and dirt slide him to the riverbed. He coughed as the cloud of dust choked him momentarily, and his eyes watered. A rein end trailed free, wrapped itself about his ankle, and caught him up. He fell with a grunt to the ground and let out a yelp as the saddle horn gutted him.

It saved his life.

A dark, scaled arm, taloned and vicious, cut the air above his head just where his throat had been. Dar felt the body heat and smelled the tart musk as he rolled and drew his sword, and smoldering red eyes glared at him. He rolled to one knee, his leg braced to bring him to his feet, and faced the demon who danced in the blue-shadowed side of the wash. His mouth went dry.

The beast had no weapon—needed none, with the twelve curved talons on his two hands, and spurs the size of Dar's fist adorning his hocks. The creature grinned, baring fangs as big as a falroth's, and he chuckled, an odd sound issuing from the broad barrel chest.

"I have you, Aarondar."

Dar pushed himself to his feet, flexed his knees and his left wrist. The silver stiletto in the wrist sheath was still there; its rigidity answered his movement. He swallowed as the red-hot bruise from his fall spread like a blossoming flower from his stomach throughout his body. "Maybe. Maybe not. I thought your master wanted me alive."

The demon shrugged. Ear flaps spread open, hooding the sides of his brutish head. "He does. Perhaps we have an accident, you and I. Like the happening at the witch's cave. You nearly beheaded me. Sometimes I think more of myself than I do my master." At the last word, the demon spat in the wash, indicating what he thought of Valorek.

Red heat tinged the black scales of the demon's body. He steamed as he stood there, and the sands heated under the clawed pads of his feet. He stretched his talons. "Come, boy, to Mnak now, while you still pound with hot blood, and your spirit is strong. I will wear you down. Let me devour you now, while you are still a man. Do not make me wait until you are but an impotent shadow."

Brand neighed then, a shrill sound of fear. Dar clenched his sword tighter, and a small animal burst out of the copse, its ears flattened to its skull, large feet propelling it in hopping leaps past the man and the demon.

Blood, thought Dar, and he swung his sword in a chop at the softfoot. It severed the head from the furred body neatly, and the creature fell in two pieces at their feet, large paws still twitching in its flight.

Mnak groaned and went to his knees as crimson juices splattered the sand and the fur and his own scaled form. Dar turned and ran as the demon knelt to lap up the blood he could not resist, for his own power was exhausted from the long trailing to catch up with Dar . . . else he would never have ignored Valorek's wishes and tried to kill Dar instead of capturing him.

Brand tossed his head and shuddered as Dar threw on the saddle and bridle, tightened the girth, and hurled himself into the saddle. He kicked the horse out of the wash in a cloud of grit and dirt as Mnak roared his frustration. Dar took the long way back, crossing running water three times, just to be safe.

He returned to the waterfall with full waterbags, a saddle lined with a woolie skin for extra comfort, and a bridle with feathers laced into the headband that Brand had snorted at suspiciously before he took the bit and let Dar ease the headstall over his ears. Sharlin was saddling up her gray stallion in the dark, pulling viciously at the girth until the horse let out a tired groan and shifted weight. She wore the pallan hood over her hair again, but the veil hung softly by the line of her set jaw.

She said nothing as Dar rode up, but took up her reins and swung aboard with a strange hopping motion, first planting her boot toe in the stirrup, then swinging her leg over. She watched as Dar unsheathed his sword, cleansed it in the spray of the waterfall, and took an oil rag to it, wiping down the metal with a caressing motion.

She turned at the sight of the blood on the blade and choked, "Did you have to kill him for a *saddle?*"

He frowned. "I didn't kill him."

"By the gods, that's worse, then . . . wounded and left behind."

Dar's mouth opened and closed in silent frustration for a second, as he had no intention of telling her what he really had left behind them. Then he forced out, "Let's at least show some pleasure for the return of my half of the map."

She stabbed a finger at him in answer. "That was a stupid thing to do. Now Nabor and the others will know we were behind them, instead of ahead of them—and for what? So you could sit comfortably for a day or two! We could have bought what we needed when we reach Murch's Flats and look for the wizard, but no—you had to alert the whole countryside. And as for the map, I had a good enough look at it. It might interest you to know that I have the half pertaining to the last of the trip. Even a thick-headed swordsman would understand that I have the portion showing the end of the trail!"

With that, she kicked the gray, hard, and reined past him, while Dar sat his chestnut, and an odd expression broke over his face, somewhat akin to a smile. He wheeled Brand and set him after the gray, but not without a look over the back of his shoulder. Nothing stood in the darkness, but the back of his neck prickled. He shouted after Sharlin's disappearing back, "Maybe you'd like to answer the questions that would've been asked if I had ridden in bareback!"

A whipping branch hissed through the air and cut off any further argument as he ducked low over Brand's neck.

The Shield hung low in the sky, a silvery beacon that told Dar exactly where he was going. He placed it at his right elbow and steered Brand through the lowlands, passing by Sharlin, who seemed confused in the dark and kept looking at the Shield as though it were a ghost. As he rode past, she shot him a look he couldn't fathom, her lips pressed together thinly. She reached up and fastened the pallan veil in place as though to keep him from reading her further, then Brand surged past the tired gray and Dar turned his attention to the terrain, always treacherous in the dark.

When the Shield weakened and let Little Warrior pass it, Dar circled Brand and blocked the gray from passing.

"We've ridden far enough. You can be sure the hazers are camped, and their extra man won't be discovered on foot until midmorning, if then."

The girl slid down without a word, cared for her horse, hobbled him, and then lay down to sleep on an evergreen bough that curled upon the ground. Dar hobbled Brand, then stood for a moment, watching her sleep on the bruised pine needles that wafted a gentle fragrance into the night air.

He lay his bared sword between them, hilt close at hand, and rested his head upon the woolie pelt of his newly acquired saddle.

She didn't remove the veil for the next two days, saying little except occasionally to ask for a rest stop, until they rode to the bluffs and halted, looking down at the river flats, and a booming wood-shack town that must be Murch's Flats.

Her remark gusted the veil out. "The pits of humanity."

Dar smiled and urged Brand down the bluff and onto

the main road. "Not quite. This looks to be a trade center . . . and the hazers can't openly attack us once within the gates, without themselves becoming targets for thieves. And once we have our wizard, a good spell or two, and the witch should be confused enough to lose us entirely—unless you enjoy the idea of riding the rest of the way looking back over your shoulder." And a gold piece and a quiet word aside should take care of the problem of Mnak as well . . . at least for a while.

"The way you do? Not hardly!" Sharlin flicked her reins against the gray's neck and sent him plunging down the soft ground on Brand's heels.

Dar ignored her remark and headed down the main road, which was rutted deep and caked over with a dry crust of mud that would turn to slop with the next brief rain. He took a deep breath. The heavy smell of smoke and dung hung in the air, but there was another smell, too, that of freshly plowed fields along the side of the road where farmers bent their backs readying for the short crop season ahead. The newly turned earth smelled deep and rich. He could smell the green grass shoots torn up by the plow and almost hear the plunk of seeds being dropped into the furrows and then stamped firmly into the earth.

Empty carts rattled past them from the city gates, farmers hunched onto their butts, pipes gripped between their teeth or maybe a free hand filled with a mug of ale, as they clucked to their shaggy horses and sent them home. They looked once at Dar, and their gazes flicked away. Nothing remarkable in a mercenary and his pallan on the road, and Dar was satisfied. He would be worried only if they saw more, instead of less.

He twisted toward Sharlin. "As far as anyone here is concerned, you're my pallan. Address me as you would a master."

"But—" She choked down a second word. The hood nodded once, brusquely.

At the city gates, a great bear of a man with a purple scar along the back of his right fist stopped them.

"What do you do here at Murch's Flats?"

"I'm a free trader, man, and I'm here seeking a new line to work, or a gentleman to stake me and buy new traps. The floods got my line, and it's been rough going since."

The guard's heavy-lidded eyes closed once, tightly, then opened. The flat black eyes stared unwinkingly, and the man said, "Th' floods were bad, right enough. Do much trapping with a sword like that?"

Dar laughed. "What do you think I am, man? This is the badlands . . . I'd lief cut off my leg as leave my sword. What would you do if a falroth came after you? Tap him on the head and say, 'Pardon me, but I'm a trapper and can't use a sword'?" He made as if to knee Brand past the guard, but the man's beefy hand wrapped itself around the toe of Dar's boot.

"You can enter, right enough," the guard said. "But I have to report your entrance to Trader Joe. He's the boss of this town, and no one comes or goes without his knowing why."

Dar saw a flicker in the guard's lidded eyes and leaned down to say equally quietly, "My visit is one that requires discretion. I'm a lowly free trader, too unimportant to disturb the likes of the boss man about." He fetched out a half-crown piece from inside his tunic and pressed it into the guard's hand. "Forget you saw us."

The guard grunted and let go of his boot. Dar straightened and kicked Brand through the gate. The guard called out, "But dismount. No riders allowed on the street."

With a shrug, Dar motioned for Sharlin to get down, and he did the same. They led their horses through the gates.

Murch's Flats sprawled before them, wide, dusty streets, filled with citizenry, and Dar paused to search the pathways, looking for familiar colored banners to let him know which lane he wanted.

He pointed out Treefrog Lane to Sharlin. "Merchants, kava houses, and a few temples. Looks promising enough."

She stayed frozen to the ground as he moved forward, her eyes wide above the veil. He mentally cursed the absence of a pallan mask, which would hide her much more effectively. He unlaced his saddlebags and threw them at her. "Here, pallan. Carry these and keep an eye on your own goods while I find a stabler."

Sharlin coughed as though choking back an angry retort. The veil fluttered, but she threw the heavy bags over her shoulder, ducked her head, and followed in his footsteps.

Gnats buzzed about fruit stands as Dar paced the street, steering wide of a garbage dump that drew loud black flies and squirmed with white maggots. Sharlin made a gargling sound at the back of her throat, and he turned on his boot heel to see her face pale as she gagged a second time. He raised an eyebrow, and she ducked her chin, refusing to look at him, and strode purposefully by the heap, leading her mincing gray stallion past.

"Freeman! How about a new cloak to protect you from winter's breath? I see your horse is blanketed with the comfort of a woolie hide . . . why not do for yourself what you do for your animal?" a merchant called, leaning comfortably out of his shop on a window shutter that served also as a counter. Dar shook his head with a laugh, pleased that the man had sized him up as a potential customer. Not a word was shouted at his pallan, who stumbled miserably along after him.

His feeling of cheer diminished somewhat when he got a look at the weapons of the other citizenry bustling the streets. Long knives, wicked swords with double tangs, sharp, gleaming . . . while his darkening blade held nicks and the leather-wrapped handle was worn and sweat-stained. He turned sharply when he spotted a long-striding man with a weapon cradled on his hip that he had only seen a few times in his life—a stinger, a small bolt-shooting weapon, the darts usually tipped with drugs or poison. No law-abiding lord allowed stingers in his domain, yet from what Dar had seen of Murch's Flats, anything went, as long as Trader Joe knew about it.

He stopped Sharlin abruptly in her tracks. "You said you had enough gold to buy a saddle."

"Yes, but the wizard . . ."

"The wizard can wait. And if he goes with us, he'll take the same chances we do as far as a share goes. I need my sword sharpened, and can use some other tools . . . a hand ax, and something I saw earlier that may take a hefty bribe to buy."

Her eyes narrowed. "What's that?"

"It's called a stinger. It shoots bolts at close range, and it's deadly accurate. If Nabor or any of his men can get one here, I want to have the same advantage."

Her gaze flickered from his set jaw to his belt. "What about breaking into your own purse?"

The pouch she eyed he palmed quickly, to ensure himself that the ashes were still there, and he shook his head. "I paid a half-crown to get us in this city without the local boss knowing. I'm going to be tapped out quickly at that rate."

She sighed. "All right."

"Good. Then our first business is to find a forge and a weapons dealer."

A rumbling voice from about thigh level broke in between them. "Then, bucko, you should follow me to the part o' town that'll serve ye best."

The two of them looked down in surprise to see a bald-headed, long-bearded, gnarled man grinning up at them. He hooked his thumbs in his wide belt.

"Toothpick at yer service," he said, in the basso profundo tones of a mountain dwarf. He plucked at Dar's knee. "If it's a forge ye want, and the likes of a stinger, you follow me."

And he burst from between the two of them, his crooked legs churning, as he shifted his way through the crowded street. Dar looked at Sharlin, shrugged, and they followed the being's lead, while Dar tried to keep track of the twists and turns, for he didn't trust dwarves very much and wasn't sure if the man had overheard talk about their need for a wizard.

Angling through Murch's Flats after the dwarf took fleet footwork, and when the dwarf paused triumphantly at the corner of a lane and waved them on, Sharlin caught up with Dar, puffing, straining under the weight of the saddlebags.

"I'm not sure I like this," she gasped.

"Nor I." Dar looked around. "With the exception of the lack of banners, this street looks like many others." He shrugged. "We followed him this far; we may as well follow him on in."

The lane ahead was shadowed and narrow and winding, and no merchants leaned comfortably from their stalls. A cold feeling prickled between Dar's shoulder blades. It was a feeling he didn't want to have, but he hiked up his belt, palmed his sword guard, and smiled at Toothpick as he caught up with the dwarf.

"So where is it you've brought us?"

The dwarf jumped up, snarling, "To the end of the line, bucko," reached out and tweaked the pouch from Dar's belt with the flash of a dagger, and then was churning dust before he even hit the street again, running.

"Dar!" Sharlin cried hoarsely as Dar cursed, "God blast him," and took off after the gnarled being.

Toothpick knew the area well, but he hadn't counted on Dar's ability to keep track of his surroundings, for when he turned a corner, the swordsman knew instinctively how to cut him off. He swerved sharply to his right, Brand clopping after him, and then the alleyway echoed with Sharlin's light bootsteps. No one else paid attention to the chase except for one merchant who put out a booted foot in Toothpick's way. The dwarf went sprawling.

Dar gasped, "Thank you, freeman!" and jumped on the gnarled man. The merchant smiled thinly and walked on without a word. Sharlin puffed up, still carrying the saddlebags and this time holding the reins of both horses.

Her eyes widened at the sight of the two rolling on the ground, the pouch grasped in all four hands as Toothpick grunted and tore to keep his booty. The drawstring snapped open and the dwarf fell back onto the ground, the pouch spilled out over his homespuns.

Gray ashes everywhere. Toothpick blinked and coughed as Dar shouted, "Don't move a muscle!" His wrist stiletto flashed into sight and touched the dwarf's throat under the wagging beard, and the little man lay still. The swordsman carefully scraped the ash off the dwarf and tucked it back into the pouch.

The beard wagged as the dwarf burst out laughing until his snappy black eyes turned red-rimmed, and his lips flapped soundlessly when he ran out of wind. Then he sucked air back in and gasped, "So I says to meself, it's now or nivver, and look what I pinched—a bag full of ashes!"

Dar's hand trembled as he pulled the drawstring taut and returned the pouch to its rightful place at his belt. Sharlin bent to help the dwarf to his feet, and the swordsman's hand shot out, fingers curling about the gnarled man's shoulder in a white-knuckled grip. "You'll take me to a forge, and when my business is done there, I want a witch or a wizard—the most powerful one in Murch's Flats—and you'll march along with me step by step, because I think I may have you turned into a toad while I'm there!"

Sharlin's gasp was shadowed by Toothpick's grunt of wonderment. He twisted in Dar's grip until his dark eyes met Dar's.

"A wizard, is it, bucko?" the gnarled man said in undaunted triumph. "Then ye'd best come with me first, for my master is a wizard."

"Not any wizard," Dar husked. "We want someone without the taint of dragonmagic."

Toothpick sucked in his breath sharply. "Ahhhh . . . so that be the way o' it. Well, my man fits that requirement."

"Dar," Sharlin said under her breath, for the scene was beginning to draw some curious onlookers, and the horses stamped restlessly. "Let's try the wizard first."

"Good thinking," Toothpick answered, as Dar loosed him, and he shook off the fist. He flexed his shoulder, winked, and took off down the street, with the others following hastily.

The short troublemaker led them to a stable at the far edge of the town, steeped in purple shadows though it was noonday, and the pungent smell of the establishment rode the street heavily. Sharlin coughed and ducked her face, her eyes tearing at the stink, which Toothpick seemed not to notice. He beckoned to the stable.

"Ye can leave your mounts here, for I works for the stablemaster. A penny a day fer the two of them."

"Fair enough," Dar answered. He took the reins from Sharlin's cold hands, and as their fingers touched briefly, he looked into her startled blue eyes and read something unfathomable there. He moved away uneasily to turn the horses into a common box stall. Both the chestnut and the gray snorted and moved to the mangers.

Toothpick perched on the railing of a rickety outside staircase, boards warped and cracked by weather. Sharlin mounted the first step and looked back at Dar. Her gaze flickered to his pouch, and he saw an unasked question pass over her face and fade away, and for that he was grateful. He took her elbow, and they followed the dwarf up the staircase, all of them swatting at flies that bit viciously.

He said quietly, "Not much of a wizard to be found here," and Sharlin nodded in silent agreement, for the abode could not have been in a worse part of the town. Either the man had little power or he was in bad graces with the boss, Trader Joe. He withheld further judgment as the dwarf knocked, and then swung open a creaky door.

Inside the weathered second-story room, the air bloomed like a spring field after a new rain. Dar straightened unconsciously and took a deep breath, and beside him, Sharlin sighed gratefully. As the door shut behind him, he became aware of the many candles and lamps that lent a golden sunlight to the room, and he reassessed the magic-worker, for he had taken a stinking dungheap of a building and turned it into near paradise.

As though reading their thoughts, a man arose deliberately from his chair and table as Toothpick tugged on his robe and bragged, "Paying customers, master. Or at least I wager one of them carries gold—t'other carries ashes!"

The wizard nodded. "I'm Thurgood, freeman." The sleeves pulled away from his wrists as he limped forward and stretched out his right hand in greeting.

Dar took the shake suspiciously, for the hand was gentle and mild, and he frowned as he watched the wizard turn toward Sharlin, and then he cursed himself. The wizard's face was smooth and unlined, but it pulled in the corner of his right eye, and his mouth drooped slightly on that side despite the smile, and the lame leg, though hidden by wizard's robes, was also on the right side. He looked at the ash-blond hair shot with much gray, though it was neatly cut and groomed, and the beard and mustache newly trimmed, and he let out a slight groan. He'd seen this before, and knew the man's heart had gone bad . . . leaving him with muscle weakness and paralysis on the right side. Thurgood, no matter how enchanting a wizard, could never make the trip to the land of legend they sought.

Sharlin and Thurgood both heard the sound of dismay escape him and turned with inquiring faces. He licked his lips and shook his head.

"I'm sorry, Master Thurgood. The business that brought us here will have to be transacted elsewhere."

"Dar—" said Sharlin in a hard voice, but he overrode her protest.

"We have a long way to travel, and cannot take an invalid."

The wizard's face tightened, and the smoky gray eyes flared a moment, but he nodded abruptly as their gazes met. "Be that as it will," Thurgood said in a mild but resigned tone. "Luck be with you, fair lady," he murmured to Sharlin, as though his eyes pierced the pallan veil easily.

Dar turned on his heel to leave, but Sharlin threw the saddlebags down with a resounding thump. The two of them glared at each other, though she barely chinned his shoulder, and neither of them noticed Toothpick's dive to the floor, where he pinched something up quickly and tucked it away in his breeches. The swordsman said quietly, "I'll not carry a man to his death," as Sharlin sputtered, "My choice! I have a say in this, too, remember," and came to a halt as she heard Dar's words.

She looked at the wizard, and he inclined his head. "It's true," the man said softly. "Not my death, but my infirmity. If you will not give me time to prove myself, then you must go, for trust is all."

Dar picked up the saddlebags, slung them over his shoulder, grabbed Sharlin's elbow, and steered her outside the room. As the door slammed behind them, the stupefying stink of the dunghill inundated them.

Later that day, after the sword had been sharpened and unsuccessful inquiries regarding stingers had been made, and a witch or two recommended, though they did little but make love potions, Sharlin rubbed her forehead wearily, smearing a mark on her forehead.

She halted in the middle of the street. "I'm not going a step farther without lunch and a cold mug. You can walk Murch's Flats until you drop, or something guts you, but I'm eating . . ." She paused dramatically as she looked up and down the street. She pointed. "There."

Dar hesitated, though his shoulders ached, and one heel felt as though stone-bruised, and his stomach rumbled. "All right then," he answered. "Since you're buying."

"Me?"

He shrugged. "It's your idea."

"Oh, all right." She stumbled toward the inn, her veil fluttering as she mumbled something additional under her breath that he did not quite catch.

She came to a stop just inside the shadowed arch, for at a table, looking as though they had been waiting for the two of them, sat the wizard and his dwarf valet.

Thurgood smiled and held up his hand. "Come and sit—you look a little street-weary, and the ale is refreshing. And . . ." His weakened hand slid a triangular object across the table, where it glimmered in a slanting ray of light from the ill-thatched roof. "We have something to talk about."

The dragon scale lay gleaming on the wooden table.

Dar strode forward and sat on the bench, and quickly tucked the scale into his pack. "Where did you get this?"

The dwarf perched on the tabletop, swinging his bandy legs, cleaning his teeth with a silver dagger. "Ye left it behind this morning."

Sharlin seated herself with a weary sigh. "What do you want of us?"

Thurgood shook his head, answering, "It's not what we want of you, but what you wanted of us." The bags under his mild eyes wrinkled as he smiled. "I think I can be of very great service to you, if we can learn each other's secrets, for the moment."

Dar snickered, thinking of Valorek and the demon Mnak—how would the wizard like knowing about *them*? He reached for a clay jug and wrinkled his nose. "What is this?"

Toothpick had taken a draught and wiped off a mustache with his sleeve. He burped delicately and said, "Yorth. Fermented woolie milk."

The swordsman pushed the jug away quickly. "I'll have ale, and meat pie, if they have any."

"They do." Thurgood signaled the tavern boy and repeated the order. He folded his hands and remarked, "Toothpick tells me you have people watching your moves in Murch's Flats as well."

"Oh?" Dar quirked an eyebrow. "Hazers?"

"Yes."

"That's to be expected. If we share secrets, I also expect you'll learn why." The swordsman visibly relaxed, stretching his arms out on the table.

Sharlin took down a side of her veil and smiled at the wizard. "He already knows some of mine." She leaned aside to let the tavern boy serve two mugs of ale and two meat pies, though their steaming aroma made her lips moisten. Dar reached for his lunch with a snort as she held out her hand to the wizard.

Thurgood placed a finger alongside his nose and looked at her wisely. "Not all secrets are that difficult to find." He lowered his hand and took hers gently, stroking the skin. "This wearing is new, and with the proper applications of lotions, your hands will once again be free of the drudgeries you undertook."

The clatter of Dar's mug to the tabletop interrupted the wizard, but he took little notice. Sharlin blushed faintly and returned his intent gaze.

"There are tiny calluses here from handling reins and weapons, and perhaps a thimble, as befits a lord's daughter, but you're no serving wench . . . princess."

Sharlin gaped in surprise at Dar, who lurched to his feet, face graying, as he turned toward the two of them. Then she stammered in confusion, "Why, but . . . no, I won't lie this time. You're right, wizard, and—Dar, you don't have to kneel to me!" This last as Dar crashed to his knees and looked at them, his expression one of stricken agony.

Thurgood jumped to his feet, knocking the wooden bench over, and shouted, "Fire the place, Toothpick!"

The dwarf swept his arm across the table, spreading lamp oil over all, and dropped a lit firestick into the puddle, setting off a curtain of smoke and blue flame. Thurgood put his shoulder under Dar's limp arm and got him to his feet.

Sharlin stood in confusion, still stammering, "B-b-but, Dar—"

She stopped as the wizard snapped, "Bring the skin of yorth, but forget the ale!"

The three of them dragged Dar outside, choking and eyes stinging from the flames, the swordsman slack in their arms. Outside, Sharlin watched as Thurgood lowered the man to his knees once more and poured the yorth freely down Dar's throat. Dar gargled and turned faintly blue about the folds of his nose.

"What is it?"

"Poison, most likely, but he's a strong one," Toothpick said, and spat to one side. "Enough yorth, and he'll be bringin' the potion back up. Stand to one side, yer ladyship, or he'll be barfin' on yer boots."

Sharlin stepped back hurriedly, and not a moment too soon, as Dar strangled and then retched, a horrible sound. His throat and mouth filled with bile and yorth, and he vomited into the alleyway. Thurgood looked at the mixture intently before kicking dirt over it, as Sharlin gagged in sympathy and stood pressing her hands to her mouth.

Thurgood pried open Dar's lips and emptied the last of the yorth down his gullet. The swordsman's lips turned from blue to white, and he gargled again, his stomach heaving. Then, with a nod of satisfaction, Thurgood hauled Aarondar to his feet and shouldered him.

"Take the other side, princess, for I can't bear his weight alone," the wizard ordered.

With a wrinkle of her nose, Sharlin took the other side, for Dar stank of soured yorth, if there could be such a thing, and the two of them pulled him out of the alley, boot tips dragging in the dust. After a moment, he coughed, and the pink came back to his face. Thurgood slowed as the swordsman gained his feet and coughed until his face glistened bright red.

Dar said feebly, "I . . . can't . . . stand . . . yorth."

"Be that as it may, it saved your life this time."

"Bad ale?"

"The worst," chimed in Toothpick as he hurried after them. "'Twas poisoned, young master."

Bells clanged and the street filled with shouts as the fire alarm was sent out. Dar, staggering away between the wizard and the princess, thought of another inn burning, and he looked back, thinking to see something impervious to flame watching him, but nothing was there in the ripple of hot air and orange flame except figures running back and forth to the well with pails of water.

They dragged him down the street, turned the corner with Dar stumbling between them, and hauled him up the outside stairs to Thurgood's stable loft, and he noticed in surprise that they had evidently been walking in circles all afternoon, for all the ground that they had covered. A compulsion spell, perhaps, to bring them back to the wizard? He gulped as the pungent odor overwhelmed him, and he leaned over the stair railing to retch yet again. Toothpick grabbed him by the belt or he would have pitched over and landed head first.

Thurgood's face swam into focus again, and Dar blinked as a cooling cloth moistened his face. The wizard nodded in satisfaction and said, "There now. It's just a matter of your own constitution, young man . . . and lucky I was there."

Dar burped faintly, and Sharlin giggled, her pallan hood removed from her fair hair, and leaned over him.

"I'd say the wizard has plenty of skills we could use," she remarked, her eyes twinkling at his discomfort.

He raised his hand. It shook, and he sat amazed at his own weakness. He protested, "It's not that . . . princess. Ah . . . our needs will take us on a long and difficult journey . . . and Thurgood here—"

"—is capable of anything he sets his mind to," the wizard interrupted.

"Oh yeah?" Dar answered, looking sharply at the man. He was recovering his faculties more completely by the second. "How do you feel about handling a—"

His response was shattered by a heavy thump on the roof above them. Wood splintered with a howl and a growl as ebony talons ripped through the lumber like kindling, and Sharlin screamed.

With a guttural laugh, Mnak jumped through the gaping hole as Dar finished weakly, "—a demon?"

Chapter 4

Toothpick jumped the study table with a warcry as he pulled his silver dagger and a wicked longknife appeared magically out of his boot top. "Git behind me, princess," he called, waving her out of the demon's path. The tart, musky odor of the beast pervaded the room, breaking down all the wards set, and as the scent from the stables downstairs flooded in, Dar's eyes watered.

Thurgood staggered back in astonishment, his arms flung wide, robe sleeves rolling down thin white arms as he stood face to face with Mnak. Both demon and wizard hesitated.

Dar took advantage of the halt to roll off the crude straw bunk and grab his weapons belt, hands trembling as he fought to get the sword out of the twisted leather sheath.

"The devil you say," Thurgood murmured. "There's more to you than I thought, lad," he added, as he and the demon circled each other warily.

Mnak said nothing, but his coal-red eyes glittered and his talons clicked against one another as he flexed them. The heat of his body rolled off like steam in the dusk of the room; even the candle stubs flickered and threatened to gutter out. Fangs glistened as he grimaced an unfriendly smile.

"Do it, boss," the dwarf urged, Sharlin cowering behind him, her face drained of color even as she pulled her own dagger and readied it.

"No," said Thurgood.

"Do what?" asked Dar, who was trying to get behind Mnak, but the demon snarled loudly and fenced him off. The best he could aim for was a good flank shot, and then hope he could get out of the way before his sword melted and left him completely defenseless.

"Kill th' beast," Toothpick growled.

A tremor went through Mnak's frame, but not one of fear. The beast straightened, muscles rippling across his back in triumph.

Thurgood smiled, lopsidedly of necessity, as he could not lift the right corner of his mouth. He fingered the pouch at his side and flung a puff of white powder into the air, drifting over Mnak. "But I can send him back. Demon, thy master summons thee!"

Boom! A thunderclap shook the wooden frame building to its very foundation, and horses down below whickered and shifted in fear, as the demon disappeared from sight.

Dar lowered his sword. "Where did he go?"

Thurgood looked at him and quirked his eyebrow. "Well, now, lad . . . that's the bad news. The beast was returned to whoever sent him after you, and he will be back, though we have some time. I think perhaps you and I had better talk. Hazers I am prepared to deal with, but demons are another matter."

Dar let his sword tip dig into the wooden floor. He watched as the timber splintered and gave way. Back to Valorek! After all of the ground he had put between the sorcerer king and himself since the last meeting with one of Valorek's minions. And now Valorek would know exactly where, and with whom, he had been. He considered the waiting wizard as Sharlin helped Toothpick to right the furniture.

Thurgood didn't yet know who the demon's master was. He had used no names making the spell . . . probably one of the reasons he couldn't hope to kill the demon was not knowing its name, and whatever it was, Dar was sure it wasn't really Mnak. No beast would give away its soul that easily. He would tell Thurgood enough, but not all.

The wizard's gaze flickered then and dropped away, and Dar was certain that Thurgood guessed he would not tell him everything. "As you wish, master wizard," he said.

"Good. We have work to do. Toothpick, get up and reshingle that—we may have another night or two under this roof, and I don't want any leaks. I'll set the wards back up—" this as Sharlin coughed faintly and sniffled— "and then we'll discuss the journey you two have in mind."

Day had gone to dusk by the time the dwarf finished his task and the wizard his, and they sent the bandy-legged man out for smoked ribs and piping hot tubers and folded fruit pies. They sat about the table wiping their sticky hands clean with a great deal of satisfaction after eating. Thurgood tapped the tabletop.

"Give that scale here."

Dar hesitated but a second before handing it over.

The gold flakes and emerald light danced in the room's illumination. Thurgood sucked on a tooth, worrying a string of meat, but his attention was all on the scale.

He looked up at last, forgetting the tooth, and his mouth tightened. "This is from a dragon . . . the underbelly, unless I'm much mistaken. The emerald will do you some good—it is smallish, but you should be able to pry it out and use it for trade. What are you doing with this?"

"It was given to us," Sharlin said eagerly. "By a peddler."

"The same man who was killed by the hazers following us."

"I see. And what else did he give you?"

"This." Sharlin pushed her half of the map over the tabletop, and Dar followed suit.

Thurgood stared at the illustrated hide as though afraid to touch it. Then, with blue-veined hands that shook a little, he pushed back the sleeves on his robe and rolled them into place before reaching out for the map and matching its edges.

Dar stared at the wicked scar on the underside of the

wizard's right arm—a jagged white line stretching from the wrist almost all the way to the man's armpit. Even the needle holes from the instrument used to stitch it together were harsh dots of white skin. Studying the old wound, he realized the man must have stitched it together himself, even while he sat bleeding on the ground.

He wrenched his attention away and his gaze met Sharlin's, and he knew that she had seen the same thing, for her lips were drawn, the color gone faintly pink. He grinned for her benefit.

"It's good to know we have a fighter in our midst."

"What? Oh," Thurgood said. He pushed the sleeve down a little, hiding the worst of the scar. "I hope I didn't offend you, princess."

She blushed then and ducked her head away. "Bravery never offends me," she said softly in return, then tucked a lock of hair behind her ear and turned her attention back to the map.

"What do we have here?" the wizard demanded, his abstraction deepening into an imperious tone. "Just what are we talking about?"

"This map leads to the place where dragons go to die," the swordsman answered as he leaned forward on his elbows.

"Gods don't die."

"Dragons are no gods."

"Say you," Toothpick put in. He had been using his dagger to advantage on his blunt white dwarf's teeth, and he wiped it now on the knee of his trousers and secured it in a wrist sheath.

The man ignored his valet and shot back at Dar, "And you think this scale is proof of that?"

"I think no such thing. I know only that everything has its time, of birth and death and rebirth, and if a dragon can be killed, it's no god. I've never spoken to a god, though I've prayed to one. Gods are like the wind—everywhere is touched, even the edges of the great seas, but never are they seen. Never captured. Never pierced."

Sharlin looked at him in surprise. She closed her open

mouth hastily, then added, "I don't believe in dragon-gods, either. And neither do you, for Toothpick told us you were the man we were looking for."

Thurgood rocked back. The candlelight made his ash-blond hair and beard even more golden, and his bagged eyes more shadowed in his mild face. "He is right—I don't believe in dragongods. This peddler, did he tell you anything else? How far? Did he see dragons, or was this just a tale told to him?"

"He said he saw the dragons fall from the skies," Dar answered, "trumpeting in anger and spite as they plunged to their deaths. And he saw hoards of treasure among their rotting bones. Think of it . . . think of the jewels and gold and silver and more they have collected for generations until their time comes to die, and they go to that place!"

"Even shares," grunted Toothpick. "We're layin' our lives on th' line."

Sharlin looked at him. "If the wizard goes with us, all right—three ways even."

"Four."

She blinked, then smiled at the bald-headed dwarf whose pate gleamed in the candlelight. "All right."

Thurgood thrust the map toward Dar and Sharlin, one half in each hand. "Then we have goods to buy and weapons, and plans to make regarding the hazers, for the hazers must guess that you have what they wanted from the peddler. We must make ready, if we intend to go after dragons. They will have the place guarded with all their cunning and might and sorcery. There will be traps, perhaps, and riddles, and illusions. I'll do what I can to prepare for that . . . and if we're all wrong, we go to defy the gods themselves."

Toothpick swaggered up to Dar and tugged on his vest. "I've found th' stingers for ye. Keep yer mouth shut and yer eyes open and follow me."

The swordsman turned, but the dwarf was gone in a puff of dust, and with a faint curse, for he had been bartering, successfully, for a fine cloak for Sharlin, he took to his heels to catch up with the gnarled man. He caught him at the corner of Blue Flame and Bent Twig lanes, the crowd brushing around Toothpick as though he weren't there.

Dar had been in Murch's Flats only three days, but had come to despise the place. Pallans and dwarves were treated worse than stray dogs here, which was not saying much, for roast dog was a delicacy on many of the barbecue spits. He caught up with the dwarf, for only his own size and looks could afford Toothpick some protection.

The dwarf rumbled, "Three alleys forward and then take a sharp right into th' next one, and yer seller will meet you there."

Dar nodded and walked through the crowded street, Toothpick hobbling next to him. If anything could be said about the citizens of Murch's Flats, it was that they had a fine sense of what they could sell—which was just about anything. Three times he'd been offered mercenary jobs, one lady wanted to buy him to decorate her bower for the night, and he'd had to bribe two additional town guards to dispel their interest in his business in Murch's Flats. He had a feeling Trader Joe even had a percentage of bribes and that if he appeared to be reasonably harmless, the boss wouldn't get too interested in him, as long as he paid dues one way or the other. Trader Joe kept the Flats relatively clean, though—he'd run into Nabor face to face on the street and merely been nudged aside by the man, though he'd run his hand through his cockscomb of hair and muttered, "Later," as he'd done so.

He turned into the alleyway marked by Toothpick and spotted a lanky man leaning against the slat side of a building, gnawing on a cold meat leg of some kind. The man dropped his bone into the dust, wiped his hands on his trousers, and straightened up as he saw Dar approach.

"I hear you want a nice hand weapon," the man said. His beady eyes sparkled from the deep setting in his bony face.

"That's right. How many do you have and how much?"

"Two, with a full set of bolts each . . . and I want two crowns for each of them."

"Two crowns?" Dar repeated, his thoughts racing. That was high-priced indeed. If it hadn't been for Thurgood's selling the emerald for twenty-five crowns, the stingers would be beyond purchasing. He chewed his lower lip, then responded, "A crown and a half."

"Done." The ferret-faced man pressed a brown-wrapped bundle in his hands, and Dar fumbled for the gold coins. He made as if to turn away, but Toothpick grabbed the knee of his breeches.

"Don't go away until we check the goods," the dwarf warned.

Dar opened the bundle. Two stingers gleamed, cradled side by side, with holsters and full bundles of darts, ends red- or black-tipped, strapped to their barrels. "How are the darts tipped?"

The ferret man's lip curled. "Red for poison and black for stun," he answered. "And don't forget the tax."

Shadows danced in the alley as Dar said, "What tax?" Two brawny arms seized him, and a cold blade bit into the skin at the back of his neck. "Trader Joe's tax."

The stingers were spread across the desk top, lumpy from objects cluttering the desk below the cloth, and Trader Joe leaned back in his chair, crossed his arms, and looked down his nose at the two of them. He was a short man, compact, not an ounce on him of fat or flabbiness, and Dar was willing to bet he could have taken on any one of his burly guards and gutted them in seconds . . . and that he wouldn't hesitate to do it.

He kept his gaze locked with that of the town boss, though Toothpick huddled like a miserable object in the middle of his chair. He was glad the dwarf had finally stopped whining when Trader Joe walked in and sat down.

"My men tell me you've been here for three days," Trader Joe said, in a high, fluting voice that didn't match the square body of solid muscle.

Dar looked stolidly at the dark hair flecked with gray

and refused to let his facial muscles twitch in amusement. The last man who had laughed at Trader Joe probably wore a grin from ear to ear . . . below his jaw.

"You came in with a pallan, and now we find you on the streets with a mountain dwarf. You keep strange company."

"I keep my own company," Dar answered. "We've broken no laws."

Trader Joe nodded briskly. He reached out and stroked the barrel of the stinger. "No, that's true. Not even these beauties are illegal in the Flats. There is another matter, which you are rumored to be involved in, that has come to my attention. Nabor and his crew are watching you."

"There's been no trouble in that quarter," Dar pointed out.

"Not yet," the man agreed. "They've even filled the coffers of two of my gambling pits. But Nabor has made it plain that my guards are to tell him the moment you set foot beyond the gates. You're dead meat then, my friend."

Dar felt a flicker of surprise that the town boss would warn him, and wondered what he wanted in exchange. "Thank you for the information."

"It's not necessary. I need to keep the roads free and open, or the citizens won't even get close to Murch's Flats. No, swordsman, I want you far and away from here before Nabor catches up to you. That much I will do for you . . . but you must do something for me."

Toothpick looked up from his spot on the chair, and his flinty black eyes appeared to be signaling something to Dar.

"My abilities are limited," Dar answered warily.

"This is within them. One of my inns was fired a few days ago, a small alehouse, modest in size but profitable. I'm told you're responsible. In my town, you understand, I can't let a thing like that go unpunished."

"What kind of fine?"

"Don't let him badger ye, bucko," Toothpick growled,

animating suddenly. He twisted around in the chair as he glared at Trader Joe. "You and Thurgood have an agreement."

The man's posture changed suddenly. A ripple of tension straightened him in his chair, and he leaned forward, looking closely at the dwarf. He sat back then, and his lips tightened.

"I didn't recognize you, Toothpick."

"Ay, I know you dinna," the little man snarled. He jumped out of his chair and shook a fist.

Trader Joe snapped his fingers, and one of the huge, statuelike men lining the wall picked up Toothpick by the scruff of his shirt. "Get him out of here."

The guard and Toothpick disappeared, and Dar stiffened.

Trader Joe waved a hand. "He'll be outside waiting for you." He glanced around the room. "Leave us."

Boots shuffled and clomped, then they were left in silence. A prickling at the back of his neck reminded Dar of unpleasant things, and he kept his feet under him.

Trader Joe pursed his lips, quickly rewrapped the bundle of stingers, and tossed them into Dar's lap. "Keep them—you paid for them. And as for the fine for wrecking the alehouse—"

"Let's not, and say I did," Dar interrupted smoothly.

The man's sharp jawline tightened, then he nodded abruptly. "All right. But there is another matter to take care of. You said your abilities are limited, but you wear a sword that is well used, and newly sharpened. Swords rarely plow fields, or grind grain, or set traps, or work in the counting houses."

"There is that," Dar answered slowly. He didn't like the feeling that began to build in the room.

"What is your connection with the wizard Thurgood?"

He weighed the options before saying, "I've hired him to guide me and my pallan on a journey."

"So." The man's breath sighed from him and he tilted his head back to look at the ceiling. "Half your job is done then." He looked sharply at Dar. "Kill him once you're far enough away from Murch's Flats and your own purpose served, and there's fifty crowns in it for you."

Dar held his surprise, reflecting that he reckoned something of the kind would happen. Thurgood was obviously not in the town boss's graces, and yet this was the kind of town where the wizard would not be suffered to stay unless the man had no way to force him out. Trader Joe opened a drawer in the desk, pulled something out, and slid it across the desk.

"May the dragongods forgive me," he said. "But use this on him."

A silver dart lay gleaming between them. Dar picked it up without a word and slid it into his bundle. A faint glimmer of perspiration glistened on the man's forehead as he watched Dar secure the dart.

"How will I be paid . . . and how will you know?"

"I'll know," the man burst out emphatically. "Make no doubt of that. And as for how you will be paid . . ." A bulging purse slammed onto the desk top. "Take it! Now! That's how sure I am you will do it, because once out on the open fields, Thurgood is free to summon Jet."

Dar's hand froze, covering the purse of gold, at the name of the dragon. Then he smoothly finished picking it up and tying it to his belt. "Jet will never know," he vowed. He stood and left the town boss's office, got Toothpick, and walked back through the streets, unmolested in body but deeply troubled in his mind. The gods help him, too, if they left him no choice but to dispatch Thurgood. He lied to Toothpick about being fined for the damaged alehouse, and although the dwarf's bushy eyebrows wiggled in disbelief, he said nothing further.

That evening, while packs were being loaded and bedrolls wrapped, a package was delivered to the wizard's apartments. Toothpick answered the rapping at the door as he jumped and skipped past the cluttered floor, but no one was there when he pulled it open. A bundle lay wrapped at his feet, and he picked it up with a sigh.

He uncurled the cloth, and a shimmering blue-green wool cloak, decorated with curling fringes of deepest blue, shook out from his hands. Sharlin gasped, "What a beauty! Where did it come from?"

"Uh . . . I bought that earlier," Dar said. "I was wondering when the merchant would deliver it. It's for you."

Sharlin grabbed it from Toothpick and held it up, then twirled it about to lower it over her shoulders. The three men appraised her silently, drinking in the pleasure of her beauty and happiness.

She flashed a rare, unguarded look at Dar. "Thank you."

"Think nothing of it. You needed a cloak." He ducked his head, missing the hurt expression that replaced pleasure, for his concern wasn't Sharlin's gift. He had bought no such cloak, though he had been haggling for it when Toothpick interrupted him. The cloak was a message, clearly written. Trader Joe was watching him . . . would know every step that had been taken and would be taken. It could not have been clearer if the man had written it in stone.

Thurgood cleared his throat. He stood up and arched his back as he said, "I think we're done here, for now. An early morning, and we'll be off."

"Good," rumbled Toothpick. "I've had enough of this godforsaken dungpile."

Sharlin laughed, and the dwarf blushed and apologized for the language. "I couldn't agree with you more," she said. She fumbled with the catch on her new cloak, determined to fasten it.

"Let me help you," Thurgood said smoothly and reached around to help her, brushing away her fall of curls. His fingertips lingered on the curve of her throat. "You are bruised, milady."

"What?" She grasped the cloak and pulled it tight, moving away from the wizard in confusion, two bright spots of pink on her cheekbones. "It's nothing."

Dar stood, kicking aside the bedroll he had just tied. "I'll kill Nabor for that," he said.

"It—it's not Nabor. It's nothing, an old mark. Don't worry about it."

But Toothpick nudged the wizard, and Thurgood looked down with an abstracted expression.

"Whut is't?" the dwarf whispered.

Dar heard the low answer given by the wizard, "The mark of the Dhamon," before he turned away and began to pinch out the candles, lowering the apartments into twilight.

"It will be an early morning," the wizard said to no one and everyone, as they made ready for sleep, deep thoughts bothering all of them.

True to Trader Joe's word, no one marked their going in the gray mist of fog, not even the hazers . . . but then, they weren't looking for a train of four dwarves and six mules stumbling out of the gate of Murch's Flats.

Chapter 5

"Illusion or not," Sharlin grumbled, scratching at her chin, "I'd swear this was real!"

Dar looked to her face, seeing not the young woman he'd come to know, but a young dwarf with a short, silky black beard and unlined face. The being wrinkled his nose at Dar. His own face suffered a similar discomfort, though he had been reassured by Thurgood that the transformation was only an illusion in the sight of the beholder. The doubt the two of them felt was not their only worry about the wizard and his valet—despite the necessity for speed in leaving Murch's Flats, Thurgood insisted on taking his own good time. Dar finally gave in to that, agreeing to the logic that the hazers would be looking for departees riding hard, not four deliberate, slow-moving dwarves. It would only be a matter of time, however, before Nabor and his crew ferreted out the information that the two of them had hired a wizard, and wizards meant magic and illusion. Even more, there was a good possibility Kory would be witch-tracking them successfully, illusion or no.

"Take heart," he said to the uncomfortable Sharlin. "It's only for a few more days."

"Besides," rumbled Toothpick, "I ne'er seen a beard so soft and fine as that un. My master outdid himself."

"Thank you, Toothpick," the wizard said. "I had a good subject to begin with."

The dwarf lad with the silky beard flushed pink, but

the wizard's keen gaze had already gone on to Dar. "You, however, were another story. I take it your clean-shaven aspect is due to something other than a sharp razor."

Dar nodded. "There's a sap from a tree that grows where I was born—it's the custom to use it instead. It keeps the hair away permanently, or nearly so."

"I see," the man said. "And what is it called?"

"Hairroot."

"Of course."

"How do you keep warm wi'out a good beard?" Toothpick asked, his own white chin hairs fluttering indignantly.

"We manage," Dar answered with a grin. "Of course, it doesn't get so cold there as it does on this side of the mountains." He paused, seeing a light flicker in the wizard's eyes, and he knew he'd given the man a fairly good clue as to where he'd come from. He tightened his lips and kicked Brand around the other bunched-up animals. "I'm going to scout ahead a little and see if I can pick up some softfoot for dinner."

The wizard and the girl marked his going. He was broad-shouldered, taller than most dwarves, with brown curls blowing in the wind and a short, neatly trimmed, curling beard. Sharlin sighed.

Thurgood looked at her, seeing through the illusion he had provided, and said, "If you like, I can remove the beard."

She'd seen and sensed the effort that had gone into the disguises and shook her head gently. "No, it's all right."

The wizard kneed his mule closer to her mount. His beast needed no disguise, for it was a real mule, and its dark-cream-colored ears flopped as it strode along. Toothpick's mount and the two pack animals were actually donkeys. "Remarkable young man, that."

"Yes, I know. I learn more about him every day," Sharlin said, not looking from where her gaze still followed the figure on the ridge ahead of them until he crossed over and disappeared from sight.

"And that frightens you."

Her eyes widened, and she took extra care in wrapping the reins about her fingers. "I wouldn't say that, exactly," she answered finally. "When we first met, I thought he was nothing more than a renegade, like those hazers, and then he did something . . . like what he did last night. He caught three softfoot in his snares."

"But he brought in only two."

"That's right. The third was a female, roly-poly with young. He let her go, saying that the softfoot is everybody's prey, and needs all the chances it can get to survive. So we all ate a little lighter last night than we wanted to."

The animals plodded along in relative silence for a moment. Birdsong surrounded them, and the puff of hooves on the dirt, and a light wind rustled the scattered trees. Then Thurgood said, "Toothpick told me he carried a pouch of bone and ashes."

"So it would appear, but I don't know why. He's never said anything to me about it. I do know this: I think he would have killed Toothpick for stealing it."

Thurgood nodded sagely at her remark. "Toothpick said as much." He pursed his lips. "Riddles on top of riddles, but the truth I'm searching for is why he would have a demon set on his trail. A lot of power behind that; yes, a lot of blind, corrupt power."

The two of them lapsed into uneasy silence, until Toothpick decided the quiet of the day needed a little something and broke into a saucy dwarfish tune that made Sharlin blush, and the master wizard twisted in his saddle to censor a few of the verses by adding his own pleasant if flat voice to the dwarf's proud bass.

Three weary days on the trail left Dar lying quietly on his saddle and blankets, listening to the heavy, rhythmic breathing of the girl as she slept, aching and sore in every bone as he was, no doubt, but driven as though it were she the demon trailed and not himself. His arms crossed at the back of his head, he cradled his skull, deep in thought that wouldn't let him rest. She pushed them to the limits of the animals' stamina, and there Dar drew the line, for grazing animals had to have time to eat as well as sleep and rest . . . and when she had yelled at him sharply earlier that day to go a little farther before making camp, he'd snapped back at her to grow wings if she wanted to go faster. The look on her face made him almost believe for a moment that if they had been riding the mountainous ranges of the legendary east, she'd have made him trap and tame a griffin to carry her on their task, if such a thing could have been done.

And she'd been subtly questioning the wizard about the moons—she called them Big Sister and Little Sister—until Dar had no choice but to think she was as much a stranger in the region as he was. The only thing that seemed to give her comfort was the season, the mellowing summer days that stretched forever, the actual heat of the summer gone. She worried as much about the time of year as the length of the road they had to follow, and Dar read the signs. Sharlin followed an inner timetable, for some reason. It was not only important to her to find the dragons' graveyard, but imperative to reach it *in time*. In time for what?

His thoughts buzzed off a moment, and he almost thought he drifted into sleep, then he recognized Toothpick's hearty tones, hushed. The wizard answered briefly, saying something Dar couldn't hear, but he concentrated harder.

Thurgood comforted the dwarf, "Don't worry so about me. I need my strength to work my sorceries, and need to work my sorceries to keep my life, but I'm doing well enough. Never fear, Toothpick—he won't trouble with me now. He likes to keep me dangling, like a fly at the edge of a spider's web, powerless or nearly so. One day, perhaps, he'll cut the thread of my power, but not now . . . especially not now."

"You read him, then?"

"Yes." In the silence that wrapped those words, Dar nearly forgot to breathe, but he forced himself to imitate

Sharlin's deep sighs, realizing the wizard listened for them before speaking again.

"Yes, I was able to read them tonight. Ah, Toothpick, I'm older than my years and I'm no seer, but I did it! There has been an immense battle . . . one of his pawns, and he was called to aid the man, and did so, to his grief. He's been injured, my little friend, injured badly . . . and must make his way to the lands we seek!"

"Now?" Apprehension edged the hearty whisper.

"I don't know when. I don't know yet," Thurgood said. His robes rustled. "I'm no seer," he repeated. "I don't know when! Now enough whispering. Our young friends sleep deeply, but they have doubts, and I don't wonder our young swordsman is as curious about me as I am about him. And I need my rest, old friend."

Branches crackled as Toothpick evidently stretched out his stocky body, and Dar relaxed, letting his own body drop into the deep-breathing rhythms he'd been pretending to. Whom had the old wizard been talking about? The town boss of Murch's Flats? He dismissed that thought, for all that Trader Joe wanted the man dead, if anything, Trader Joe dangled at the edge of the wizard's powers. Whatever it was, it affected all of them, for he'd seen the wizard grow more frail each day. Sorcery took, not gave, and the man weakened every moment. Perhaps Sharlin had seen it too, and knew what was happening, and that was the timetable she followed—to make it to the hidden lands before Thurgood died and could guide them no longer.

Dar dug his knuckles into his temples and massaged them a moment before rolling onto his side and drifting into sleep.

Mnak relaxed and enjoyed the hot, gray nether regions of his birth and existence as the wizard's geas threw him back to the master that had sent him forth. He smoldered as he tumbled, and drank in the air, and drew out that which he needed to devour and was fed, for the trailing had been long and difficult, but the ride back was free

. . . and so would be the return to the site of the enchantment, for Mnak had marked it well, and had limited sorceries of his own to use to return to it. Yes, what had taken him moons would take only a matter of a few days once he dealt with facing his master again and explaining his failure.

The return took time, but since the demon swam in the nether regions, time did not exist for him as it did when he traveled Rangard. He would have delayed his arrival if he could, but had no control over the enchantment. The powder thrown over him by the unnamed sorcerer made his skin itch, tingling at first until it grew unbearable, and that was when Mnak tore through the skin of his own world and burst into that of his master.

It was late dusk in his master's study, and the *whoosh* of his entrance made the lanterns sputter and the orange light dim, then flare up wildly, as the man sitting at the desk looked up, unsurprised.

Mnak braced his hind legs and studied the other, aware that not too many men threw the shadow of a dragonlord, but there it danced on the far wall, the black sinuous shape of man and beast entwined. The demon flexed his shoulders as his heat rolled off him, wondering only briefly how man could endure such a cold world.

"What are you doing here?" said Valorek wearily. He rocked back in his chair and dropped a quill pen to the tabletop, then rubbed one eyelid as though to clear his sight. "Where's my boy?"

The tone of Valorek's last words sent a chill even through Mnak's body, though the demon's skin barely twitched, revealing nothing of the monster's thoughts. "I was close, master. Too close. He has a wizard now, and the wizard sent me back."

"Do you know where you were?"

"Yes. A region just east and north of the borderlands called Murch's Flats."

Valorek studied a finger tip and neatly clipped off a hanging flap of skin with sharp white teeth. He had never heard of the area. "Can you get back?"

"Yes."

"You've been gone for months. How quickly can you return?"

Mnak shrugged, uninterested in the importance of the quest. "A handful of days, perhaps. I could go faster, if your dragon bore me."

Valorek thrust himself to his feet. "He's not *my* dragon, and to refer to him as such will mean the death of us both!" The sorcerer picked up the quill pen, threw it down, and picked it up again. "The boy means nothing to the dragon."

"The boy means nothing to me, either, master. Only to you."

"I want him back!"

Mnak bowed and took a step backward, preparing to leave. "As you wish."

"I haven't dismissed you yet," Valorek said with sudden recovered composure. "I can use you for the next few days until the siege is broken . . . then you can hunt again for me."

The demon made a fist and pressed it to his forehead as he bowed. "As you wish. Good hunting to us both, King Valorek."

Valorek echoed the sentiment, and the demon disappeared into the shadows, for the moment. Mnak's dark form melted until only two glowing red eyes glared balefully out of the corner, and then were gone.

Sharlin dug at the ground with her boot toe, muttered to herself, and twisted on one leg to glare behind her at the tethered animals. Her image as a young male dwarf wavered for a moment, and Dar saw her fully as the young lady she was, large blue eyes and tumble of honey-colored hair, anger flashing across her face.

"He stops earlier and earlier every day to set the wards," Sharlin snapped. "We're getting nowhere."

Toothpick looked up from his sentinel posture over the wizard's kneeling form, and his dark eyes flashed back at her, two bright spots of red on his cheekbones. "He does

as well as he can, lady! Ask the lad there how to git rid o'
his demon, and we wouldn't have to take these mea-
sures."

Sharlin's anger deflected to Dar, and he shrugged.
"Thurgood figures that the demon trailing me has probably returned by now from wherever he was sent. We need
extra protection."

"You need extra protection." Sharlin hugged herself
against the crisp wind.

The illusion rippled again, and Dar found himself
caught by a dilemma he had hoped not to face. He shifted
away from her, subtly putting himself between her and the
breeze, protecting her with whatever bulk of frame he
owned that was real or granted him by the illusion.

"I tell you what—I'll put up a tent, and start a fire now.
I can spend the extra time heating water for you . . . I
can't guarantee a bath, but you should have two or three
pots of nice hot water."

The girl looked at him, silenced by his show of concern.
She smiled tentatively, then her face was replaced abruptly by the black-bearded dwarf lad. "I'd like that." She
turned away and went to her mule/horse and began to
search through her pack while Dar made good his promise.

Evening fell, and the three men turned their backs on
the tent as the girl bathed, silhouetted like an ebony
shadow against the golden lanternlight surrounding her,
thrown against a canvas screen, which they studious-
ly pretended they either could not or did not want to
see.

Toothpick's beard waggled as he talked to himself while
sweating over a spit which roasted the body of a young
antelope, the pink of the dwarf's skull shining in the light
of the two moons. Dar lay on the ground, leaning against
his woolie-covered saddle, listening to the animals shift as
they cropped the grass diligently and murmured in the way
grazing animals have when seeking one another's company.

"Get close enough," he said to the wizard, who also lay

comfortably back, though one elbow propped him up, "and the illusion does no good. Our horses sound like horses while your mule and donkeys sound like just what they are."

"True." Thurgood sucked on a long stem of sour grass. "But the point of the whole exercise is to keep Nabor and his boys as far away as possible, isn't it? And so far, it appears to have worked."

"Then," the young man mused, "it will do no harm to face the tent, for if the illusion is a good one, we'll merely see a young dwarf scrubbing himself . . . nothing we all haven't seen before."

An eyebrow arched. "Lad, I've seen a dwarf scrubbing, and many a young maid bathing, too, for that matter . . . but I've no wish to intrude upon the princess's privacy. Nor should you."

"Oh, I don't."

The sputter of dripping fat over the open fire broke the silence. Neither man shifted as Toothpick picked up his short, keen-bladed paring knife and began to chop up onions and wild vegetables for a side dish. The aroma was enough to bring tears to the corners of their eyes, but did not, though Thurgood fished out a handkerchief and blew his nose.

He sighed and tucked the handkerchief back into a pocket. "She's quite a girl, that one. Not a word of complaint about the hard riding—in fact, I gather she's quite impatient to finish the task. Why don't you speak to her, Dar?"

"I talk to her."

"Ah . . . but not in the way you'd like to. I've been watching the two of you long enough to understand the way of things."

Dar sat up suddenly and crossed his legs under him, heedless of the sharp corners of the falroth boots. "There is no way of things! Wasn't before we came to Murch's Flats and certainly not now. She's from a noble family, and I'm—" He broke off, aware of the wizard's keen interest. "I'm a wanderer," he finished.

"Ay," Toothpick agreed. He hung a pot of the onion stew on a tripod over the fire and deftly basted the venison with a carefully portioned ration of his ale. "Th' spot on your falroth boots now—that be goblin blood, or I'm nae a mountain dwarf."

"How did you know?"

The dwarf smiled at Dar's surprise. "Be a purrr dwarf if I didn't . . . I can still pick up the stench. Up to yer heels in't you were. I heard tell of the goblin wars up north . . . though you look a little young to have been in them."

No one noticed when Sharlin emerged from the tent, wrapped in a soft blanket of pallan spinning, and sat down by the fire to dry her hair, no sign whatever of dwarf illusion about her. "Is that right, Dar?" she asked gently. "Did you fight goblins?"

In astonishment, they turned as one to stare at her, but Dar never got a chance to answer, for an arrow cut the firelight, whistling past his cheek and ripping through the side of the tent.

"Down!"

A second arrow cut the night air so close it nearly parted Thurgood's hair, but he sat steadfastly and put an iron hand around Dar's wrist as he grabbed for his sword. "Stay where you are . . . the wards are set. They aren't missing us on purpose."

Dar's heart pounded once or twice in his chest as he listened for another shot, but nothing came. He uncurled from the dust and grass and wiped himself down, saying, "That's too close for comfort. Can your wards be losing power?"

Sharlin's face paled, and she murmured, "No . . . but the wizard can be."

Thurgood waved a hand. "Never fear, children. My powers may rise and ebb as the tide, but they're enough to take us where we want to go."

Sharlin held out a hand to Toothpick, who sputtered, "Clothe yerself, gurrl. D'ye think we're all eunuchs here?"

She looked down at herself and muttered a curse when

she realized the illusion was gone and the blanket clung to her damp figure. She dove for the safety of the tent. "Toothpick! Throw in my pack!"

The gnarled valet did so, despite the fact his first charge, the dinner, sizzled a little too blackly over the campfire.

Dar heard no more late-evening conversations between the dwarf and his master, but he rode with sword loosened and bow slung at the ready during the day, for the wards were violated twice more that night, and he knew the hazers lay just out of sight, harrying at them. Tired and nervous men make mistakes . . . and Thurgood could not restore Sharlin's illusion no matter how he tried. Finally, Dar had chopped his hand down into his palm.

"Drop the illusion on the whole party."

"But—" Then the aging man had nodded. "Of course. They know who we are already, or they wouldn't be sniping." With a sigh, he added, "I won't mind it . . . the effort was beginning to wear on me."

So now Dar rode as himself, his alert-eared chestnut dancing under him. Cloud, as Sharlin had named the gray stallion, bore her, and the cream-colored mule carried his master. A nondescript shaggy gray donkey conveyed Toothpick, and two donkeys, like enough to the first to be its twins, bore a pack of supplies, which dwindled steadily.

They passed from the grassy meadows and flats outside Murch's Flats into the hilly and heavily forested region which hosted the many trappers and traders who made Murch's Flats their center. Then the hilly region gave way to drying, sharp-aired mountains that carried the chill of coming fall in the night air, and dark clouds rumbled about day and night, their edges limned with lightning that threatened but hadn't yet struck.

Brand's hooves struck against the rocks as he pulled on top of a ridge, and Dar twisted in the saddle, looking over the terrain. He didn't like it. This was ambush area, and the hazers were expert at ambush—that's how they made their living. Yet, he couldn't see how they could have gotten ahead of them, unless . . .

His chain of thoughts broke when Cloud scrambled onto the ridge behind him, Sharlin talking softly to the wizard, who trailed her.

"When are you going to read the magical writing? You haven't examined the maps once since you agreed to come along."

"No need to, yet. We know that we need a ship, and we're headed in the direction of the biggest, most open seaport available. As to the writing, there's a time and a place for everything. The moons must be right, and I rested, before it can be deciphered."

"The moons?"

"Don't fret. They won't be far out of phase when we reach the Nettings . . . a few days at the most."

"Every day counts," she answered tensely, with sorrow underlining her words.

"Perhaps if you told me more, I could help," the wizard said. He stopped abruptly as his mule and Cloud jostled into Dar's horse, and the three of them glared at each other a moment.

"What's going on?" demanded Sharlin.

Dar flexed his shoulders, feeling the heat of his half helm pressing into his scalp. "I don't like the looks of it down there."

Thurgood's gaze ran over the valley and narrow pass and clicked back to him. "Ambush?"

"A likelihood."

The wizard snapped his fingers. "Toothpick, ride ahead. See if you can tell what they're up to." He flung his weak right arm in front of Dar, holding him back. "Let my man do his work. Those sharp dwarf eyes can often see things we cannot . . . particularly in shadows or night."

They watched as the gnarled being on the shaggy donkey passed them by and kicked up dust, descending the trail into the rocky pass, where the long blue-and-purple shades of night were already reaching across the expanse.

Toothpick rode deliberately, leaning on first one side and then the other of the animal, sifting through whatever clues he might be finding, his beard moving as he talked to himself and encouraged the donkey, which had slowed to a walk and took each step ever more reluctantly until he came to a complete stop between each step.

Sharlin snapped her reins at the gray's neck, breaking out of her near-trance watching the dwarf. "We're sitting ducks up here!" A *whoosh-thunk* toppled the wizard from his mule before she finished her sentence. A feathered dart stuck from the side of his neck, and his face froze in a mask of surprise.

An arrow struck the ground between the gray's front hooves, and he bolted, plunging off the ridge back down the trail they came from. Dar cursed, hauled Brand around, and kicked him, forcing him in a bucking jump over the fallen mule and his rider. He caught a glimpse of Sharlin hunched over the stallion's neck, his whipping black mane clutched between her hands as she tried to haul him back into control. At least the girl knew how to ride, he thought as he bent over, trying to urge speed into Brand's tiring effort as they entered a grove of trees.

A net dropped suddenly in front of him, and he threw himself to the right and stood in the stirrups, pulling Brand off balance and stumbling to avoid the tangling lines, snorting and nostrils flaring. The net dropped harmlessly to the dirt. He saw a line of men converge around the gray stallion, heading him off, and Sharlin was lost to his sight. Dar turned his horse around and rode back to the pass, teeth clenched in self-anger for missing the most obvious point of the hazers' plan—to pick them off while they conscientiously searched for ambush before heading into the mountains.

The dwarf sat on the ground, tears streaking his grizzled and dirty face, as he stroked his master's temples. "I shoulda known," the little man mourned.

Dar dismounted and tied the reins to a shrub so that Brand could join the mule and donkeys grazing. "Me too," he said dispiritedly. How well he should have known! He watched a crimson drop of blood ooze from the wound left by the dart and run down the wizard's neck. "How long will he be out?"

"I dinna know. We'll camp here?"

Dar nodded grimly. "Of course. I want to stay exactly where they know we are. They want the map—they'll be contacting us soon enough to get my half."

"And then?"

"And then it's my job to get Sharlin back."

The dwarf nodded wisely as Thurgood took a labored breath, and a little color flooded back into his faded face.

Chapter 6

Dar checked his swordbelt one last time before looking at the dwarf and man who sat before the fire, even as thunderclouds threatened again, and the night air crowded heavily about them, promising rain and cold. "You know what it is you have to do?"

"He'll do it, a'right," the dwarf said for his master, in his basso profundo burr of a voice. "And I'll hover over yon lump of blankets as though Thurgood himself rested there."

A shiver touched the back of Aarondar's neck despite himself as he looked at the man, for it was his own face he looked into, though the body sat with the weariness of the wizard, who had barely recovered enough to attempt what Dar had asked of him. Did he look that tough and grim—and young? he asked himself, before looking away. He'd left his armor and half-helm for Thurgood's wearing, and kept only the falroth boots, changing trousers, shirt, and cloak for his second set. Toothpick scratched his chin and was as good as his word, hobbling over to the blankets which looked as though a man lay down by the fireside, and fussed over the dummy, ignoring Thurgood in his illusion as Dar. Dar brushed his hand against his pouch, checking that it was secured as well, and hesitated yet a moment.

"Bring her back," Thurgood said, his voice a weak husk of his normal tone, and their eyes met. Only the eyes were different, Dar told himself, for he recognized the mild eyes of the other, a flat, washed-out blue.

"I'll do my best."

The two men took a measure of each other, then Thurgood nodded. "And I'll do mine," he returned. He warmed his hands by the flickering fire, dismissing Dar.

Dar ducked into the night shadows, wrapping them about himself as best he could, and made his way down the ridge on foot. He expected no action until the dawn, but Nabor and the others were unpredictable at best, so he and Thurgood had agreed it was best to stay awake during the night, hoping to hear ransom demands for Sharlin. In the meantime, Dar would attempt to break into the camp and bring her back.

The Shield was hidden by the massive buildup of clouds they had encountered, though the Shield was not in its full phase anyhow, and would be little use to him, a silver crescent hanging in the sky, and Little Warrior, as was always the case when the Shield was overcome, would not be out at all. The wind blew ceaselessly, tugging at his shirt and cloak, and his bare head, telling him that the days of travel in the late mellowing of summer were nearly done, for now the nights would be cold and the rains sweeping in. He stumbled at the bottom of the ridge when a tree root tripped him, righted himself, and looked across the landscape, dark shapes baffled by darker shapes, and pulled his sword, for the hazers could be out there anywhere.

It was in the dark, hunting in the night, that he felt the part of him that Valorek had stained tug at its leash of restraint. He clenched his teeth and gripped the handle of his sword tighter, denying it expression, yet knowing that it helped to guide him through the shadows of a moonless night, to set him after prey, to true the aim of his arm. Worse, it invaded his mind with a feral sense . . . a lust of the kill.

Bile rose in his throat, not from the bare meal of hard biscuits and jerky he'd shared in earlier, but from the animal lurking in the corner of his thoughts. Dar had thought he had purged it forever, exorcised it, but knew that he had not—could not—not until he had Valorek or Valorek had him. His hand clenched so tightly about the sword that his nails bit into the side of his hand, drawing flecks of blood against cold white skin. It was for this he had ridden against all common sense to find the Witch of Kalmar, and failed in what he had ridden there for, unless his quest to the graveyard of dragons led him to the severing he desired. Not even death would be enough, he knew, for Valorek would simply use sorcery to repair his body and inhabit it all the same.

Dar's thoughts grated as he neared the campfires of the hazers, driven by that which tried to possess him. The site crossed his vision with an orange-red heat, rippling through the darkness of his thoughts where he wrestled with his dread enemy, and he stopped, crouching in the bushes, his heart pounding like a drum. He listened to his breath whistle and wiped sweat from his brow, unsure of just how he'd gotten there so quickly, and gathered himself until his pulse steadied and that thing called Valorek was reined back.

It grappled with him, hands of slime and acid. He crouched doubled over in pain, his sword dropped in the dust at his feet, his hands knotted and pressed against his temples, his breath sucked in, until it *gave* and he knew he'd won again . . . for the moment.

Dar took a shuddering gasp and retrieved his sword. He blinked, surveying the camp before him, wondering again how he'd gotten so far, and if he had passed any sentries— and if they'd spotted him. Six figures were seated passing around a skin of drink, another attended animals at a tethering line, and two more passed by in a blur. The witch was nowhere to be seen, and neither were Nabor and Sharlin.

If he'd hurt her in any way . . . The sword grew hot in his grip. Dar shifted his weight, settling his thoughts again. It wouldn't do any good to charge in like a berserker. No, his best bet was to find the sentries and silence them, then single out the girl and get her horse and her pack. He wanted Sharlin, but he also knew, after his wrestling match with Valorek's imprint, that he had to have the second half of the map, too.

In a half-crouch, Dar left the safety of the shrubs. He found the first sentry and nailed him with the pommel of the sword, and the hazer collapsed to the dirt with a grunt. Dar hauled him into a twist of tall grasses and left him for the night biters to feast on until he awakened with a headache. Then he made for the horse line.

Showing his dislike for his companions, Cloud was nipping at the nearest horse even as Dar found his location. He watched the gray stallion shift uneasily at the line. They hadn't been unsaddled. He was grateful for that, though it indicated that the hazers intended to beat a hasty retreat in the morning. At least he wouldn't have to worry about stealing a saddle again.

Having located the gray, Dar circled behind the horse line, intent upon finding Sharlin. He knew the girl was resourceful and wondered if she hadn't given the hazers so much trouble that they had her strung up by the thumbs somewhere. He involuntarily flinched and looked upward to the trees overhead, even as thunder rumbled darkly again.

He jumped and stilled himself as a soft voice said, "An' when you have what it is you want, you'll buy a new scrying bowl for me, Nabor?"

The soft tones of the swamp witch drifted from the other side of the thick-trunked tree. Any closer and Dar would have stepped on her. He caught his breath as Nabor grumbled, "I told you before, witch. Get me the map and I'll be buying you whatever you want. Soft kid boots for your feet. Fine wool for your weaving. A new bowl, and all."

Bodies shifted in the dark, and Dar sensed that they lay together closely, and he inched about the rough bark of the tree, not daring to hope he could get from there without being seen. Something scraped his head, startling him, and he looked up to see boot soles dangling over him. He followed the fine leather boots up slim ankles and legs to where Sharlin, bound and gagged, eyes snapping with unsaid fury, kicked the air for his attention.

He smiled in spite of himself. He'd be damned, but the hazers *had* put her up a tree!

She stopped swinging her feet, and her eyebrows arched in surprise at his smile. He put his fingers to his lips, shushing her vigorous movements indicating a need to have her hands free immediately. The gag bobbed up and down, muffling words he was glad he didn't have to hear. Dar nodded and continued about the tree trunk, one cautious footfall at a time, holding his sword across the front of him defensively.

The sight that met his eyes when he leaned around the tree trunk stopped him and made him swallow, for the witching woman positively glowed with sexual power. Nabor lay in her naked lap, nuzzling her peaked breasts like a nursing baby, himself disarmed, but not unmanned, as Dar took stock of the situation quickly. Though he looked over her bared shoulder, the fragrance from her cloud of dark-brown hair drifted over him . . . a musky, heady scent of exotic promises, and he was stirred himself, and then shook his head, knowing that the woman bewitched Nabor, and not just with the oldest promise in the world.

He swung his sword hilt-first, felling him without a sound, and the hazer rolled off her lap, caught literally with his pants down, and never knowing what hit him. The witch stared up at him, her full mouth in an O of surprise.

Kory pushed Nabor's slack form aside and stood up slowly, bracing her naked back against the bark of the tree, tilting her head and looking at him unafraid. She gave no alarm, but half smiled.

"You are a thief in more ways than one," she murmured and rocked her hips at him, as her waves of hair settled about her form, setting off the mellow color of her skin, and her nipples peaked, sending a jolt through him as if she'd stabbed him. "I've called no one for help. You can have what you want, if I can have what I want." And she reached for him, stepping out of the shadowed embrace of the tree.

Dar leaned forward, swayed by something he could no more control than he could the moons, as a wild thumping tried to break into his thoughts. His weapon sagged in his hand, and he reached for the woman, his heart racing. A shower of bark rained down upon his head. He looked up, blinking, and barely broke the fall of the girl from the fork of the tree, knocking the wind out of him as they both hit the ground.

Kory pulled Sharlin off Dar roughly, the girl's blond head snapping back against the tree trunk, and said, "You've been enough trouble tonight."

Sharlin glared viciously and drummed her heels against the ground. Her wrists bound in front of her, she reached for the knee of Dar's trousers as he stood, shaken, and tried to dust himself off. The musky aroma that was around him thickened his throat so that he could barely speak, and he saw nothing unblurred but the beckoning form of the brunette woman.

He stepped over Sharlin's form, heading for Kory's embrace. The woman ran her fingers through his hair, drawing him near.

Boom! Thunder broke, smashing the quiet of the camp, and the sky lit up, illuminated, but not by lightning. Kory jumped away, tearing loose a lock of his hair. Dar cursed in pain, trance shattered, and he stumbled back as a rent opened in the very air and a black form began to swim its way into being out of nothingness. The witch let out a guttural scream.

"Holy shit!" Dar grabbed his weapon and got ready to run. He fell backward over Sharlin, and the two of them clutched at each other, pulling themselves to their feet as Mnak emerged from the nether regions, steam and stink rolling about him.

Kory dug at the ground, picking up her clothing and bags, fumbling desperately. The demon rolled his glaring red eyes and tore at the air, being birthed from nowhere, only his spurred legs yet unseen. The witch placed herself between Dar and the demon, and he took advantage of the moment to pitch Sharlin over his shoulder, the cords on her neck straining with an unheard scream, as the witching woman shook out her bags and feathers.

As the swamp witch tossed her potions over the demon and prepared to do battle, he sprinted around the tree and took off for the horse line, even as the beasts reared and screamed in fright, snapping the rope and bolting from the campsite.

He grabbed the gray and threw Sharlin headfirst over his withers, then pulled himself on and spurred the beast, leaving the hazers behind in the night and the dust to deal with Mnak, who, from past experiences, had a tendency to maim first and ask questions later.

He dismounted on the run, bringing Cloud to a plunging halt, and Toothpick jumped up to catch Sharlin. His wrist dagger snapped into the open, and he slit the gag from her mouth.

"Slung over the beast like a sack of meal," she sputtered, spitting and coughing, and she turned on Dar, fingers curled to scratch, her wrists still bound together.

Dar slapped her hands aside impatiently. "Toothpick, get her wrists." He strode to the wizard, who sloughed off the illusion as he approached. For a sickening moment, Dar saw himself melt into nothingness and Thurgood reappear. His stomach turned. "Mnak came through."

"I know. I felt it." Thurgood stood, his head tilted to one side, listening. Then he nodded. "The witch has held him. We are safe until, oh, this time tomorrow night, unless I am much mistaken. Congratulations—you came back much sooner than expected."

The side of his head burned and smarted where Kory had torn her hand free, and Dar put his fingertips to it and drew his hand away, staring at the flecks of blood in wonder. He shook his head, but the pain increased until his vision swam.

Sharlin stood and rubbed her wrists. "Well, thank you,

anyway—though what you see in that lumpy woman, I'll never . . . Dar, what is it?"

Toothpick was steadying the terrified gray. Jerked about at the end of the reins puppetlike, he still managed to curb the horse's head, and he spoke to him quietly, finally soothing the beast. Dar frowned at them.

She pointed at his sword. "Put it back—you got me free. They didn't even search the pack, they were so certain you had the map. Gods forbid a simple woman could have something that valuable, and Nabor didn't lay a hand on me. . . ." Her sentence trailed off as Thurgood suddenly jolted into motion.

He came after Dar, but too late, as Dar tore the horse away from Toothpick and mounted the foaming beast.

"I have to go back!" he cried, spurring the animal. Sharlin choked and turned her face to the wizard's embrace.

Strands of his hair remained curled about the witch's fingers, and she laughed as she pulled him back to her, and only he could hear the laughter as Cloud reared and plunged into the night.

Chapter 7

As Cloud skittered into the hazer camp, Nabor was half into his own saddle. The man roared and jumped down, crossing the clearing in bounds, to tear Dar off the horse before he could pull his sword.

Five bows trained on Dar as he drew the blade clear of the leather sheath, and the hazer crouched in front of him, breathing heavily, his chest still bared.

"Leave him!" Nabor ordered, running his fingers through his cockscomb of hair, making it stand even straighter. Slowly, he pulled his sword free, and its dull iron length was no less work-worn and businesslike than Dar's own. "Let's see how well you fight face to face!"

His crew relaxed, arrows unnotched but the bows in hand, as their faces glittered greedily. They wanted the fight, Dar saw. He had humiliated them too often.

"Some of us fight mean, Nabor—and others of us fight smart," Dar replied, firmly wrapping his fingers around the grip, feeling the leather warm to his touch. Heat flared about his head—couldn't they see it? Couldn't they feel the crown, the aura of his injury, staining the night? He circled the hazer, thinking of him only as an obstacle to cut down to get to the witching woman.

Right-handed even as Dar was himself, the hazer circled to his right, the light of the campfire flaring up when one of his men stoked the logs, sending illumination throughout the clearing. Dar sized him up and let him take the first cut.

Blades rang as he parried it, and the shock of the blow jolted into his elbow. Nabor rocked back and met Dar's next stroke, sliding the sword edge off his own as he stopped in his tracks. Dar watched his eyes, noticed that the feathered fetish on its tight strap bobbed as the man swallowed or breathed deeply.

The fetish bobbed just before Nabor lunged. Dar sidestepped him easily and cut at the plunging hazer, who went down as though knowing he was in mortal danger, and the sword barely clipped him, a flap of skin letting a thin trail of blood run down his arm. The hazer rolled and got back on his feet.

"You're the one," Nabor rasped. "You ambushed my man and left him in the wastes for that—that thing to get."

Surprise flickered through Dar. It must have shown in his eyes, for Nabor rushed him, and the swords clanged loudly as they thrust, parried, and thrust again, each trying to drive the other back. They disengaged, and Dar stood breathing quickly.

"I left your man for no one. A walk back—that's all he had to suffer."

"That thing got him! My woman has the demon contained now . . . but I saw the claws on him, just as I saw the claw marks on Eustus's body. Never saw a beast pull a man apart like that to get at his vitals. You left him for that thing to slaughter, so that he would stay off your trail."

It could have happened. The softfoot might not have been enough to slake the bloodlust of the demon. He could have gone after Dar and been attracted by the helpless form of the waylaid hazer. The sword wavered in Dar's hand.

Nabor feinted with his sword arm, cutting the air in front of him in a pattern, ignoring the trickle of blood from his thick shoulder. "I'm going to bring you down," he said. "I should have done that first, but I listened to the witching woman too long, and we thought the girl would do the trick. But I'm going to cut you down in your tracks, sling your body over th' horse, and give what's left of you back to them . . . and have the girl anyway. The lamed

man and the dwarf"— he spat to one side contemptu-
ously—"they can't hold against me. Kory knows the
lamed man. He's the walking dead, that one."

Dar saw the look in his eyes a second before he lunged.
He parried the blow, though it rattled him clear to his
teeth when the blades engaged, then he whirled away and
sliced at the man's knees. Nabor met him, and the swords
rang against each other. Dar's slid away awkwardly, and
the hazer leaned in, the edge of the sword razoring down
his thigh.

Dar pulled away before the edge slashed deeper, but
the pain of it cleared away the haze of his thoughts, pulled
him back from the mention of the witch, even though he
could feel the twitch of his locks in her hands as she willed
him to her. He sensed her watching in the dusky shadows
of the trees beyond, waiting for him alone.

With a cry, Dar raised his sword high and charged,
whirled to his right, and cut below Nabor's guard, slicing
inward at the thick marble of leg, and crimson spurted
into the air.

Nabor screamed in pain and anger and curled down into
the dirt in a fountain of blood.

"Let him go!" Kory ordered. She stepped out of the
shadows, one hand held palm up, a bead-and-feather
fetish rattling. "He's mine now. Take care of Nabor." She
tossed a pouch to the nearest man. "That will staunch the
bleeding."

Already the hazer's face had gone gray, and a veil of
sweat beaded his forehead, his eyes rolling so only whites
showed. His men dragged him out of the way to work on
him.

She wore a thin linen blouse now, its low neckline off
her smooth shoulders, and a full skirt of many colors that
shimmered as she walked away, as sure that Dar would
stumble after her as she had ever been sure of anything.
The curve of her waist into her hips swayed ever so slightly
with her walk, and he blinked hard once or twice, unaware
of his own wound as he followed.

A second fire burned in a clearing, and he recognized

the tree Sharlin had been stashed in, though now candles decorated the trampled grass. He stopped dead when he saw the demon Mnak, surrounded by a gold-green aura. The beast snarled and flexed his talons.

Kory laughed. "He can't break loose . . . at least, not yet. And by then"—she shrugged—"our business can be finished."

"Business?" asked Dar weakly. He sat down suddenly on the bruised grasses and wiped his forehead.

"We want the map."

"I know."

Kory stood before him. She put her hand on her hip, gathering up the full skirt slightly as she did so, flashing a glimpse of her slender leg. "Nabor wants it only so that he can sell it, for whatever it's worth. It's a treasure map—he told me—and we both know that men seldom find treasure, though many are willing to take the chance. Such a map can be easily sold."

"Then you . . . don't want to go there yourself."

She laughed sharply. "If such a place existed. No, I only want what is owed me . . . fine clothes, warm shelter, a woman to wait on me, and a new scrying bowl, so that I may do what I do best. There will be those who will seek me out then, that shunned me when I lived at Kalmar. Yessss . . ." her voice faded away in a hiss, and Dar shuddered. Her fingers stroked the strands of hair in her hand, and he felt a caress alongside his face, a loving caress.

He shook his head. A feeling of loathing crept over him, and it must have showed in his face, for Kory leaned forward suddenly and snarled, her lips pulling back over her teeth.

"Damn you," she grated out. "Don't think you're too fine for me!" She turned and strode to the pulsating aura that imprisoned the demon. "I did that! My powers." Her eyes narrowed. "All I have to do is throw him what I hold, and he will have you, not I!"

"Then you'll have nothing," Dar gasped, as her fingers clenched the fetish she had made of his braided hairs, and his head felt as though caught in a vise. "I have the map hidden from the wizard and the girl. They don't know anything!"

"Oh?"

The grip relaxed minutely, and Dar fought to breathe. He hoisted himself to his feet, leaning on his sword. His pants clung wetly to his leg. A pain streaked through his right biceps, and he looked, in surprise, to see a blood-stain spreading there as well. He hadn't even noticed when Nabor cut him there. He took a deep breath.

"Come with me, then."

Kory tilted her chin up a little, and the flames lit her face. "With you? All the way to this graveyard?"

"The dragons will watch you then. There is power there."

Her eyelids lowered slightly in consideration.

Mnak roused inside the aura. His red eyes smoldered as Kory swayed close . . . too close!

Dar jumped as the witch fell back toward the aura, only her left arm holding his hair fetish clear. Mnak roared and clawed her inside. Dar grabbed her hand and booted feet to pull her clear, but the beast swiped at him.

Fire lashed his brow. Sobbing with exertion, he lifted the woman and threw her from the aura, then turned to see Mnak coming for him, arms spread.

Kory screamed, "No!"

Dar staggered back, a puppet on a string, as the witch manipulated the fetish, jerking him out of reach of the demon and free of the aura. He stood in the clear, weaving, feeling the tide of warm blood wash down his forehead over his brows and to his cheekbone, as Mnak gnashed his teeth and howled in frustration. The sound echoed throughout the clearing, broken only as Nabor's men rushed in to see what was happening, their bows and arrows ready. He saw the glint of silver, and knew the beast feared, and was silent, crouching at his back.

Kory whirled on them. "Get out! All of you! Tend to your leader and your duties!"

They stared at him, then shuffled away reluctantly, but not before he had seen the fear in their eyes. What kind of man had a demon following him?

She looked at him. "Tell me why I should join with you instead of with this beast. Tell me why I shouldn't hunt you down, if you won't give me what I want."

She had truth-read him, then—throwing herself into a trance—and that was how Mnak had gotten hold of her. She knew him, and nothing he could say would make any difference.

"I can't . . ." His voice trailed off.

"Love me?" Her fists clenched, and she shook her head, throwing the waves of deep-brown hair over her shoulders. "Why not?" Her voice caught. "Because of these?" And she held one bare foot in the air, swollen and knobbed with warts, the legacy of her years in the Swamps of Kalmar.

"No . . . because I . . . because I . . . Let me go, Kory." He leaned on the sword like a cane, and knew that he would drop if he couldn't get himself a-horseback soon. The vision of Sharlin swam before his eyes.

The witch tightened her jaw. "I could have any man I want!" she cried. "Any man!"

"Then take any man, and let me go."

"I want you. From the first moment I looked into your brown eyes when you came to me for help. There is more to you than you know, swordsman. I looked into my scrying bowl, and I *saw*. Share your destiny with me!"

He shook his head, wordless now.

The witch held up her hand, her whole body trembling with her passion. "Then run for it! I will give you a start . . . but run for it, as fast as you are able . . . because I will be coming after you, and I will have what I want!"

Kory tore the fetish apart and scattered it above the fire, where it lit in a *ffft* and spark, and was gone, that quickly, and the band about his head fled, though the throbbing pain of his wound remained.

Dar pivoted and hobbled from the clearing, thrashing into the brush. He surprised the hazer holding the gray stallion, ran him through, and pulled himself into the saddle. He kicked the horse toward the mountains, even as Kory's voice followed him.

"Run for it!"

The thin edge of dawn tipped the mountain pass when he reached the others. Thurgood was already mounted on the cream-colored mule, and Sharlin was coaxing Brand to accept her, as she hopped about with one booted foot in the stirrup, trying to get the chestnut to stand still long enough to let her swing aboard. Toothpick finished lashing the supplies as Cloud clattered onto the ridge and pulled to a stop, horse and rider sweating and shaking. The others looked at them.

The dwarf raised an eyebrow. "Looks like a rough night o' it, bucko."

Dar mopped the slash on his forehead gingerly, his legs trembling as he clutched the gray's flanks. "I'm glad you didn't wait any longer for me. They'll be after us as soon as the demon is free, and no quarter given."

Sharlin pulled herself aboard Brand finally, as the stallion flared his nostrils out to sniff suspiciously at Cloud. "The witch . . . did she . . ."

Thurgood put his hand out to hers and interrupted, "Not now." The sky rumbled, and it echoed through the pass. From the dark curtains across the mountains, there would be rain pelting the high rocks. "We must hurry. Don't worry about the hazers, Dar . . . we've got to get out of here."

"Why?" He needed to stop a moment to bind his wounds, at least.

Toothpick knelt on the ground and bent over, pressing his ear to the packed dirt. He jumped up and scurried to his donkey. "Ye're right, master. Nae time to waste!"

The three of them kicked their mounts into a run, and Dar urged his tired horse after them as Sharlin looked back and flung the warning over her shoulder. "Flash flood, Dar, and coming right down this valley. We'll have barely enough time to get through . . . but it'll stop the hazers for a day or two!"

Lightning sizzled blue fire above them, spurring the horses down into the valley with fear, and the very earth rumbled.

Chapter 8

Cloud put his ears back and surged over the terrain with all of his flagging energy, his black mane whipping into Dar's face as the animal stretched his legs out, digging his hooves into the sandy wash of the valley. But his efforts of the night told, for Thurgood's mount was far ahead, and Sharlin on Brand led the charge. Even Toothpick and the two pack donkeys showed their heels to the gray stallion. Dar leaned over his neck and whipped the rein ends as they overtook the squealing gray beasts. He caught a glimpse of the dwarf's face, panic etched in the map of wrinkles, white beard flying over his shoulder, his arms and shoulders pumping furiously as he urged his donkey onward.

Thunder rumbled again. The black-and-purple miasma covered the peaks ahead and swept down over the valley, yet not a drop fell, though the veil of clouds hung to the twisted trees and grasses. By the time the rain fell here, they would be up to their necks in floodwater from the peaks. They swept under a low-hanging tree. Dar put his hand to his face as the branches whipped through his hair. He caught one twig, and it came off in his hand. He used it to flay the pack donkeys as they stumbled near him, bawling in their fear.

Sharlin disappeared ahead as the wash turned out of sight. The wizard followed, his robes flapping about his elbows. Toothpick tried to shout something, but their race tore the words out of his mouth.

"High ground . . . ahead . . ."

High ground, and a wall of water that would sweep them all off their feet and send them plunging to their deaths. Dar snapped the branch at the nearest pack donkey when it faltered, and it spurted ahead, pain lending wings to its tiny black hooves. The second he couldn't reach, and it dropped steadily behind.

His vision blurred suddenly. He dropped the branch and grasped Cloud's mane with both hands to steady himself. The wash twisted. Dust flew as Cloud stampeded around the turn, Toothpick pounding his donkey at Dar's heels, and a bank loomed above them, taking them out of the flood's central path.

The soft ground crumbled under their sharp hooves as horse and donkeys flung themselves at the bank. One of the little pack animals gave a squeal, lost its footing, and rolled down, head over heels, hooves lashing the air. Dar looked up and spotted Sharlin and Thurgood. They yelled through the noise of the rumbling which now thundered continuously in his ear. Toothpick spurred his donkey up the second bank to the rock ledge, and the remaining pack animal followed.

The wind howled and the ground shook. Dar pivoted Cloud on the lower bank and watched as the fallen donkey got to its feet and stood, head lowered, trembling in every limb like a newborn colt.

"Dar!" Sharlin screamed, cupping her hands to her mouth. "The water!"

He looked down the wash and saw it, a steel-gray foaming wall of water, uprooted trees twirling in its curl, death to all in its path. He slipped off Cloud, slapped the horse's flank, and slid down the bank to the donkey. As he grabbed its reins, the beast rubbed its soft muzzle along his wrist, and he looked into the big brown eyes.

"Balk now," he told the animal, voice raised above the roaring, "and we're both dead!" He jerked on the reins, and it lurched after him.

The two of them scrambled up the bank as the flash flood hit, and the earth churned beneath them. Dar

half-pulled, half-whipped the little beast onto the rocky
ledge. They gained it just as the waters foamed up and
their first foothold crumbled away.

Dar went to his knees, and the donkey snuffled his hair.

Then the rain began to fall, cold gentle drops that soon
turned into a pelting curtain, and they all huddled together on the ledge and watched the river churn past where
seconds before there had been nothing but a narrow
valley, trees and grasses upon a sandy ground. The
donkeys stood close about Dar, warming him, until
Sharlin gave a small cry and came to him.

"You're hurt!"

Then Thurgood sat down beside him and ordered,
"Toothpick, put up what's left of that tent, and see if we
can't scare up a fire."

The fire was small and smoky, and the tent sides sagged
with the heavy rain, but they did purchase a little bit of
comfort. Dar stretched out, his arm and leg bound tightly
by Sharlin after Thurgood whipped up a plaster from one
of his pouches.

The forehead he gave a bit more attention to. He *tsked*
as he dabbed a cloth on it one more time, and Dar winced
from the stinging pain.

Thurgood focused on him instead of the talon wound,
and frowned. "Hold still. These demon wounds can be
tricky . . . a lot of poison can fester here, if I'm not
careful." He rocked back on his heels. "Toothpick, get me
the purple glass vial from the packs."

"But that's outside," the dwarf protested, as he stopped
chipping at his teeth with his thin silver dagger.

"I know. It's what I require, and be quick about it!"

The dwarf ducked outside the tent with a grumble.
Sharlin grinned. The smile fled from her face as the wizard
said, "Dar, the demon can't have been on your trail
long—you've had three encounters with him since we met,
and all of them so badly botched that you should be dead
meat. Therefore, I can deduce that Mnak hasn't been
after you long."

"What kind of thing is that to say?" Sharlin retorted.

She sat up, uncrossing her legs, her back stiffening in anger.

Dar braced himself on one elbow as Toothpick entered, shook off rainwater like a dog, and handed the vial to the wizard with a sniff. "It's true, Sharlin. Mnak's almost had me every time. It's only thanks to luck, and a little help, I'm here." He winced sharply as the wizard dabbed the vile-smelling purple medicine on his forehead, but then a cool numbing spread over it, and he smiled in relief.

Thurgood noticed. "Not so bad, is it?" he grunted in self-satisfaction, as he began repacking his items. As he finished, he added, "I think it's safe to say that, rather than killing you, as I first thought the demon had been assigned to do, his purpose is to fetch you. Am I right in that?"

Sharlin looked at him from the other side of the wizard. A tiny streak of mud crossed her brow, and her blue eyes looked bloodshot, as though she had not slept well, which indeed none of them had, yet. "Who is hunting you, Dar?"

He shook his head. "I can't tell you that. Knowing that puts you in even greater danger."

"Maybe we can fight him together."

"I have my own ways."

"Then whoever it is must have power indeed, for it's nothing less than miraculous you've gotten this far." Thurgood's eyebrow arched. For a man with the appearance of a dead man at dusk, he'd made a good recovery, and Dar decided it was time to change the subject.

He stirred. "If we're discussing miracles, let's discuss you. I saw the dart hit home, a red-feathered little devil it was, and I'd given you up for dead. But since then, I've done a bit of talking with Kory, the witch maid, and remembered my conversation with Trader Joe, and I realize it's nearly impossible to kill somebody that's already the walking dead. Am I right?"

Sharlin rocked back, her eyes wide, her hand covering her mouth, as Dar pushed on. "And that's why a man of power such as yourself was considered next to nothing in Murch's Flats, and why setting the wards took so much

energy, and even their protection 'ebbed and rose,' as you
put it—because the bulk of your talent goes merely
toward keeping yourself alive, and though you can risk an
outlay now and then, such as sending the demon back or
cursing Trader Joe, most of the time you're just keeping
yourself together."

"I think ye've said enough, bucko," Toothpick snapped,
and the silver dagger gleamed in his hand. "I took th' dart
out, and it was a black-feathered dart, for stunning."

Thurgood stared back at Dar levelly, then waved a hand
at his companion and sat back with a sigh. The rain above
them stayed a little, and the tent seemed deathly still.
"Leave him be, Toothpick. He's right, of course."

Sharlin's hand trembled, and she made a tiny noise, as
though she couldn't stand listening to what she was
hearing.

"It's a little more complicated than that," Thurgood
added, smoothing his drying robes out about his knees.
Patched trousers showed as he did so. "As you may or
may not know, only the dragons hold the true powers of
Rangard. Those few of us others have talents that are
meager compared to what they can do. Witches such as
Kory or wizards such as myself must barter for sorcery
from the beasts . . . and occasionally, one of us is granted
the boon, and is channeled a certain amount of power. I
was one."

Sharlin pointed at him. "But you told us you didn't
believe in dragongods!"

"And I don't. No, the beasts aren't gods . . . just
enigmatic reservoirs of power that can change the very
shape of this world, if they wish. And still, for all of that,
they are very ravenous, spiteful, and generally evil creatures. That, Sharlin, is where I made my mistake. I made
a bargain with an evil beast for power, and thought I
could take that power and mold it into all the good I
wanted."

Dar said, "A sword in a man's hand is just a weapon.
Whether it does good or evil depends on the man wielding
it."

"So I thought about sorcery. But I was wrong, and it nearly killed me."

"But there are good dragons!"

"Assuredly." Thurgood smiled at Sharlin. "The legendary gold dragon Turiana was one such. But the evil in the beasts far outweighs the good, and I was caught in the trap of thinking that I knew better. You see, I thought I could break the alliance between dragonlord and dragonmagic, and not be burned."

She reached out and touched his scarred forearm, saying, "Then that's when this must have happened. It nearly killed you."

"It tried. It thought it had. And so I am allowed to totter through the world, my presence a tiny speck at the back of the dragonlord's mind, allowed to roam at the length of my chain, so long as I don't tug at it very hard."

"And one day, the dragon will let go of you completely," Dar said thoughtfully.

"Yes, and that day, most of my power will be shorn from me. I'll die soon after." And the wizard grinned, surprisingly, adding, "Unless grand adventures such as this don't kill me first! You need me, and I need you. The dragons have secrets, Dar, secrets that we can learn."

Dar coughed. "I don't want secrets," he mumbled. "I want gold," and he turned his face away before it could be read. "And before any of that, I want sleep!" He pillowed his face on his folded hands and closed his eyes. Which of the nine great dragonlords had Thurgood battled? Was it possible they would have a dragon on their trail as well as a demon? He shivered at the thought.

Sharlin misread his shiver and draped her new cloak about him tenderly, before she went to a corner of the tent and curled up herself.

Her fingertips brushed a trail of fire across his shoulders where she touched him, and he was awake long after the gentle snores of the others purred in the rain-soaked tent.

The morning after—for they slept all day and most of the night—Toothpick fished a dead falroth out of the floodwaters, skinned it, and made a fairly good meal out of the disagreeable beast.

Sharlin toed the skull, its lips pulled back in a horrible snarl. "It's got two rows of teeth!"

"Ay, and all of them good at chewing," Toothpick answered. He bent over the fire and spit, having worked another miracle at coaxing flames from wet wood, and without smoke, to boot.

Sharlin smiled at him, guessing that he had a touch of talent about himself, too, for all that he fussed at the wizard. She looked back at the tent, flexing sore muscles. Dar slept still, and his heavy breathing broke the stillness of the dawn.

Toothpick followed her gaze. "Let the bucko sleep . . . he needs his strength. Those cuts were deep enough to sap some o' th' blood out of him."

Sharlin settled down on her heels, and the dwarf handed her a stick with falroth meat curled upon it. Her nose wrinkled as she sniffed it delicately. The scent was good, of fresh roasted meat. When she bit into it, the juices dribbled down her chin, and she used her fingers to mop it up appreciatively.

Thurgood laughed as Toothpick handed him a string of meat and then took one himself. "Falroth is an unexpected delicacy?"

She nodded. "We don't have them in . . . where I'm from," she finished lamely, and held her stick out to be refilled, then grilled the flesh lightly herself.

"No, I wouldn't guess you do," the wizard answered. "I've been asking myself about you, and come up with few more answers than I guessed at the beginning of this quest."

She looked at the man then, his too aged face with a sagging of skin and muscles, the slight drooping of one eye. "Nothing I've held back endangers us," she said finally. "It's just that—that I know I'm far from where I need to be, and that I don't need any protectors right now to slow me down. What I need is . . . a hero, I guess. I need to find that graveyard, and then I'm going to go home, before it's too late."

"Too late for what?"

She shook her head at the wizard then, smiling wryly, for she had said enough.

Toothpick grunted around a mouthful. "It's obvious, master—the only reason a princess needs to go treasure-hunting is to buy an army." He licked the peeled stick clean without getting a drop on his beard. "I'd say the gurrl comes from a kingdom that's been overrun. She was sent out for safety, and with an escort whose job was to secure mercenaries. They were ambushed, she escaped, and here she is."

Both Thurgood and Sharlin stared at the dwarf, astonished by his lengthy statement, and he stared back at them, flinty eyes blinking.

The wizard looked at her. "Is that right?"

She shook off her surprise long enough to stammer, "Part of it."

"Which part?" They turned as Dar crawled stiffly out of the tent, squinted at the morning sky, and stood up.

Sharlin bit her lip. The swordsman flexed his bandaged leg, a flicker of pain running through his expression, and he looked at her again. "Well?"

"My kingdom is far from here, is besieged, and my escort was killed. And that's all I'm going to tell you! I don't want to run the risk of being held for ransom, and the only reason I'm telling you this is that I'm the equal of any one of you here. I can protect myself."

Toothpick *tsked*. "As if you would have to with us around, gurrl."

She cried, "Ouch!" as she pulled off a too hot string of meat and blew on it and her fingers to cool them. Dar grinned.

"I can protect you from anything but yourself," he jibed, and she glared at him before getting up and moving away from the fire.

Thurgood looked into the fire's leaping colors pensively, muttering, "Riddles upon riddles."

Dar kicked the falroth skull on the way to the fireside, remarking, "A young one." He sighed and eyed the purple mountains ahead, still veiled with rain and clouds.

"I didn't know there were any in this region. We'll have to ride carefully . . . they'll be out scavenging the floodwaters. How far to this seaport?"

"Five days will take us in the gates . . . and we've got a two-day start on the hazers, I'd say, by the looks of that river. When it stops raining in the mountains, it'll lower enough to cross. We won't have any more time than that."

Dar picked up a stick of meat and bit into it crisply. "Then let's not waste any more. I'm able enough to ride, if you are."

"Always," Thurgood answered mildly.

They made the seaport in four days, horses and mule and donkeys staggering out of the rounded mountains in the late afternoon, all stiff and sore and caked with mud.

Sharlin sighed with pleasure at the sight. The mountain pass led down to the main road, and the dim line of the sea could be seen. Gulls cried and wheeled over them, heralding what she could not yet hear, but would soon enough. "Bed and bath first," she said firmly. "Then we can go out and check the shipping lines."

"Bed and bath," Thurgood agreed. "Then we read the map, for tonight will be the first of the three days of the conjunction—never mind what I mean by that; just trust me—and then we go dicing."

"Gambling?" she asked incredulously as Toothpick grunted in anticipation. "Thurgood, this is really no time to indulge in vices."

"Who said vices? I don't carry a full purse of gold—do you? And we all know yon swordsman carries bone and ash instead of coin. Just how do you propose we buy passage for the four of us, and our mounts . . . or do you have another bejeweled scale I haven't seen? No? Well, then, leave it to me."

Dar gave a short laugh, interrupting, "Only a fool would gamble with a wizard."

Thurgood eyed him sharply. "True, true. That's why Toothpick is such a valuable companion. Dwarfs are practical creatures—they deal in concrete absolutes. Very few, if any, dabble in the black arts. No one would guess the tricks he can do with dice and sticks and stones, when he wants to.''

The dwarf grinned from ear to ear and scratched his neck. ''Ye're embarrassin' me, master.''

Thurgood picked up his reins. ''I guarantee you, we'll have passage before long.''

''While we're talking about plans, I think it wise for Sharlin to put on her pallan hood and veil. Seaports can be rough trade, and I don't want her attracting any attention.''

''Hooded again?'' Her voice trailed away in protest.

''Good idea. She's purty enough to cause trouble.''

''Am I?''

Dar glared at her. ''You know you are.''

''Well, after all these days on the trail, and caked with mud . . .''

He ignored her as the wizard nodded and coaxed her, ''Sharlin, this is no time for feminine wiles. On with the hood and veil. I want to make sleeping arrangements before dark.''

They watched as she fetched the pallan cloth from her saddlebag and attached the hood. She left the dark navy-blue veil trailing by the side of her face. She looked at them defiantly. ''I won't put the veil on until I have to! It's hard to breathe.''

''As you wish, my dear.'' Thurgood sighed. ''It's a shame to hide you, but I agree that it's best. We don't need any trouble.'' He kneed his mount onto the main road.

Sharlin kicked her horse after his mule, raising her voice so that all could hear. ''And I guarantee you that I will personally make it very unpleasant for any of you who comes back to the inn in his cups!''

Toothpick sighed as he followed her. ''Ah, gurlie. Ye take all the fun out of life!''

Chapter 9

Thurgood paid the modest toll for the party to enter the gates of the Nettings, and he sighed as he patted his lean purse.

"There's more where that come from," his valet muttered hauling the two pack donkeys after the wizard, their long ears flopping, and the tiny one stopped long enough to utter a bray that shattered even the cry of the gulls.

The Nettings was a veritable metropolis. The sight of it opened up Sharlin's heart, and she swallowed with difficulty, swept by homesickness and concern for her own holdings, as she reined the gray stallion after. Beyond city gates lay many roads, all leading to farmlands, orchards, lumber mills . . . a kingdom of many riches and people. They had come down out of the mountains into a near-paradise.

A high-pitched screaming that grew shriller with every note of terror broke her thoughts. Dar jostled his chestnut stallion close to Sharlin, their knees touching, and he murmured, "Look down," but he couldn't hide the sight on the streets of the Nettings that drew Sharlin's stare.

She fumbled to put her veil on as a pallan stumbled from the front of a shop, its clothing torn, and it stopped, holding up trembling hands in appeal to them, to *her*, as they rode past in the street. Its master burst from the doorway behind it, strap in hand, yelling in fury.

"Burn the loaves, will you? Two days' work in the

kitchens blackened, dungheap!" The strap fell again, and the pallan collapsed to its knees and began screaming again.

Dar kneed Cloud and clucked for the stallion to move on, for Sharlin's hands were numb on the reins. No one else on the busy streets paid attention to the cook as he beat the pallan into a bloody heap on the floor of his stall.

She took a sharp breath, sick to her stomach.

"Stay close to me," the swordsman ordered, moving his broad-shouldered frame to hide her from most of the curious stares of idle onlookers. But he could not keep her from seeing the pallans—dirty, bent, frightened—that scuttled about the streets doing errands and working for their masters.

A rattling of chains made her look sharply in the other direction. She caught the last glimpse of a line of pallans, shackled to one another, shuffling down an alleyway and into oblivion beyond her vision.

She was used to pallans being considered unimportant —but here, they were hated. A shiver danced down her back, and she barely noticed when Thurgood reined in under a sign, "Red Dog Inn," and signaled them to wait.

The innkeeper came out, a dwarf, with flaming red hair. He frowned at her, thinking she was a pallan, but Thurgood pressed an extra coin into his hand, and he nodded reluctantly. A pallan stableboy darted out from the shadows to take the reins from them and lead their mounts to the stabling in the rear yard.

A hot bath and a pot of herbed tea later, Sharlin basked in the fire-lit glow of their room. Thurgood and Dar had gone on some mysterious errand of their own, after leaving Toothpick guard outside her door while she bathed, and as she sat at the tub's edge now, she could hear the deep-toned humming of the gnarled man as he sat whittling.

For the first time since Gabe's death, she felt human again. The nicks and scars of her servitude in the borderlands were nearly gone, and the wild panic that had stricken her at being lost in an unknown land had faded. Instead of being caught by circumstances, she was on the offensive at last.

She strode across the room, her hair heavy and damp upon her back, and stopped at the jumble of packs. Hers, naturally, was thrown on the bottom. She tugged and tugged to get it loose, and stepped back from the avalanche when the leather bag pulled free. The forest-green trousers and full-sleeved shirt came out smelling like the potpourri she had folded in with it, and Sharlin shook the garments out, trailing the sweet scents across the rude wooden flooring of the room. A matching hood and veil drifted down to rest at her feet. She toed it.

She owed the pallans more than even her life. The enigmatic and mysterious people had found her wandering the wilderness, parched with thirst and alone. They'd taken her in, giving her food and shelter, and eventually directed her to the inn where she worked as one of them, taking some abuse, but surviving nonetheless. Though they clothed her and taught her their ways, she still knew little about them . . . and had never seen beyond their skillfully woven cloth and masks. Being a pallan had saved her, and yet here, in this part of Rangard, being a pallan was almost less than being a rodent in a grainfield.

Sharlin bound her breasts lightly for comfort, then pulled on clean linens and the forest-green clothes. The navy-blue clothes needed a thorough scrubbing.

She shook her hair out over the collar of the full-sleeved shirt as she tucked in the slim waistband and then fastened her belt over it. With a smile, she fingered her money pouch. Yes, she would take Toothpick and go to the bazaar, and buy decent clothes . . . for going as a pallan would no longer benefit her. She'd been touched by the sight of them hiding in the shadows of the street, watching her ride by with the others as though she were some foreign creature.

Here in the Nettings, the proud and graceful pallans had been broken like dry sticks and tossed into the fires of man's hatred. Like it or not, Thurgood and Dar would now have a full-fledged princess on their hands!

Sharlin bent over and picked up the hood and veil, refolded them, and placed them back in her pack. If the last few months had taught her nothing else, they had taught her that everything changes. Even the moons of her childhood no longer rode the sky in the same path or went by the same names.

Toothpick nearly fell off his chair when she yanked the door open. His slate-dark eyes popped open. "Why, princess . . . " he sputtered. "Have ye taken leave of yer senses?"

"No, Toothpick. I am what I am . . . and surely even you would agree that being a pallan in this place might be more dangerous. Come on, I have some shopping to do."

Toothpick pensively slid his dagger back into his wrist sheath and stood up. "My master and th' swordsman said not to go anywhere . . . they'll be back soon, and there's th' reading of the map to be done. Thurgood says at dusk."

Sharlin peered down the crude hallway, where the late-afternoon light filtered in through the slat sides of the building. "I won't be long! I spotted the stalls I want on our way here. We'll be back in time. Come on . . . or I'll be going without you."

Toothpick clicked his teeth, galvanized into action, racing to keep up with her long strides. "That wouldnae do, princess. Not at all!"

Salt tang rode the air the way the lean-breasted gulls did, sharp and keen, flooding her senses. It was strange to look down the sloping hillside of town and see the horizon of the water, gray and flat, as far as she could look, she who'd been raised in a landlocked kingdom. For a moment, a dizziness tinged her, as though she might slip and fall away down to the nothingness of the ocean. Sharlin halted in the street.

"Here there," panted Toothpick. "Are ye all right?"

"Yes." She smiled at the dwarf. "Over there." She

pointed out the stall of a bootmaker, his leather ware displayed on wooden racks, cloth banners rippling overhead. The journey-thinned soles of her own boots reminded her just how far away home was.

The balding man straightened his lanky form and patted his few wisps of hair out of the way as she approached. His frown gave way to a grudging smile when she leaned over the stall front. "Yes, miss? What might I do for you?"

"I need new boots, and these resoled."

He bowed, leather apron crinkling. "Come in and sit, whilst I take a measurement."

Sharlin shook her head. "I have no time for measuring. Perhaps you have something already made that will do?" Balancing, she swung her leg up and placed her right foot on the counter.

The merchant shut his gaping mouth quickly and ran his hands over her booted foot, then quickly circled it with his knotted tape. Satisfaction replaced astonishment. "I have just what you need!" He bent over and rummaged around under his shelves, came up with a finely wrapped parcel, and handed it to her with the air of a man bestowing a great treasure.

Indeed, the boots appeared to be just that, when she had undone the string and laid the cloth covering aside. Finely tooled, a rich dark-blue leather, the boots glistened. The scent of well-tanned leather, leather fresh and new, reached her.

Sharlin ran her hands over them. "These are . . . much too fine for me." She began to rewrap them. "I'm sorry—"

"No, no!" He waved his palms in front of her. "Try them on first."

Toothpick eyed her warily as she entered the stall and sat down on the three-legged stool the cobbler dragged out for her. The boots slipped on, as they both knew they would, as though made for her. The cobbler grinned.

She shook her head again. "I won't insult you by bartering for these. Your handiwork is exquisite, and I already know my purse won't bear the price."

The cobbler laid his calloused hand on her wrist when she bent to take the boots off. "Milady, the price is meager. These boots were made for another—the younger sister of the duke—and the price is already paid."

"What—"

His face closed in sorrow. "There was an accident. The boots will never be worn by her—I should have burned them, I know, I got my price out of them—but the workmanship—I had hoped another would come along—and see! You have walked right into them!" He straightened and dug his hands in his apron pockets, rattling tools of his trade. "Would half a silver piece for the resoling and the new boots be too much?"

Sharlin gaped. The man must be a pauper if he bargained like this. She changed her expression to a smile, fished out the coin, and pressed it into his palm.

The cobbler smiled widely, saying, "Leave your boots. I will have them ready by tomorrow noon."

"That will be fine." Sharlin stood, marveling at the calf-high boots, slightly heeled for riding, but not too high for walking. Even her own high arch was met and supported by the curving sole. The cobbler bowed, his pleasure fed by hers, as they left the booth.

Toothpick made a low sound in his throat. "Th' man fair gived them to you, princess."

"I know. But I can understand why he did it." What she didn't understand was the look of pure hatred that he had first worn until he'd seen that she wasn't a pallan, after all.

At a clothier's stall, she bought two well-sewn and heavy riding skirts, stepping into them and trying them on over her trousers, and twirling, glad to feel feminine again. The embroidery was subtle, gold threads on dark-blue fabric and pink tracings on brown. She haggled long and hard to get a price she could afford, then the hard-faced woman surprised her by throwing in a vest that matched the brown skirt. Two blouses she found in another stall, and well worth the money they asked, though the daughter checked the coins with a sharp bite before handing over her bundle.

Toothpick gave a mock stagger as they left the booth. He flushed as Sharlin laughed at his antic, and the top of his head shone pinkly. He squinted at the skyline. "'Tis getting late."

"I know . . . I know. But I need a hat or a scarf, and then we'll be off." Sharlin sighted another stall that drew her like a magnet. The headcoverings adorned puppet heads, and she laughed at the cleverness of the craftsman who had carved them, for instead of bland round heads on a stick, she stared at thick-headed farmers, and arrogant swordsmen, and seasick fishermen, and fair ladies and shrews.

The lad who stood up and stretched in a corner couldn't have been the tradesman, she thought, as he yawned and came over. Curtains parted at the back of the shop, and another man stepped out, took the lad by the elbow, and sent him back to his corner. The thick, burly man bowed. "Can I be of assistance?"

"You already have," she told him. "Your creations are marvelous."

The man blinked, then smiled. "Why, thank you. My little people—pardon me, dwarf—appreciate the attention. There is, alas, more money in showing my goods than in performing, however."

She'd seen puppets only once before in her life, and the performance had drawn people from all over her kingdom, to shout and laugh with delight and shower the troupe with coins, so that Sharlin found it difficult to believe him, but she nodded. She wasn't in her kingdom now . . . how could she judge?

"What would you like to see? A net of links and jewels to coax the sun from your hair?"

Sharlin tilted her head, then shook it wistfully. "No . . . a good riding hat, I think."

"A practical lass, ummmm?" A square hand plucked off a hat from a plucky forest lad. "How about this? Broad-brimmed against the sun . . . the rain will run off it thus . . . and delicate enough to be borne by a princess."

Toothpick choked. Sharlin ignored her bodyguard and nodded. "What will you be asking?"

"Three copper pennies, or five sticks, whatever you carry."

She fished the pennies from the bottom of her pouch, leaving her precious little, but she didn't care. Once they were on a boat, she would be so close to her final goal that she could almost taste the mountain air of home. Curtains rippled at the back of the stall, and someone tall peered out . . . a customer, perhaps, whom the man had left. "I'm sorry to have disturbed you."

The milliner shrugged. "For your fair face, I'd have left a dragongod waiting." He tipped his own cap. "Good day to you, miss."

Toothpick grumbled all the way back to the inn. "Ye're being too chancy," he said. "Showin' yer purty face all up and down the street. Thurgood'll have my scalp."

"You worry too much. And besides, you were with me every step of the way." Sharlin refused to let her happiness be dampened by the dour man. She took the back stairs to the inn and sniffed hungrily. Fish chowder and roast gunter were sizzling over the fires, reminding her that she hadn't had a decent meal in weeks, Toothpick's cooking notwithstanding.

She took the bundles from Toothpick's arms. "Wait outside for me."

"But . . ." Then the dwarf's face wrinkled in a smile. "A'right, Sharlin—but hurry. My stummick can't take much more hunger."

She wore the brown skirt and matching vest downstairs, and a silken blouse the color of fresh cream, and her new boots, and the innkeeper's bearded jaw gaped open when he saw her and Toothpick.

He hurried to meet them by the food spits. His smoky-green eyes appraised her openly, and he remarked, "Ye've traveled far indeed, miss, if yer companions considered it safer to have ye ride as a pallan with them than as a lady."

Toothpick hooked his thumbs in his belt and rumbled,

"Having thought an' said that, countryman, ye'd be wise to keep your beard from a-wagging any further. We're travelers, an' that be enough." His heavy frown kept Sharlin quiet, too, as the keep gathered two trays loaded with drink and food and handed them over.

Sharlin took the tray and asked quietly, "Why are the pallans hated so here?"

The flaming red hair of the dwarf's head and beard seemed to spark with fire. "They have mocked our dragongods too long, milady, and now brought disaster on all of us. It wasn't two weeks ago that the duke's good sister, bless her soul, was drownded when a serpent attacked the sailing ship she was on. Th' creature has poisoned our waters and driven most of the fish away, and all because the gods are angry. We'll let no more pallans scorn us, if we have to beat them into th' dust!"

With a sputter, Toothpick elbowed her away from the innkeeper and nudged her up the stairs. He didn't speak until he kicked the door shut behind them and slammed the tray down on the tabletop, and she slid hers next to his.

His flinty eyes glared at her. "Sometimes, princess, ye got a big mouth."

"What? Me? How else would you know what's going on?"

"There be ways." He drew up a stool and snapped his dagger out, to suck on the point reflectively. "I'll have to tell th' master soon's possible."

"What's a sea serpent, anyway?" She pulled up another stool.

"Like a seagoin' dragon . . . big an' nasty. Bad noos for us."

Unable to resist the smell any longer, she pulled her own dagger out to cut the bread and line it with slices of meat from the roast. "Again, why?"

"Because it'll be tough goin' to find a sailor who'll ship out wi' that beastie layin' about the harbor."

The door kicked opened with a bang and Dar and Thurgood entered, each carrying bags and baskets.

With a sniff, the young man stopped and lowered his bundles to a straw cot. "Dinner smells good."

Sharlin picked up her sandwich. "I wouldn't know—yet." She sank her white teeth hungrily into the meal.

Thurgood dropped his bundles with a sigh, and his valet poured him a foaming mug. "Just the thing. Quickly now. Dusk will be here soon, and I have to set this up."

Full stomachs and empty mugs later, the wizard squatted in front of his warding cubes all lined up inside the closed door. Dar flexed his shoulders uneasily.

"All this just to read the map?"

Thurgood laughed softly. "To read the map—and keep out demons. Mind you, I don't know that the hazers have caught up yet, I doubt that they would have . . . but this time, I would rather be safe than sorry." He straightened carefully. "How was that bath, m'dear?"

"Wonderful."

"Good. I think I shall avail myself of the same facilities later. These old bones and muscles would be grateful, I think."

Toothpick's beard flagged as he muttered, "Ye'll catch yer death of cold."

"Nonsense. Now, clear the dishes and spread those maps out. No . . . that way . . . yes. Use the mugs to hold down the corners if they curl. Good." Thurgood approached the table and folded his arms. "Bring the baskets."

Toothpick jumped up to do his master's bidding. The wizard selected several vials and a large earthenware bowl. While the dwarf held the bowl in his grizzled hands, he passed the vials over several times and then began to pour a portion of the contents into the bowl. When the liquids hit one another, smoke began to rise from Toothpick's hands.

"Quick, man, to the table," Thurgood snapped, and puffed gently so that the colorful cloud of smoke, streaked pink and yellow and purple, drifted over the map and descended like a fog.

When Thurgood gently waved the smoke aside, the faded inks stood out in renewed colors, and the oceans were filled with runic letters in brilliant crimson. The four of them crowded about the table to look at it.

The wizard shook his head, laughing at himself. Dar frowned as the man pointed at the lettering. "What is it?"

"The joke is on us, I fear. The man who drew this was clever indeed."

"What does it say?"

Thurgood looked at Sharlin, his eyes twinkling with mirth. "It says, among other things, that the direction is reversed. We've been traveling tail to head . . . and should have been traveling head to tail."

Dar stabbed a finger at the skins. "You mean . . . we've been going north, from the borderlands to Murch's Flats to here . . . and where we need to be is in the south?" He looked incredulously at the landmass in front of him. "That's not funny, Thurgood."

"No, but shrewd. Very shrewd." He traced the journey facing them, from the anchorage of the Nettings, along the coast and around the cape of the land. "We must sail not to this land in the north, but down here to the south."

"Glymarach," Sharlin whispered, as the newly revealed writing labeled the island. "The Cradle."

Dar sank down onto a stool, his jaw tight. "The peddler has sent us nowhere then . . . for I know that area, a little, and there's no island down there but a handful of rock. This"—and he tapped the drawing—"doesn't exist."

"I know," Thurgood said smoothly. "I have seen many mappings of Rangard as set down by dragons through the ages. No such island exists, except for this tiny outcropping here."

"That can't be!" Sharlin protested. "It's drawn here . . . it's almost as big as Kalmar, which we just crossed."

"A jest. An old man's fancy or dream perhaps."

"What else do the runes say?"

Thurgood looked at her with a kindly tilt of his head. "I don't mean to disappoint you, Sharlin. Nothing that makes sense. It says to 'walk a day upon the water.'" With a puff, the cloud faded away entirely. "I'm sorry. I've done my best."

A tremor ran through Sharlin as she sat. She looked up. "It's not good enough. We'll sail there, and then we'll see."

The three men considered her, face pale, blue eyes as dark in her face as sorrow, hands clenched, her chin pointing at them defiantly.

Dar shifted. "All right then," he said slowly. "We know we may face illusion and deceit . . . if there is a grave-yard, the dragons will have gone to great lengths to hide it. South it is."

"Then," Toothpick rumbled, rubbing his hands together, "we've a lot o' gambling to do, master. That's a considerable voyage."

"Indeed it is." Thurgood straightened and patted his robes down. "I think it best the two of you stay here . . . neither of you have somber faces. Expression plays across your innocence like lightning across a dark day. We shall return."

Sharlin waited until the footsteps of the two had echoed away down the wooden stairs, and Dar had carefully replaced the wards, before relaxing her hands.

"Thank you," she whispered, but he heard it, nonetheless. He crossed the room and unbuckled his belt and lowered it to his cot, sword, pouch, and all.

"It must be important to you."

She stood up and busied herself clearing the table. The crude texture of the earthenware sent a shiver through her as her fingers touched it. It was nothing like the fine plates and drinkware of home, and for the second time that day, she was flooded with thoughts of her land. Did the House of Dhamon still war? "It's more important than you could ever guess."

"Then we'll go. Whether Thurgood wins enough money to buy passage or I have to steal a ship, we'll go."

Their gazes met. "It's important to you, too."

"Yes. It's one of the ways of getting rid of the demon."

"You have other demons besides that."

Dar watched her gracefully perform the ordinary task of cleaning up, thinking that the dark brown of her skirt and vest lent gold to her hair, and he watched it shine in the room's illumination. He cleared his throat uneasily. "I think we all do. I trailed Thurgood throughout the town center. He gleaned facts as a hungry farmer gleans his fields. He wasn't at all surprised to hear of a sea serpent off the coast . . . in fact, I think he would have been disappointed if he hadn't heard tidings of it."

"I'm not talking about Thurgood," she said, mildly reproaching him. "Tell me why you carry a pouch of ashes."

"They're the remains of my parents."

She dropped a mug, and it shattered into thick wedges about the room. Dar quickly bent to his knees to help her pick up the pieces. When they finished, they knelt very close to each other, so close that she could smell the horses and woodsmoke of the past day's traveling on him, and he the sweet scent of the potpourri which clung to her skin.

"I'm sorry. I shouldn't have asked—it wasn't any of my business."

He straightened up and held a hand out to assist her. "It's all right. They died when I was younger . . . a farmhouse fire. It happens."

"Nothing about you just happens."

As she got to her feet, he pulled her close without warning, and kissed her. Sharlin stood very still within his embrace, then shifted her weight, tilted her chin up higher, and returned the kiss, and the room was quiet for a very long while.

She rocked back on her boot heels when he let her go. He grinned, then strode away, dropped down on his cot, and threw his sword out onto the wooden flooring, between the two of them.

"You're safe for now, princess," he said, the smile still lighting his face and his eyes. "But if you cross that, you're mine tonight."

Sharlin opened and closed her mouth wordlessly, then

shoved the empty trays outside the door for the innkeeper to collect. She wrapped herself in the woolen cloak he had bought for her, lay down to sleep on the bunk farthest from him, and rested, staring at the door long after he gave a gentle snore and went to sleep.

Bam! Bam! "Open up in there!" A heavy fist shook the door.

Dar rolled from his cot and picked up his sword. Sharlin got to her feet, still wrapped in her cloak, her eyes puffed with sleep. Two of the four clay lamps had burned out, and the room lay criss-crossed in dark shadows. It was late night, and Thurgood and Toothpick hadn't returned.

Bam!

Sharlin looked at him. "The hazers?"

He shook his head quickly. During the afternoon's outing with the wizard, he'd grown used to the accents of the Nettings. These were locals. He gestured to her to open the door and get out of the way quickly.

The burly town guard that stood there glared down at the wizard's warding cubes and stepped no farther as he hooked a thumb into his belt, palm caressing the hilt of his short sword. "Th' duke says we're to fetch you."

"Why? What have we done?"

His beady eyes flickered to Sharlin. "Nothing, milady," he said grudgingly. "Do you know a wizard and his servant, a bald-pated dwarf?"

"Why, yes," she answered even as Dar made a sharp cutting motion with the side of his hand not to answer.

"Then you're to accompany me, for there's a game going on with high stakes, and the duke wishes your presence."

Sharlin lifted the hem of her skirts then to step over the wards, as movement in the hallway indicated a gathering of strength that would prove hazardous if they refused. Buckling on his swordbelt, Dar followed reluctantly.

An open cart drawn by a matched pair of bay ponies awaited them in the street. Dar and Sharlin seated themselves, facing the captain of the guard and an equally muscular lieutenant. Dar tried not to let his tension show, but it played through his muscles. Sharlin smiled too brightly at him, and looked away as the cart rattled through the streets.

The cart drew up before a wide-fronted pub on a graveled street, and the two of them looked at each other. If Thurgood and Toothpick had come here to do their gambling, they'd gone far afield.

The captain helped Sharlin down. He sandwiched Dar in between himself and his lieutenant, and they all marched into the well-lit gambling hall, where crowds of people lined the walls.

Toothpick knelt by a dicing pit, his head shining with sweat, apple cheeks flushed with excitement as he rubbed his instruments of fortune between his hands. Thurgood leaned against a wall, looking somewhat rueful. Seated next to him, in an elegant carved chair of wood and brocade, was an aging man, well dressed and wearing chains of gold, who was intent upon the dwarf until his guards entered.

Sharlin gave a bow as the captain announced, "The Duke of Nettings, the lady Sharlin."

After slipping away from the lieutenant, Dar joined Sharlin. The duke waved a hand. His gaze fastened on her boots. His black hair curled about his face, away from a high widow's peak. His face could not hide the gaunt look of sorrow. Sharlin flushed, wondering if he recognized the boots she wore as ones intended for his recently dead sister.

"Come closer, my dear. You are about to witness a historic event. If the dwarf throws two more quintains in a row, he'll have won his wager."

A gasp ran through the room, and even Sharlin knew enough about dicing to know that what Toothpick proposed to do was an impossibility. The quintain formation was the rarest to come up, and she saw the scoring on the boards by the pit—Toothpick had thrown it five times already!

The duke looked over his shoulder at Thurgood, and she saw then that the wizard was wrapped, head to toe, with a fine, singular thread. The older man smiled gently as he saw her gaze.

"It's nothing, my dear. Just a little wizardly precaution that I do not in any way influence the fall of the dice."

"But—"

The Duke of the Nettings took her hand, soft and cool, and warmed it between his own two great warm ones. "Don't fret. My ship is sound, and a sailing beauty, and it will be fully stocked for you."

"A ship?" She looked, eyes wide, over the duke to the wizard. Thurgood nodded briefly, but his comment was interrupted by the sharp rattle of the dice in the dwarf's palms.

The boards clattered as the dice shot off them and rolled to a stop in the middle of the pit. A quintain!

Dar moved close to Sharlin as the audience shouted, and their voices mounted to a frenzy while coins and bets changed hands until the duke lifted his palms, indicating a need for silence.

The dice were dropped into Toothpick's gnarled palms once more. His eyesight shifted to his master as he cradled them, worry creased into his wrinkled forehead.

Something seemed wrong, but Sharlin and Dar could not pinpoint the feeling. Thurgood nodded permission to his valet, and Toothpick swallowed. He rolled the dice between his hands for several seconds, then threw them sharply into the pit.

The first die dropped into formation, but the second spun on one end, seemingly never to stop. Then it slowed and toppled into place.

The room went wild as the quintain faced upward from the gaming pit, gleaming in the lanternlight. The duke sighed, his tension broken, and he signaled for Thurgood to be cut loose from the spellbinding.

The four of them were hustled quickly out into the street and into the cart, and the duke followed them out.

"Remember high tide, day after tomorrow," the man said. He smiled, a tight line across his mask of sorrow, and took Sharlin's face gently between his hands. She recognized, with a start, the man who had watched her from the milliner's curtains. He gave her a chaste kiss on her forehead before ordering his driver to return them to their lodgings.

Dar waited until the gambling hall and duke were behind them, then smacked the wizard on the knee. "You've done it! Passage for the four of us around the cape."

Toothpick mopped his brow and head with a much-folded handkerchief and a trembling hand. "Nay, bucko, he's done more than that! He's gotten us the whole ship."

"The whole ship!" Sharlin gasped. "You're a marvel!"

The wizard looked at them, his face sagged in quiet thought. "No, my dear . . . it's even more than that. You see, what I've done is won the right for us to sail out of the Nettings . . . and into a sacrifice for the serpent."

Chapter 10

"This is barbaric," Sharlin muttered, looking over the wooden jetty to where the ninety-foot-long ship bobbed and waited for them. Its deck was piled with boxes of goods contributed by local merchants and farmers, intended to be offerings to the minion of the dragonlords who lay waiting outside the bay. Among the goods she recognized carved puppet heads and finely made boots. She ducked her head, sick to her stomach, and could not force herself to look back.

Thurgood took her elbow. "Keep your chin up, my dear," the wizard said.

They sat elbow to elbow in the duke's cart, Toothpick and Dar across from them, effectively held prisoner until the ship was loaded and ready to set sail. From the looks of it, denizens of the Nettings had been working all night. A band played a low, mournful tune, solemn and fluting, and the shrill cry of the gulls shattered the melody as they wheeled in and out, and gray clouds parted to show that dawn had come at last.

"I still don't know how ye managed to convince them to put the horses and ponies aboard."

The wizard tightened the corner of his mouth grimly. "Sea serpents are known to have large appetites. And the duke and I have an understanding. The serpent might not even be in the waters now. He is giving us a chance to continue our journey unmolested, however unlikely that might be."

Sharlin's nose wrinkled as fishmongers struggled past, their baskets loaded with bloody offal. "What is that?"

"Chum. To bring the serpent to the boat. The sailors will be throwing it overboard to lay a trail to attract it."

She shuddered and pressed a fist to her chin to help keep her jaw clenched. It was cool—the long summer waning at last—and she was cold even under her pallan cloak. Only Dar was quiet. Too quiet. She alone had noticed that he kept his sword sheathed loosely, and now he palmed the pouch of ashes tenderly, his thoughts absent, his jawline tensed. Thurgood was wasting his soothing talents on her, she thought; he ought to be settling down Dar.

Crewmen scuttled off the ship in waves, leaving only ten men on dock facing the duke. Thurgood straightened.

"Get ready," he warned.

The Duke of the Nettings waited until the band fell silent, and townspeople crowded forward on the docks to hear him, pressing inward, their chafed faces red with hope, eyes bright with excitement, children swinging from their mother's skirts, men puffing clouds of sweet smoke from their pipes.

"Nine of you go willingly to your deaths, proud to sacrifice yourself in the name of the dragonlords and the Nettings. The tenth also is proud, but leaves behind his wife and children. To him I promise that his son will be raised and educated and landed, his daughter will be made a gentlewoman and dowried, and his wife will be a comfort to mine own wife."

"Big o' him," Toothpick muttered. He spat outside the carriage.

"Quiet, all of you. Thus far the people of the Nettings are convinced a live sacrifice will appease the serpent more . . . but I don't think they'll have anything against dead meat, if it comes down to that!"

Dar looked at the wizard, and an odd expression passed across his face, and Sharlin saw his well-muscled thighs tense. A shiver ran through her again—it was like standing across from a berserker, wondering when the man would explode. Couldn't Thurgood sense it?

"Dar . . ." she began, but the sentence hung on the air, for the duke had rolled up his scroll and now signaled his guards to unload the carriage.

A murmur ran through the crowd watching the strangers leave the hospitality of their own duke and approach the ship . . . a powerful wizard and his servant, a mysterious princess, and a heroic swordsman. For days the stories of the importance and prowess of their visitors had been told, inflating their value to the serpent, until the citizens of the Nettings were certain that if this boatload did not appease the dragonlords, nothing would. They held their breath.

Toothpick hopped aboard with the nimbleness of a woolie, and leaned over the side of the ship to help Thurgood navigate the rope ladder. Sharlin watched the man climb painstakingly, his weakened side hampering every movement. The duke took her hand and held it a little too long, and she looked him full in the eyes, trying to fathom his true emotions.

"I wish I were going with you," the man said. "But I have no choice."

"Choice?" Dar repeated angrily. "Are you animal enough to think that tossing food down the gullet of a big fish will drive it away? Maybe you should all jump off the docks and swim to it in droves. There are no dragon-gods."

His words rang out with the sharpness of a newly honed blade. Meant for the duke alone, they carried on the misty air of the seafront as though shouted, and the man rocked back on his heels, slapped by them, as his people gasped.

"Blasphemy . . ."

The Duke of the Nettings heard the shocked whispers of the crowd as clearly as if all stood right beside him. He paled and signaled his guardsmen.

"He impugns the gods. Take him. We'll deal with him later, rather than let his presence soil our gifts."

Sharlin hung on the ladder, her boot heels twisted, reaching back for Dar with a cry, but soldiers surrounded him, their weapons drawn even as he pulled his.

"No!" Thurgood shouted, leaning over the railing.

Dar ran the first man through, pulled his blade free, and parried a second, turned and kicked a third man down, giving himself breathing room, and the first rays of clear sunlight flashed off the bloody metal as he pointed at the duke.

A guard pounced from behind him, the butt of his staff thumping into the back of Dar's skull, and the swordsman collapsed with a grunt, his sword clattering to the dock.

Eager hands seized his limp form to drag him from the docks.

"Stop!" Thurgood's voice rang out, even as Toothpick grasped Sharlin and pulled her onto the ship, his massive shoulders bulging as he did so, and she righted herself, trying to catch her breath.

The duke glared up at them, the wind catching his fine black locks. The high tide began to ease them away from the docks. "I think little of oath-breakers, and the gods think even less," the man charged.

"We have broken no oaths! The man only expressed his mind . . . and if you believe blasphemers have brought this creature to your waters, then perhaps it is only fitting you should send a blasphemer out to appease it!"

Sharlin's breath caught in her throat. "Oh, no, Thurgood," she whispered, her words carrying no farther than herself. "The pallans! They'll sacrifice the pallans in droves if we fail."

She closed her eyes, clutching at the rope railing. The pallans had come to her in the nighttime hours, long before the other citizens of the Nettings awoke and came down to the docks, had come and filed past the carriage, their gauze masks and veils and hoods hiding their emotions, but Sharlin had sensed their gratitude. They had known when she entered the city that she was not one of them, though she wore pallan clothing . . . just as they knew she was one of their last hopes for being allowed to live unpersecuted. Because she was going, they would not have to. When she reached the graveyard and raised Turiana, first she would save the House of Dhamon, and then she would return to the Nettings to repay the debt she owed the pallans.

The duke's men heaved the bundle of Dar halfway to his feet, and the duke and Thurgood stared at each other. Then the duke shifted. He nodded. "It is fitting," he said loudly, and looked about the docks. "It is fitting that one of the blasphemers should go down to the depths and meet our god's punishment."

Sharlin's hand curled whitely upon the rope.

Thurgood let out a breath and leaned upon the dwarf as a guard shouldered Dar and dragged him up the rope ladder.

"I hope I know what I have just done," the wizard sighed. Toothpick bolstered him up, and Dar's body was thrown onto the decking like a sack of meal.

Sharlin went to her knees beside him and took his head in her lap. Shouts rang through the air, and the frozen sailors went to work, freeing the sails into the billowing morning air and throwing the anchor ropes free. With a lurch, the boat staggered into the wind, and they were away from the dock. The band struck up another tune, and cheers filled the air, but Sharlin closed her mind to the noise, stroking Dar's unruly hair from his forehead after taking off the half-helm that had failed to protect him.

Thurgood remained standing, leaning on his valet, watching the shore fade behind them. "That should cut the hazers off for good," he said.

"An' th' demon?"

He shrugged. "I don't know, Toothpick. The beast has a geas laid on him, and from what I know of the witch, she might join her powers with his—I would not be surprised if they attempt to follow us, once they have found out where we are going. Keep those sharp eyes of yours to the aft. Let me know if you see another tall ship one of these days."

He consented then for Toothpick to lead him away from the railing and to the cargo hold, where a cabin of sorts had been erected to hold the sacrificial passengers. Sharlin watched him disappear.

Her right leg had gone numb, then awoke to prickles, then become icy cold, before Dar finally stirred. His eyelids flickered and he groaned, his left hand flailing, trying to touch his scalp. She caught his wrist before he hit her, and the touch of her hand woke him completely.

A smile replaced the first dazed look. "I made it aboard," he said.

"Through no fault of your own!" But she smiled back. "Thurgood convinced the duke you should die for your sins. Can you sit up? My legs are in pain."

He struggled upward and winced. Gingerly, he touched the back of his head, where a lump the size of a cackle egg greeted him. "These past few weeks have been rough," he mused.

"Thurgood said it would take thirty days or so to make the cape. We all could use the rest."

"And if the island is there?"

Their gazes met and held, until Sharlin blushed and broke away. "Then the worst is yet to come," she said. "Stand up and lean on me. We need to go below . . . the crew's nearly stepped on us a handful of times already."

He leaned on her perhaps a bit more than was necessary as she helped him downstairs, but she was keenly aware of the strength of his arm that encircled her shoulders and the quiet way he moved. At the bottom of the ladder, he halted her in the shadows, for Toothpick's voice rumbled, and it was obvious that the two of them had not been heard entering the hold.

Dar's hand dug into her shoulder. "Stop and be quiet."

"Dar! We can't eavesdrop."

"Quiet!" His fingers bit into her muscles, and she choked off a cry of pain, and stood, trembling, beneath his hand.

". . . I couldna get a better fix on th' time than that, master. I'm sorry, but scuttlebutt around th' Nettings has the battle happening aboot the time we left Murch's Flats."

"And Jet was injured." Tired, yet still mild tones, clearly Thurgood's voice, though barely audible above the creak and groan of the ship, and the thumping and shouting of the crew above.

"Injured gravely, though 'tis doubtful the beast would die of his injuries."

"Then he'll go to spawn. To heal and to spawn, for that's their instinct. It explains my growing weakness." Thurgood sighed.

Dar made a small sound in his throat, turned and scaled the ladder, and made a great noise of dropping the grating and clambering down again, and the voices stopped abruptly. He draped his arm about Sharlin and let her help him into the meager cabin. Already the air smelled of horse and sweat, and the wizard smiled apologetically. Sharlin dropped Dar onto a bunk comprised of no more than a blanket stuffed with sweet hay.

"Ye have a thick skull," the dwarf said.

Dar shrugged ruefully. "And a big mouth. Why didn't you leave me behind? My half of the map is done for."

Thurgood looked at him, his drooping right eye tearing slightly. "What is ahead of us will take all the skills we all possess . . . and maybe more. We can't afford to be separated now. When we reach Glymarach, the Cradle, the dragons will know we're there. Until now, we've been an annoying speck, but the closer we get to our objective, the more annoying we'll be."

"Then you think we'll face their power."

The wizard gathered his robes up, swung his feet aboard his bunk, and lay back on his pack. "I have no doubt of it, princess." He motioned to the corner, where curtains were pulled back from an equally austere bunk. "I managed to persuade them to give you something of privacy. You must be tired." He sniffed. "Unless my senses deceive me, the crew has begun chumming. I suggest we rest while we can. There is still the serpent to deal with.''

"Ay," muttered Toothpick. "And I've no wish to slither down th' cold drake's throat."

The beast did not strike on the first day, nor even the second, nor yet the third, and the crew from the Nettings listened to Thurgood's argument that the dragonlords had set them free, and they turned the ship down the coast, with the wind at their back, and no misgivings, though the one man wept, for he knew he couldn't return to his family no matter what the future held.

Dar healed quickly and took to helping the crew with the rigging, his shirt off, absorbing the last warm rays of the sun, in the following weeks. He wore an odd pattern of scars, a knife wound here, a ragged tear there, but had been remarkably free of foolish encounters during his tenure as a mercenary. The sailors from the Nettings accepted him grudgingly at first, then admiringly when he showed them enthusiasm and skill. Crew and passengers held an uneasy truce, each aware that the other had not fulfilled its true purpose, but not once as the weeks passed did the sailors mention turning back from the course Thurgood had set them on around the cape.

Sharlin sat on deck and watched Toothpick teach them dicing, though the sailors already seemed expert.

"'Tis the least I can do," the gnarled man said gruffly. "Their lord sent them out to be dead men, and dead men have to learn to make their way through th' rest of the world somehow. They canna go back."

A shout from the fo'c'sle interrupted his philosophy, and both Sharlin and Toothpick scrambled to the side with the sailors to see what the lookout had spied.

The crew had kept the ship within sight of the shore, and the view that met them now was of sere brown hills, red cliffs, with a pink beach resting at the foot of it, and a huge, graying carcass awash on the sands, its rib bones hanging with meat.

Sharlin gagged and looked away, and Toothpick cursed and hotfooted it downstairs to the cargo hold, where Thurgood was napping.

Dar came up behind her and put his arm about her waist to steady her. "It must have been big."

Drawn in spite of herself, she looked at the bloated and ruined beast. "The—the sea serpent."

A crewman spat. "Not likely, miss. More like the remains of one of its meals."

"It's following us down the coast?"

He gave a brown-toothed grin. "Thought ye'd gotten away from it, eh? Yep, it's either followin' us—or we're followin' it."

She would have gone to her knees, but for Dar holding her. A soft step at her side reminded her that Thurgood had been brought up to look at it. The wizard shouldered his way to the rail and paused.

"There's no way that could be the serpent?"

"I don't think so, milady. The sailors have recognized it. The creature is feared by their fishermen, but it's not the sea serpent. And look at that." He pointed across the water, hand quivering ever so slightly. "The first three ribs are cracked, just dangling there. The only beast in the water big enough to attack that thing, and survive, would be—"

"—the serpent," she finished for him. The carcass rolled back and forth in the water as the sea tugged at it, and birds covered it, eagerly pulling off gobs of flesh. She turned away a second time from the gore, and did not miss the look that passed between dwarf and wizard. Though Dar had never spoken of the conversation they overheard, she knew he mistrusted Thurgood.

The wizard stroked his soft, ash-blond beard. "You knew we'd be followed," he admonished her. "The serpent perhaps, the witch perhaps. That both are close now should not surprise you."

"The witch?"

He nodded, even as Dar took his arm from her waist quietly, easily, so that she suddenly missed the warmth of his touch though she never heard his steps fade away.

Two days later, the dawn brought forth not only the now familiar sight of dry cliffs and strands where the ocean struck so hard that huge spumes shot into the air, but a scene of carnage. The crew leaned overboard, awestruck, as they sailed through a patch of fish—dead fish, belly up, floating on the glassy roil of the sea.

"What killed all of them?"

Dar shook his head. His shirt was off, knotted loosely about his throat, and a diamond patch of hair on his chest shone like spun gold. He took one of the rigging ropes, threw it overboard, and swung over with it, even as she screamed and the crew gaped in astonishment.

Hanging at the end of the line, he dipped his hand through the wake and brought up a fish, only to have it flake through his fingers. He wasted no more time; he climbed the rope quickly and waved a crewman to pull the rope up.

"What is it?" she asked, as he washed his hands off.

He frowned. "It was cooked . . . boiled in the water."

"Cooked? But how?"

He shook his head. "I don't know, but I'm willing to bet our friend the wizard won't be surprised by it."

And in the depths of the hold, where Thurgood rested on his bunk and read by lanternlight, and made etchings on his papers, Dar learned that he was right. The wizard laid his book aside and tapped his drawing stick thoughtfully.

"I don't suppose," he said, finally, "that you could tell how fresh the patch was?"

Dar grinned. "Dinner already cooked? No . . . but it couldn't have been too old, or the birds and tide would have swept it away. Perhaps early this morning, before sunrise?"

Thurgood nodded. "Probably. I think tonight would be a good time to pull the maps out again. According to all signs, the shoreline and the constellations, we are nearing

the end of our journey. Perhaps two more days' sailing
. . . less if we pull in a strong wind. We are rounding the
cape now. And . . . I have other things I must discuss
with you."

The sea was black before the ship was secured for night
running and supper was cleared away. Sharlin licked her
lips. Water was scarce now, but Thurgood had calmed
everyone with news that they would soon be dropping
anchor and looking for fresh water.

They made a table out of empty crates, stacking them
side by side, and knelt by the map as Thurgood smoothed
it out. He tapped the end of the lands of Kalmar. "We
rounded this cape this morning. Here"—a bare thumb-
length away—"is the island marked as Glymarach." He
sketched the thin peninsula at the southwestern end of the
island. "Have you seen maps of this area?"

"Once," Dar responded, catching the look of the
wizard upon him. "The island is rounded . . . no such
peninsula exists. Heavy fogs, like steam, veil the southern
tip most of the time. I've heard sailors say the water
boils."

Thurgood smiled. "Have you now. Well, it probably
fogs . . . we've had problems with that the farther south
we've sailed. I misdoubt the water boils."

"I don't think you doubted that this morning." The
swordsman straightened. He hooked a thumb in his
weapons belt, which he hadn't worn in days, as it was of
no use for climbing rigging.

"That is, as the locals would say," Thurgood said,
"another kettle of fish."

The ship rolled suddenly, hard to port. The candles and
lanterns flickered, and Sharlin grabbed to steady herself.

But Dar and the wizard hardly noticed. "I think you've
been holding out on us," the swordsman accused. "You
know much more than you're willing to tell us."

"Ay, bucko," Toothpick interjected. "And ye've been
known to inhabit a few shadows. Think you my sharp eyes
couldna see ye? Ye're lucky to have a man of Thurgood's

talents along . . . and ye'll pay handsomely for it, before this quest is done, take my word for it!"

"Why, you little thief—I should have cut you off at the knees back at Murch's Flats!"

"Dar!" Sharlin objected sharply, but a shrill scream from above damped her words. One of the horses bucked and plunged in its makeshift stall in the dark. A great booming thrilled the ship, and wood cracked, and the sea roared.

The deck lid was thrown back, and a man screamed down, "Serpent! Serpent!"

Thurgood paled. "Not yet." He swore softly. "Not yet!"

"We're taking on water," Dar added. He stood and turned. "I can hear it coming in."

Boots ran across the deck, and a man screamed, a deathcry cut off in midsound, and another man finished the high-pitched terror of the first.

"We're under attack!"

Chapter 11

Black water boiled about the hull of the listing ship, throwing glowing green foam, but yielding none of its secrets. The four of them gained the deck and went to the side where two of the crew members yammered and pointed.

Sharlin skidded across wet footing, and Toothpick righted her, growling, "Not even a moon t' see by!"

Thurgood threw his head back and glared at the cloud cover. "Oh, they're there, all right," he muttered. The swinging lanterns guttered and shed little vision on the waves as the ocean quieted. It drew back as though gathering its strength to assault them again—it or what its dark waters hid. The wizard pivoted. "Toothpick, go below and get a barrel of that oil—you know the sort. It was put aboard with the offerings."

The dwarf muttered and scampered off to do his master's bidding.

Dar had his sword pulled and leaned over the railing, searching the phosphorescent shimmerings for a glimmer of the beast. "I can't fight what I can't see!"

But Sharlin stood mesmerized, for she alone faced the aft of the boat, and she could see in the lanternlight what the others could not, and her scream froze in her throat.

A small moon rose out of the water. Its golden orb caught the scant illumination and shone it back faceted like a jewel, and the darkness of its bulk rose with it, and

149

for a moment Sharlin wasn't sure what she looked at—for there was no second eye, but a cavern of blackness.

She staggered back and clutched at Dar, a sound gargling in her throat. She pointed, and the others turned and saw what she saw.

"Holy shit," husked Dar. He fumbled at his belt for his throwing dagger, cursed himself for not having sheathed it, and clutched his sword desperately, fighting with himself over whether to throw it or not.

Thurgood stayed his arm even as he cocked it. "That's not a serpent. That's a full-fledged dragon, hurt and spiteful, but he's not blasted us yet. Hold your blade."

The creature opened his jaws, glowing crimson as his tongue flickered out and he hissed, the sound steaming out on the night air. Flinching, Sharlin put her hands to her ears and turned her face away.

"Now you know why we found fish boiled in the ocean," murmured the wizard.

Toothpick popped his head out of the cargo hold and assessed the situation quickly. Hugging the deck as crewmen screamed and ran, he crawled behind his master, uncorked the barrel, and poured the oil over the side, where it ran into a slick and curled toward the body of the floating dragon.

Thurgood grabbed a lantern and emptied it into the slick. The fountain of oil burned as it arched into the night, and the entire slick erupted into orange flame that turned blue as it burned.

"Jet!" screamed the wizard and threw his hands into the air. The dragon answered in fury, the burning water etching his outlines brilliantly.

Dar moved then. He shouted at the crewmen, "Get your weapons—spears, nets, daggers—we have a target!"

In the firelight, Sharlin could see clearly now the ragged socket of the eye wound, and half-seamed tears that ran down the beast's neck as he reared higher out of the water.

"Miserable worm!" the dragon roared, so loudly she barely understood that he spoke, even as Toothpick grabbed her and threw her down to the decking. "I know your voice! I thought I cut your thread long ago!"

"Not yet!" screamed Thurgood in frenzy. "We shall go together!" He clapped his hands and began to chant.

A trident clipped the dragon under the chin and dropped harmlessly into the waters, and the creature heaved, water foaming under his bulk. The boat shuddered. A taloned paw clutched it aft. Wood exploded under his grasp. The horses whinnied in shrill panic belowdeck, and one of the pack donkeys gave a shattering bray.

Dar slipped as he leaned back and loosed a spear. Jet snatched it in flight and crumbled it. Furious hissing filled the night.

"Why doesn't he flame us?" Sharlin muttered to herself, clutching the decking.

"He canna," Toothpick answered, "or he would have!" The dwarf picked himself up, "Stay there!"

The boat tilted a little, almost knocking Thurgood off his feet. Silver fire spurted from his hands, and when the bolt smashed against the dragon's breast the air shook with a thunderclap. The beast flailed and rolled, and the ocean crested, as Jet's bulk slipped below the waters.

The oil slick parted about him, then quieted, its flames still bright. All grew still, except for one man who lay over the railing, sobbing hysterically, and the horses stamping down below.

Dar straightened from his half-crouch, another spear in hand. "Where is he?"

Thurgood took a deep breath. "I don't know. He's not dead . . . yet."

The crewmen thawed slowly, looking about them in the pitch of night, trying to see the unseeable. Clouds thinned overhead. The burning slick drifted too close to the ship.

Sharlin got to her knees, her hands bracing herself. She looked up at the wizard as the man lowered his hands wearily and let the dwarf hold him up. "You knew!" she said hoarsely, and her slender frame trembled with her anger. "You knew it was a dragon all along! You knew he wouldn't stay near the Nettings . . . he was injured in battle, and he was swimming this way."

"I didn't know . . . but I hoped!" The wizard twisted to look at her, and a wild light gleamed in his eyes. "I hoped! He would go to spawn, I knew that much, to reproduce himself, as his life was threatened. That much I've learned about the so-called gods. And I waited. I kept myself alive and I waited—and now I will take that dark evil out of the world. Vengeance is given to me!"

With every word, the man's voice grew stronger and louder until the last, and then suddenly the oceans split with a roar, and Jet burst from the waters.

"You want me, man—come take me!" the creature sounded. His jaws curled open, and flame issued forth, spewing across the deck.

Dar leaped, his body parallel with the boat, knocking Sharlin over, protecting her body with his own, as blaze grazed them both. The flames parted around the wizard and the dwarf and sizzled out on the damp wood, but the aft burst into fire.

The dragon lifted his bulk onto the rear of the boat, and it sagged under his massive chest and splintered as he clawed for a hold.

"He's taking us down!"

The crewmen moved then, surged forward as one, and spears and tridents filled the air. Jet shook his head, nostrils flared like balls of fire, his spines rattling as the weapons bounced off his armored hide.

Dar rolled off Sharlin and pulled her tightly into his arms. "Can you swim?"

"A—a little."

"Take the empty barrel then." He corked it hastily as he spoke. "It'll help you float. Jump—the ship's going down. We're near enough to shore . . . you should be able to make it back to Kalmar or maybe drift down to Glymarach."

"No! I won't leave you."

"You haven't any choice!" He twisted a fragment of net about the barrel and thrust it into her hands. "Just hold on tightly. Now go!"

Thurgood laughed before she could move . . . the sound chilling. It cut through the battle fever. He moved forward boldly, leaning on the shoulder of his faithful servant, and pulled a silver longknife from his sleeve. With the grace of a born knife thrower, he drew back and threw—and the blade traced the darkness with a silvery line as it sang toward its target.

The longknife sank deep into the dragon's breast. Silver exploded from Jet's chest, and the beast screamed in agony. He thrashed, and his wings bated the air and his tail lashed about, sweeping two crewmen overboard. The dragon raised himself high. He convulsed and with a gasping hiss, sank from the boat and disappeared into the ocean once more.

Dar loosed Sharlin. The wizard stood, his body in an attitude of listening, but all the swordsman could hear was the panicked whinnying of his horse and the gray down below . . . and the pouring in of water.

"We're sinking!"

The dwarf shook Thurgood. "He's no comin' back this time. You wounded him fair mortal."

"But he's not dead!"

"Nay," the little man soothed his master. "Not dead yet, but we will be if we dunna get out o' here!"

The wizard stared down, dazed. The oil on the water reflected light onto his aged face. "It's still not over." He flexed his shoulders, as though suddenly aware of what was happening to others. "Toothpick . . . we've got to get off."

"Now ye're talkin'." The dwarf led his master to the side. "We'll jump together!"

Sharlin pushed the netted barrel into his hands. "Use this—it'll help keep you afloat."

"But princess—" the dwarf began, and spoke to her back, for she had turned and bolted after Dar, who clambered down into the hold.

Lanterns had smashed, and the hold burned in patches, casting towering shadows even as water poured in. Dar saw her, his face pale and etched. "Get out of here!"

She shook her head. "I can't leave them down here to—to die." Gaining his side, she took out her own dagger and sawed the horses free from their ties, and then wrestled down a donkey as it bucked in fear.

The horses bolted past them toward the gaping hole in the boat, and leaped into the night and air and foaming sea, their ropes trailing from them. Dar cut the last donkey loose. Crates and barrels floated past them.

"My pack!" she cried, in remembrance then, thinking of her herbs and spices. She turned and fought her way to the bow, even as the patches of fire sizzled out one by one as the waters met and passed her, tangling her skirts about her knees.

She grasped her pack. Dar caught up with her, shouting over the mayhem, "Are you crazy?"

"Maybe!" Her teeth chattered as the chill water swept about her. "But if we make Glymarach, we still need the map!"

He helped her shoulder the straps and snatched up his own pack and pouch of ashes. The flooring tilted sharply under their feet. The ocean sucked at them eagerly, swallowing pack donkeys and cargo into its roaring depths.

He literally pulled her through the waters with him, up the ladder and onto the decking, the only place where they could now safely jump.

"Pray you can swim," he shouted.

She looked at him and grabbed him, in sudden fear and terror, and hugged him close. She couldn't tell the salt from her eyes apart from the salt of the sea as she cried, "No! I pray you can swim!"

With a boom, the water reared up, knocking them both from the deck, and the ship went down.

Chapter 12

He woke, crusted and bruised, with the sea lapping still at his boots as though ever hopeful it could pull him back in. Sand gritted under his cheek. He curled up, and then sat up.

His eyes were swollen shut. It was like cracking an eggshell to open them, and the tenderness immediately made his eyes water, but the tearing was what cleared them. Dar drew his legs under him, blinking hard, until his sight cleared. The relentless sun beat down.

Haaaw-hee, haaaaw-hee . . . the air rattled as a tiny donkey brayed out its defiance of the ocean and trotted along the sand past Dar, trailing its frayed rope. He threw himself forward and grabbed it. The beast put its head down as the rope grew taut, planted its four legs, but halted.

Dar staggered to his feet and followed the rope up. He patted the shaggy mount, glad that it had stopped. It could have dragged him the length of the beach, for his muscles trembled with every movement and he felt weak as a baby. The donkey pressed against him after smelling him and crowded close, and the two stood a moment in silent kinship, for they had survived.

Dar's heart skipped a beat then, and he looked up and down the beach wildly. Rock and cliff behind him, and beach stretched out far in front of him, but there was no sign of anyone else, save crates and barrels washed up or still bobbing in the surf.

He cupped his hand. "Sharlin! Sharlin!"

Empty sky and sand ate up the sound of his voice, and he couldn't even tell if it carried far enough to be heard. The emptiness tore at him, his throat and his gut, and he tightened his arm about the donkey.

The creature brayed again, its hoarse voice shattering the quiet. Its ears flickered forward and back, and then an echo came back.

From beyond the rocks! Dar turned in his tracks and broke into a staggering run. The donkey trotting by his side, he made for the shoals that cut off the beach.

Coal-black rock greeted him, dimpled by the ages-long pounding of seawater. In tiny pockets, water pooled and feathery plants waved while shelled creatures scuttled away the moment his shadow fell on them and blocked out the sun, as he climbed over them. The rock cut at his hands. Dar cursed and paused, squatting, and took what was left of his shredded cloak and wrapped it about his hands, then continued to climb.

On the other side was a tiny bay, cut off by another arm of rocks, but he smiled broadly, the salt crust breaking across his tanned face, for pink-and-beige sands were cupped in a sheltering bay, and beyond it was a strand of high grass, and a tree waving, and two horses, a mule, and one donkey cropped tranquilly, as though totally unaware their survival was nothing less than a gift from the gods.

Then, on the pink-and-beige sands, something moved. Dar stared, then gave a shout and bounded down from the rocks heedlessly, crying aloud with a hoarse voice.

"Sharlin! Sharlin!"

The girl barely stirred again as Dar gained her side, her amber hair still damp and tangled on her face. When he lifted her up, she coughed feebly, retching up seawater and bile. He gently wiped her mouth dry. Her eyes fluttered, and beneath his hand, her pulse grew stronger.

Muscles that had been weak surged. He stood, raised her in his arms, and strode across the beach toward the grass, surer than life itself that fresh water would be nearby, and that, for the moment, the two of them lived.

* * *

"What about Thurgood and Toothpick?"

Even her question did not fade Dar's smile as he sat and watched her sip her drink from a large cup he'd fixed for her. "No sign of them." He'd bathed her, fully clothed, in the fresh water, and then bathed himself, and they sat drying in the sun.

"You haven't looked," she chided gently.

He'd gone back around the strand of rocks and forced the remaining little donkey to swim with him to the bay, and now all of the animals jostled each other, greedily eating the first fresh grass they'd had in weeks. They'd lost only one of the donkeys.

"No." As if the subject was closed, he reached across to her pack. "This thing nearly pulled you under." He hefted it, and water seeped out of it as he did so.

Sharlin grabbed for it with a cry of pain. He untied its thongs and began to air out the contents. She took away a pouch, the leather dark and stained with seawater, and horror crossed her face as she opened it.

Almost everything within was ruined. Her hands trembled as she shook out the spices. Tiny packets fell into her hand, and a concoction of seed and bud floated around in her palm. Her eyes washed with tears.

"Oh, gods," she whispered. To have come this far and lose it . . . to have come this far and have her hopes ruined.

"What is it?"

"The lyrith . . . the seawater . . ."

"Your potpourri? I'll get you more . . . the draw is full of wildflowers."

Dar blurred in her sight as he bent over her, but she shook her head. "You don't understand! This is lyrith. It's worth more than most kings. I need it to save my home."

He knelt by her and took her trembling hand, looking at the ruined herbs. "Dragon gold isn't enough, is it? You need to bring back more than an army. There's sorcery behind all of this."

"Yes." She met his solemn gaze and tried to quiet her trembling, but couldn't. So far from home, even after all these weeks in his care, could she trust him? Rodeka's powers stretched everywhere . . . the sorceress had hurled her so far from the lands of Dhamon that she might never get back without the aid of the golden dragon, if she could even raise her. And if she couldn't . . . then she would die trying.

"Dar, it doesn't grow everywhere. It's a very powerful charm."

His brown eyes warmed her as he answered, "We'll find the graveyard first. Then, I guarantee you, I'll find the answers you need. Your people will be freed!"

"I've got to have it before we reach the graveyard, or it'll be too late."

He dropped her hand, dried a welling teardrop with the rough tip of his finger, and smiled ironically. "Then you shall have it before."

He had just pledged to give her heart and home back to her . . . could she do less than believe for the moment that he had the power to do it? And there was nothing else to be done, in this he was right. Maybe the lyrith could be restored if she dried it. She laid out the spices on a rock and gently blew over them. Then she carefully repackaged what she could salvage. Finally, a little breathless, she asked, to change the subject, "Where are we?" Dar had touched her a little too closely, and she didn't know how to handle it. What would he say if he knew she intended to rejuvenate a dragon, if she could find the lyrith to do it . . . a process that could cost them their lives?

"Kalmar or Glymarach?" At her nod, he shrugged. "I don't know. East or west, I can tell, but where, I don't know. After I'm sure we can survive here, I'll have to do some scouting to determine where we are." He flexed gingerly and stood. "The beach I washed up on is littered with goods. Some may be ruined, some may be all right. We need whatever I can find. Will you be all right alone?"

Sharlin grinned as the herd of grazing animals nudged closer. "Alone? Yes, I'll be fine." She stuck her booted feet into a bold ray of sun to dry them better.

He left her with few qualms, knowing the livestock couldn't be so quiet after the night's ordeal unless the area was relatively safe.

His back ached when he had finished combing the beach for barrels and crates, and he had a fair-sized pile of them. He eyed the rocky outcropping, mentally declaring there was no way he was going to climb over the rocks one at a time. He would have to swim around them, the way he'd taken the donkey.

With what few twists of rope he could find, he lashed together a makeshift raft of broken wood, some of it natural, tree limbs bleached in the sun, and some he recognized with a pang as having been from the ship. A talon scar raked one board that he tied into place. He loaded the crates, pulled the rope over his shoulder, and determinedly walked into the surf, dragging the raft behind him.

The tide surged in, threatening to impale him on the jagged rocks, but he finally got his unwieldy craft beached. Sharlin waited for him on the sands, her split skirt rolled up above her knees, her tiny feet bared, and her hair dry and fluffed out wildly about her face. She grinned as he stood, careful not to drip on her.

"I couldn't imagine this much washing in!" Delighted, she bent and began helping him unload high on the beach, where the goods would stay dry. A veritable bazaar littered the sands as they worked.

When done, she knelt and shaded her hand and looked southward to the other side of the bay. Sunburn pinked her high cheekbones.

"You're going to have to go looking for them," she said, as her thoughts turned to matters they had both tried to ignore. "The sun is getting low." She paused, her dagger in hand, before prying up another lid to see what treasures the shipwreck had left them.

Dar arched his back. His boots were full of sand and he ached in every limb, but he knew she was right.

"I'll be all right here. But they could be hurt, or—or—" Her voice faded, and she swallowed.

"And you want to know."

"Not to know, but to . . . to help, if we can."

Dar looked down at her. For a moment, his chest felt full of emotions he couldn't quite name, nothing to do with the matter at hand. He pushed them away. "After what he did to us?"

"He tried to destroy Jet. You'd have done the same—you did try to do the same," she pointed out.

His lips were cracked, and he licked them carefully. "You know they lied to us. They tracked Jet from his wounding up north and into the Nettings, and figured the beast would come south to spawn."

"What's done is done."

He nodded and took in a deep breath to steady himself for the assault on the far end of the bay. "Take shelter with the horses then, if I'm not back before dark. Can you make a fire?"

Sharlin's eyes flashed. "Listen to you!" Her old independence asserted itself.

Laughing, he started toward the cliffs.

He wasn't laughing when he finally pulled himself to the top, the sun now blazing even lower in the sky. He cursed and spit on his torn palms to soothe them. A bonfire roared on the beach below, and a man-sized figure hunched in front of it, while a half-man-sized figure busily dragged more crates to and fro. He stood for a moment before waving and hailing the wizard and the dwarf.

Nor was Thurgood surprised to see him. Dar helped the man climb the rocky cliff to the sheltering bay and fresh water, and Toothpick scrambled nimbly behind, bracing and pushing whenever the wizard needed aid.

"I told you the spell would work," he shot triumphantly at his servant, leaning back from a handhold, his robes fluttering about him.

Toothpick's beard, stiff with salt water, stood out like a pick as his chin wagged, and he grumbled, "Ye've told me a lot o' things in all these years." He braced his shoulder under his master's rump, adding, "Now heave to, ye old goat!"

The trip down the far side was easier than Dar remembered. He helped the man start down, and the dimpled rocks gave up footholds for their descent.

"What spell was that?"

Thurgood's mild blue eyes had lost the frenzy of the night before when he'd battled the dragon, though they were as red-rimmed and sore-looking as Dar's had felt when he first awoke on the beach. Thurgood fastened a hard gaze on him.

"Did you think I would abandon you in your hour of need? I warded you as best I could . . . though, to my sorrow, I could do little for the crew. I knew the two of you well enough to attempt it, but couldn't help the others. I hope the gods brought them ashore as well."

"I found no sign of them," Dar said. "Do you know where we are?" He helped the man limp to the sand, and Thurgood smiled as Sharlin got to her feet and called out a joyous greeting.

Thurgood waved at her, then shot a sideways glance at Dar. "I think it best to save that until morning. And best that we spend the night here, where it's sheltered and there's water. Tomorrow morning's light is enough to tell the tale."

Toothpick made stew out of dried gunter strips and vegetables that had survived the shipwreck, but sweet berries picked by Sharlin made up for the stale dinner. They slept soundly. A gentle breeze fanned the trees overhead, and the horses murmured low to one another as they sought the company of their riders and the warmth of the low-burning fire.

In the morning, a little scouting by Toothpick proved it far easier and quicker to ride to the beach, as the interior opened up in that direction. They rode bareback, using bitless rope hackamores to control their mounts, for all their tack had gone down with the ship. Sharlin, however, rode on a dress of satin, well stuffed with petticoats, courtesy of one of the boxes they had opened. It didn't make for a saddle, but padded Cloud's back enough that she didn't complain as they reined forward through the trees and saw the beach, where Toothpick's bonfire yet smoldered.

"Toothpick, you stay and scavenge whatever you can. What I have to show them you've already seen."

The dwarf's mouth twisted and he stroked his now soft white beard, but he did not argue. Thurgood reined his mule south.

They rode silently. Dar was aware of his pack, which rode his shoulders instead of his saddle, and inside that pack was the stinger and darts he had procured in Murch's Flats, along with the silver quarrel Trader Joe had given him to dispatch the wizard. He had not considered it before, but now the job offered him rankled at his thoughts. The wizard had not dealt with them openly.

Thurgood talked to Sharlin as they rode, but their voices stilled, and he turned to Dar. "As to where we are, we thought we could have beached on the tip of the cape of Kalmar . . . or on the west side of Glymarach, that part of the island which we know to exist as a surety. Only days of travel would have told us which was true—and then we found that."

He halted his mule and pointed, and Dar caught his breath as he saw the sands ahead.

Something gigantic had furrowed the beach. Scarring the earth with great trenches, an object of great bulk had pulled itself from the waters, across the sands, and into the brush. Splashes of crimson stained the pink-and-white grains.

"The dragon came ashore here." Dar stated the obvious, and he squeezed his legs to quiet Brand, for the stallion had scented the blood and rank smell of the creature, and danced in nervousness.

"Yes. And this must be Glymarach . . . for the beast is dying."

"He seeks the graveyard." Sharlin tucked a lock of her hair behind her ear as she spoke, and silence fell after her words.

Dar turned Brand toward the interior, and a line of red cliffs met his eyes. "We'll have to cross that," he said finally.

"Yes. And then we'll know where we are, unless the maps are gone."

Sharlin touched her chest. "I still have mine." She sighed. "What if Jet lies in wait for us? Or alerts others, if any are here?"

Thurgood gently put his hand about her wrist, warming her arm. "What if we had not come this far at all, and never knew?" He straightened then, and his voice grew hard. "I have a task, and I will finish it."

She said nothing as the wizard kicked his mule and returned to Toothpick, to gather up the few bundles of magicks and potions he had been able to save. Even Dar could not hear her whispered comment as she kicked the gray stallion after him.

They left the beach at midmorning, heading into the sun, and climbing slowly out of the luxurious foliage that hugged the freshwater stream from the cliffs. When that faded, they found themselves riding in towers of red dust that rose from the valleys and dry lakes shimmering in the sun. Black rock boiled up from the dust and lay about, odd jewels forced to the surface of the earth.

They crested the cliffs, and Sharlin twisted around on Cloud, looking back. Many of the goods they had recrated and left behind, but she still rode on the satin blanket fashioned from a lady's gown, and now she eyed the deep blue of the ocean.

Then she blinked, reached out for Dar's sleeve, and missed, but her hand caught his attention.

"What is it?"

"Black sails . . . down the coast . . . look!"

Toothpick pulled up sharply on his donkey. The creature wagged its long ears and gave a tiny buck in protest. The dwarf strained to look out, full white eyebrows frowning, then spat in disgust.

"It's them."

Thurgood turned his mule slowly on the path, and it nudged its way between the chestnut and gray stallions. The wizard pursed his lips. "No doubt of it?"

His servant looked at him, bald pate bright red and

peeling from all the sunburning it had taken these past few weeks. It shimmied as his eyebrows arched. "Ye had me trackin' her all this way. Why question me now? Go on down an' ask her an' th' demon yerself."

The hackles rose on Dar's neck when the dwarf scorned Thurgood's question. "That's her?"

The wizard nodded, then kicked his mule forward and hammered his heels into it, making a laborious turnabout on the pathway. "If Toothpick is correct, it is indeed Kory and Mnak and the hazers."

"How could they follow us here?"

Dar tore his gaze away from the ship approaching the coastline. "You forget, princess—that demon is like a hound on a bloodscent. He knows the way." Something gnawed at his stomach, and he was afraid that it was fear . . . fear of the demon that seemed unstoppable, and the closeness once more of Valorek. He saw Thurgood roll back his sleeves, flex his neck muscles, and wave the three of them to the side.

The wizard was weaker than he cared to admit, but now the man tightened his jaw, and even his drooping eyes blazed with determination. "There'll be no going back," he warned them.

"Why?"

"I am laying traps for them, Sharlin. They'll ensnare any of the unwary who fall into them, but they'll cover our trail and, with fortune, slow down our trackers. Once cast, they will remain until tripped."

She put her chin up a little, a gesture Dar was growing used to, and answered, "I won't be going back until we've found what we came for."

"Good." Thurgood closed his eyes then and began to recite in an odd-cadenced voice that reinforced Dar's uneasiness. After long moments, he dropped his arms wearily, gathered up the mule's reins, and whispered, "Let's be on our way."

Dar took the lead, as he often had, for there was no natural trail through the mountain pass, and whatever brush tangled ahead, his swordwork cleared.

Sharlin urged Cloud to Dar's heels, and he dropped back to let her join him. Her brilliant blue eyes, frowning now a little against the high sun, held sympathy.

"On the run again?"

"I'm used to it," he said briefly. "I'm only sorry that you've become a part of it." He had nothing to offer her now that the demon tracked him again.

"You could have sold the map to me, if it's gold that you need to get him off you."

He shook his head. He'd left his ancient half-helm in his pack, and the sun had lightened his hair, and it fell over his eyes when he moved. "The graveyard holds more than gold for me. I was told that only a dragon's claw could sever me from what follows me."

"And the graveyard should be full of the onyx-and-ivory claws, cast by the dead. Dar—you'll be free!"

He did not answer that—it seemed pointless to—and they rode in quiet companionship along the cliffs until the land broke and spanned away from them, and they sat overlooking a great plain, where only a solitary tree dotted the expanse here and there, and fleeting clouds above left running patterns of darkness upon the golden grass.

The wizard and dwarf drew up with them, and Dar said, "It will be nearly impossible to hide ourselves once we're down on the plain."

"We can travel at night. I can maintain an illusion by day."

But Toothpick reached up to take his master's arm, saying, "Master—"

The wizard interrupted him sharply. "Hold your tongue."

The dwarf stayed silent, but Dar saw the rebellion. His uneasiness increased. He said nothing, just kicked Brand forward, and the chestnut stallion flicked his ears before picking a way down the sloping cliffs.

They took the last light to make a camp and read the map, and Thurgood charted the first edge of the Shield to come shining up the horizon. Though his assessment took longer than Dar's, they came to an agreement on their position. The wizard took steady pulls on a hide of a potent alcohol, part of their booty from the shipwreck. Dar had shared a drink—it was like golden fire, rippling down his gullet—but he refused a second, and frowned when Thurgood didn't. He said nothing, though, for Toothpick had seen his disapproval and stared at him in a silent plea. The wizard had met a nemesis, and was frightened, and for the moment, Dar would allow him this weakness—until it threatened all of them.

Sharlin stared at the map laid out on the grass and held down by rocks. "Then we don't cross the plains."

"No. Nor do we, I think, cut into the mountain range. See, this path is plainly marked . . . we skirt the mountains and then double back."

"Which brings us to the edge of the island where Dar says Glymarach ends."

"Yes."

"That looks to be about five days' riding, then." She hunched closer. "What's this?"

"It's nothing." Hastily, the wizard moved to roll the map up, but she caught his hands.

"You're betraying yourself by protesting too much."

He looked at her. The pulse of her temper flickered in her throat, and Dar noticed that the wizard's gaze dropped to the small marking on her neck, and then to the ground.

Thurgood took a breath. "It has nothing to do with our journey."

"It looked like a building! We might need to take shelter, if staying at the foot of the mountains doesn't hide us well enough. May I remind you, wizard, that you're in our employ, not the other way around."

Toothpick's dagger stopped in midmovement, the last rays of the sun glimmering on it, but the dwarf made no move. Thurgood held up a hand. He inclined his head graciously. "As usual, princess, you're right." He smoothed the map out again. "It appears as a building, but the runic writing identifies it as an abandoned city . . . very old, ruins mostly."

"A city?" Dar echoed. He craned his neck to get a better angle on the map. "Whose?"

"I don't know. The writing states that the place is dangerous, and to avoid it." Thurgood gently took the hide from her, examined the etching, then returned it.

"What's it called?"

"Lyrith. Named for an herb grown around ancient cities wherever the climate allowed . . . a rare herb, given to—"

"Dar!" Sharlin broke the wizard's speech, crying the swordsman's name as though it were a plea.

He looked at her. Then he said quietly, "The hazers have to be stopped. I'm going to the ruins. When we rendezvous, I'll have dropped behind them." His voice rang with enthusiasm. "For once, they'll be the hunted."

"No, you mustn't!" Thurgood staggered to his feet, tottering a moment as his weakened leg threatened to give out on him, then he caught himself. "Fools! Jet is out there somewhere, wounded and spiteful. And the trackers behind. We can't afford to split the party up now!"

"We won't be splitting up. You'll draw the trackers after you, with illusion. They'll never know the difference."

The wizard stopped in consideration, then shrugged. "This is madness, but it's your life. I'll do what I can do."

"It can't be more than half a day's ride. I'm coming with you," Sharlin added.

"No, no!" Thurgood protested weakly. He moved away from Sharlin and the map and drew Dar into the shadows with him. He lowered his voice. "You can't do this to her, Aarondar. Throw away your life, if you want to, but leave her behind."

"I'll leave her in the ruins. I've no intention of letting her face Mnak with me."

The wizard's hands shook as he implored the other, "Don't do this!"

"It's just a ruin."

"Not any ruin. This was a place of long-ago pallans

. . . and the pallans are great historians. I know more of Sharlin's past than she's been willing to tell us. I can't tell you more, but you're taking her into disaster!"

Dar looked over the wizard's bare head and saw Sharlin watching them. "We ride at the first light of morning. Ward yourselves. I'll take care of Sharlin."

"If you love her, you'll stay away from the city."

Their gazes met and held, and Dar was not the first to look away. He answered, "Because I love her, and she wishes it, I must take her."

Chapter 13

They left before dawn. The Shield had dropped quickly in the sky, with the Little Warrior chasing after it, so the darkness covered them as they saddled and rode out the way Dar had marked after looking at the map once more. Thurgood watched them go, and when Dar twisted around on Brand's bare back in farewell, he saw the wizard's features shape into an uneasy rendition of his own.

The hazers had no idea who had survived the shipwreck and who hadn't, so the illusion Thurgood had to maintain to pull the demon was simply Dar's. The trail was confused enough that it would be impossible to tell how many mounts had been ridden. The wizard agreed to maintain Dar, himself, and Toothpick. The girl, it would be presumed, had not made it.

The girl in question flashed Dar a brilliant smile when he turned away from the camp. "Lyrith! Thank you for taking me."

"If I hadn't, you'd have come anyway, later."

Her smile warmed. "You know me well."

"Not well, but better than I did," he answered. Brand put his ears back and lengthened his stride to pace the gray horse closer.

They made good time. The sun had just moved past midday when the lathered chests of the horses pushed through wither-high plains grass and they crested a hillock, and below, the ruins of the city wavered in their sight.

Sharlin pulled her waterskin off her belt.

"Take it easy with that," Dar warned her, before stretching his legs and looking on toward their destiny.

In answer, she merely licked a few drops from the end, to wet her lips, and put the waterskin back.

"How much farther?"

"Another league, perhaps. It's hard to tell in the desert."

"Then I can take a bigger drink."

He shook his head. "Those are ruins, Sharlin. There's no way of knowing what remains of the water supply. The wells may be dry. The map shows a river, but I don't see any signs of it."

With a sigh, she kept the waterskin tucked away and instead brushed her hair from her neck. Damp curls fell from her fingertips, and Dar looked away, back to the ruins.

They kicked the horses forward onto the desert stretching in front of them. The grass soon gave out and their horses trod barren ground. Yet Sharlin could see where fields had been worked once, and her heart soared. A sprig or two of lyrith was all she needed, and she'd comb the whole city for it!

As they drew closer and closer, the city sprawled before them, a civilization as great as any the two had ever seen. The walled buildings covered more land than any place Sharlin had seen before, and she reined up at the gates in awe, Dar just behind her.

Great cracks yawned in the hard-packed ground before her. Dar slid off his foamed chestnut and knelt to look at them. He touched the scaled ground. "This was the river. Probably gone underground, from the looks of it. They must have had ample water to do anything they wanted." He stood up, but didn't remount his horse.

He walked Brand around the cracks. Sharlin booted the gray with a sound thump and the stallion responded by leaping the dry riverbed. The two of them stopped again, caught by the sight of the city gates.

Two great dragon heads yawned before them. The teeth gleamed, rows of real teeth, polished by desert wind over the ages, still sharp and potent. A chill ran down Sharlin's back at the realistic skulls, spines, and gleaming eyes not dulled by time.

The builders of Lyrith had built in rock and stone, most the red of the canyons they had ridden through already, but some in a dark-blue stone that gave the appearance of serenity and shadows and coolness. The city rose, layer upon layer.

"Thousands must have lived here once," she murmured, nudging her horse forward. When he neared the gate, he rolled his eyes and stopped, and Dar took his reins to lead him in along with Brand.

Once inside, she felt the heat diminish, and the whistle of the wind died away. She slid down and joined Dar. His heat and scent rippled over her.

Their footfalls echoed as they walked down the city street. Leaves and dried weeds skittered away, and every movement drew her gaze as she looked for the precious herb. Would she find it growing in a courtyard? A window box? Or in fields outside the walls?

She toed a weed growing near an open doorway. Green had wilted, but it still lived. "Some rain," she said.

"Enough for that, anyway," Dar responded. He looked up at great eyeholes of windows looking down at them. "I think we'd better find a place to hobble the horses and rest, and then we can begin searching. We'll spend the night here, and in the morning I'll catch up with the hazers."

His grim voice faded, and he walked away. Sharlin had to hurry to catch up with him.

Tiny birds flitted through the air, their bodies a pale gray and yellow, their whistles an imitation of the wind the travelers had left behind on the plains. Other creatures, furred and sleek, leaped and crashed away through the ruins when Dar and Sharlin approached, but she never caught more than a glimpse of their eyes flashing just before they ran. Small animals. Dar eased his sword in his sheath and adjusted the hang for an easier pull, but never bared the blade.

And, of course, softfoot watched them, noses quivering, balanced on their large rumps and hind feet, ears alert, before hopping away. Dar grinned.

"Damned pests are everywhere."

"The meat of the world," Sharlin said. She patted Cloud on his bowed neck when he sniffed suspiciously at the beasts scampering away practically from under his nose.

Brand snorted and shook his head, mane rippling. Both horses seemed to share the same opinion of the nearly brainless softfoot.

Sharlin stroked the gray's nose and urged him forward, then let him trail her at the end of his reins. She looked around the great city. The dwelling rooms opened to what must have been shops and crafting centers. The interior of the city divided into a hundred roads. Dar picked one at random, and they headed down its shadowy length.

"I wonder who lived here, and why they left."

Dar shrugged. His leather breastplate creaked, and his shirt was soaked damp under it. "Water, probably. The grass out there is ample pasture . . . they would have had grazing animals, and fields. Perhaps too many lived here to be provided for."

She laughed softly. "And what do you know about pasturing?"

"My father was one of the best dairy herders in his kingdom."

She stopped in astonishment on the street and looked at Dar. "A dairy herder? You milked gunters?"

His face flushed at her astonishment, then he lowered his gaze and gave a lopsided grin. "Yes, I milked gunters." Brand's reins were looped over his arm, and he held his hands out, calloused and scarred by years of soldiering. "I don't think I could touch one now. They're sensitive, you know. My father built a good herd . . . sweet-faced chestnut gunters, with short nubby horns, so you didn't have to worry about being gored." He winced in memory. "They could kick, though."

The two of them began walking again, shoulder to shoulder.

"How did you turn to this?"

He shrugged. "My dad was also a soldier." He looked at her, considering how much to tell her. If he mentioned the name of his enemy, she probably wouldn't recognize it. "Ever heard of Valorek?"

Sharlin shook her head, and golden sunlight waved down her hair as she did. "No. Who is he? The one who set the demon after you?"

"Yes. My father was one of an army sent after him, to root him out of the earth like a weed. They failed— Valorek's never been defeated—and my father was wounded. He was lucky. My mother's father took him in, and they hid and nursed him, because Valorek doesn't take prisoners. Anyway, they married and my father eventually took over the dairy."

"And Valorek learned about him, and came after him."

Dar shook his head and smiled ruefully. "No. One day he came after me."

Sharlin waited for more to be said, and nothing was. She prompted him, "Were you very young?"

"Eight or so, the first time." He stopped. A jumble of rock lay across the edge of the street, and the side of a building sagged inward, the first real destruction he'd seen in Lyrith.

He fished Brand's reins off his arm and handed them to Sharlin. "Wait a minute. I want to take a closer look at that."

She followed after him when he stepped into an archway and ducked under the rubble. "What is it?"

A hail of stones followed her question, and she dodged the cascade as Cloud snorted and danced, a rain of dust choking them all.

Dar looked out of the ruin, and she could see the gleam of something behind him . . . like yellowed bones, a huge skeleton, still intact, poised on immense hind-leg bones, its skull grinning with ivory fangs.

"What is that?"

He came out and dusted himself off. "A landstrider, second cousin to a dragon. A big fellow, too. He evidently got into the shop and couldn't get out, and brought the roof down on himself when he tried." He kicked the street, and a small bone crunched under his boot. "He wasn't killed, but trapped. Must have starved to death in there after a while."

Sharlin looked through the peepholes at the skeleton and shuddered. "It's big!"

"Not as big as they get." Dar looked around, wondering if they were in strider country. If so, once out on the plains, they had better be a lot more cautious. Striders, though wingless and dense as a stone, were rapacious killers. "Come on."

Sharlin stood there for a moment, paralyzed by the sight, then she hurried to catch up with Dar. "Do you think there are any more around here?"

"Not inside the city, or the softfoot population would be a lot smaller and more cautious."

"Oh." Mollified, Sharlin paced him once more. She returned to the subject at hand. "What will you do when you're free of Valorek? Go back to the dairy?"

"It's not there anymore. It burned with my parents."

"I'm sorry."

"Don't be. It's what they wanted." He cleared his throat. "What will you do when you have enough gold and the lyrith?"

"Go home . . . if I can."

"You're not even from up north, are you? Can't be, or you'd know who Valorek is."

Sharlin tossed her hair from her shoulders. "It's not even on the maps. I'd hoped it would be. I guess it must be east, beyond the seas."

"And you'll go back to being a lord's daughter."

"Yes." She smiled gently. "I guess I'll have to, if my father will ever talk to me again."

He looked at her sharply. "They didn't send you out."

"No. I—I decided this was something I had to do, to help against Rodeka. She sounds a bit like your Valorek. I couldn't just sit and wait for her troops to lay siege to our lands, my home. She doesn't just war. Her powers are awful. Things . . . are twisted under her. People, even the land. I knew I needed magic of my own to stand against her, and so here I am."

"Just like that."

"Of course not! No more than you just left the dairy one day and ended up here. But, eventually, here we are." She paused again and looked him full in the face, and he was struck once more by the lustrous dark blue of her eyes, and her high cheekbones lightly dusted with freckles from the weeks under the sun, and the point of her determined chin. Her brows arched delicately, dark like her lashes.

He found it difficult to breathe, and he stepped away from her, shaded his eyes, and pointed down the street. "There. It's a temple or something. Looks as good a place as any to hobble the horses."

They took shelter in the columned building, its cool interior a welcome change from the dusty streets. Sharlin endeavored to give both the horses a handful of water while Dar stalked the temple for safety, his blade drawn and gripped tightly.

His steps echoed, muffled by the bluestone architecture, until she could barely hear him. Then he said, "Sharlin . . . come here."

She paused, then left the packs behind, drew her own dagger, and stepped after him, calling gently, "Where are you?"

"In here."

She followed him, and smelled it before she saw it, the cool air of water, and she heard the bubbling sound. Dar knelt by a pool of fresh water that fountained upward from the depths beneath the floor. He had already washed his face in it, and his hair had fallen about in damp curls on his forehead and temples.

"As pure as any water I've ever drunk." He straightened. "After all these years."

Droppings scattered about gave testimony to the use of the fountain and pool by softfoot and other creatures. Sharlin knelt and drank herself, the cool liquid washing away the soreness of her parched throat.

Sunlight glanced downward, saber rays touching the bluestone flooring. She got up and followed the nearest bank of rays and saw the boxes of soil on the floor, filled with dried leaves and buds, and went to her knees with a cry, for she knew that little flower.

"It's here! The lyrith!" With trembling hands, she picked the boxes clean, filling her leather pouch with the lyrith's muted scent, unmindful of the tears flowing down her cheeks until Dar pulled her to her feet and wiped them away with his roughened hands.

Then, before she could say anything or move away, he made a low sound from deep in his throat, pulled her to his chest, and kissed her fully, taking undisputed possession of her lips.

As his warm mouth took over her trembling one, his hands rose to her shoulders and unfastened the pallan cloak, the soft weaving tumbling to the floor behind her. She scarcely knew when she went to her knees upon it and his strong arms encircled her, pressing her to his armor, or even when they lay down upon the blanket, and she answered his kiss with one of her own . . . seeking, demanding, her hands fumbling with the straps of the breastplate, to take it from him, so that she could feel the warmth and strength of his body in her embrace.

He shook as he buried his hands in her thick, warm hair . . . hair that smelled of the sun and dust, of her gentle fragrance . . . and groaned as she answered his kiss and pulled his body down to lie on hers.

"Stop me now," he told her roughly, pulling his mouth away, breathing harshly.

Sharlin smiled as the shadow and sunlight dappled her body, and he saw the nipples of her breasts quicken under her blouse. He reached out to stroke them, and she gave a soft laugh and pulled him down to her.

Afterward, they bathed in the fountain. Dar washed her hair for her and combed its drying length against her naked back, then pulled her close and kissed her again, this time with none of the pulsating urgency of the first time, and they knelt in the balmy pool and made love a second time, slowly, tasting each other's flesh and answering each other's needs more fully. Then they dressed and walked back to the horses and packs. Dar watered the horses and Sharlin washed out her clothes, and they returned to the outside where the sun slanted deeply in, and they lay down on the pallan blanket, this time to sleep curled inside each other's arms.

When she awoke, she found him sitting up, a fire started on the bluestone, his pack spread out beside him. He fastened a silver quarrel into the stinger and looked down its crude sights.

"What is that for?"

He started. "I didn't mean to wake you."

"It's all right. Is it silver?"

"Yes. In Murch's Flats, the town boss gave it to me and asked me to use it on Thurgood."

She took in her breath sharply. "Are you going to?"

"No. I think the demon will make a better target. It might even work." He had taken a lyrith bud, pounded it to a yellow smear, and rubbed the silver tip in the juice until it looked like burnished gold instead of silver.

"I had forgotten," she said quietly, and looked away as she crawled out of her pallan cloak and stood up.

Dar looked at her, creases at the corners of his eyes wrinkling as he smiled at her. "I'll be back."

"You had better be," she threatened, and then took a long breath to steady herself. "And if you don't come back, I'd better find your bones scattered. If you go with Kory, I'll come after you myself!"

He laughed and pulled her down into his lap, and the

two horses snorted with offended dignity at what happened next.

She woke to night, the fire burned to embers, nearly out. She crawled from his encircling arms carefully, not wanting to wake him, and rebuilt the fire, though the warm air was enough. Habit, she thought. Fire makes you safe against the unseen.

Sharlin tucked her hair behind her ears, wishing a hundredth time for combs left far away in her vanity at home. Then she looked around at the temple.

Clay lamps, with stoppered jugs beside them, rested still in high niches. She went to one and opened the jug. The oil, slightly rancid, still remained. She fueled a lamp, lit it from the fire, and started into the temple, the orange aura blossoming about her.

There had been writing on the walls around the fountain, but she had been too busy to read it, and now her curiosity drew her. What people had lived here—and where had they gone? Had they been driven away, too?

She reached the fountain. A softfoot leaped in startlement, its pointed ears erect, then bounded away between her feet. She jumped too, and nearly dropped the lamp, and stood a moment, her hand to her pounding heart. Then she took a deep breath.

The courtyard walls were carved as high up as the top of her head and down nearly to the floor. She held the lamp high, its bare light just enough to read by. What were the odds, she wondered, of being able to read what this ancient city left behind?

She leaned close to trace the letters, and a chill lightninged down her spine—for she could read, most of it, for this was written in a language she knew nearly as well as her own, a language once called the tongue of the gods. Most of the lawbooks of her father's kingdom, and those of the high king, were written in this speech, called High Rangard. She felt a pang of homesickness as she leaned close and began to read.

She had followed the panels halfway around the courtyard, when suddenly the breath caught in her throat and her eyes widened in shock. She fought to hold the lamp still enough to limn the words.

"No," she moaned, and tears welled up. "No!" She dropped the lamp. Its crash echoed throughout the temple as her chest swelled and she began to scream, and scream, and scream, until all thought fled from her, and she heard only the sound of someone screaming hysterically . . . insanely.

Dar leaped to his feet when the first scream tore through his sleeping. He left the stinger gun lying across the pack, but grabbed his sword. Sharlin's voice cut through the night. She was in the direction of the fountain. He didn't even take time to pull on his boots, just dashed after her, wondering what sort of predator she'd frightened at the watering pool.

The cries built to a crescendo. He skidded into the courtyard and saw her lying in a heap on the stone, beating it with her fists, screams ripping from her hoarse throat, and she didn't stop until long after he took her in his arms and tried to rock her, to comfort her, any way he knew how.

At last, the screams gave way to ragged sobbing, and when even that quieted, he lifted her face to his, trying to make sense of her babbling.

"Sharlin, what are you saying?"

"Time," she sobbed. "My mother and father dead . . . dust . . . it's written in the stone. Oh, Dar, I wish I were dead, too!"

"What do you mean?"

She swallowed, then clutched at his shirt, burying her fingernails in the cloth and flesh, not noticing his wince. "Don't you see? My family's history is written on these walls! Ancient history, written here . . ."

". . . in these ruins," he finished for her. "But how—"

She shook her head, kneading his forearms desperately, as though he were the sanity she was trying to grasp. "I don't know! When we fled . . . I was riding Gabriel, and

Rodeka struck at us, a lightning bolt or something, I don't know—we fell from the sky. . . . My griffin died, and I was left here. I knew . . . I knew we'd been thrown across seas . . . I knew I was a long way from home . . . but—time!"

Her words confused him. Riding griffins were legend. He shook his head, unable to make sense out of most of what she said, but he freed his right arm from her grasp and smoothed her hair back from her forehead. "It's dark . . . maybe you misread it."

"No." She gulped. "The House of Dhamon conquered by the sorceress Rodeka. It's all here . . . graven a hundred years or more ago. The map, the journey, the lyrith—all for nothing!"

He pulled her to her feet. "Sharlin, don't give up! You're alive . . . was your death written there?"

"I . . . I don't remember. I dropped the lamp." She wavered in his arms, but even in the twilight of the temple, he saw the sanity glimmer in her eyes, and strengthen.

"We'll come back in the morning and read the rest of it. You could be wrong. Names are repeated in history."

She nodded tiredly. "All right. We'll come back in the morning." She leaned heavily on him, and he walked her back to the fire.

Her vulnerability struck him as he held her close through the night, breathing in the fragrance of her hair, feeling the silken play of her muscles under her clothing, liking the warmth of her body close to his, listening to her ragged breathing return to normal as she took assurance from him . . . he who had no right to give it, a homeless man running for his life . . .

. . . and so it was that he never had a chance, never saw the black shadow leap at him from beyond the fire as Mnak struck.

Chapter 14

Too limp to scream, Sharlin fell away from Dar as Mnak raked him across his left shoulder. He staggered back, bringing up the swordblade, and twisted out of a second assault, and the demon paused, red eyes blazing in the dark of the temple.

Dar clenched his jaw as fiery pain throbbed in his shoulder. He felt a cool dampness and knew that he bled. Sharlin crawled away from them, picking up a branch from the fire as she did. The horses were gone. The packs had been knocked away. He dared not look for them, for Mnak stood there, talons flexing, waiting for him to waver.

The beast grinned, white teeth flashing. "First you, and then the girl," he said hoarsely. "I will gut you, and take you back to my master while you are still breathing. He can fix you then. The girl . . ."

Dar didn't listen, knowing the demon baited him. They began to circle each other, the foul breath of the demon grazing the air as he told Dar, act by act, what he would do to Sharlin before killing her.

"Try it," she husked from the fireside, "and I'll cut your balls off, then your spurs, before sending you back to your master!"

Dar grinned in spite of himself, as the black skin of the demon lightened to a charcoal gray, then deepened again. Dar jumped into the open. The blade rang against the talons as Mnak defended. Dar swung the blade around and laid it along the beast's back, and a thin line of crimson welled up from the scaled body.

They sprang back, each breathing heavily. Mnak gave a barking laugh. "I will have you. You can't stop me—ask your wizard what I did to him. Better yet, ask your little man there. I brought him to you."

Sharlin staggered upward, holding the firebrand up, and it limned a bundle at the temple's edge, a bloody figure in shredded rags. The dwarf stirred then and sat up, white beard running with crimson.

"Toothpick!" She ran to him, even as the swordblade rang off stone as it missed its quarry. The demon and Dar wrestled with each other, then broke free, Dar with a low cry of pain.

The dwarf looked at her, his chest heaving. He had crawled over the top of the packs. "I'm sorry, princess. Thurgood . . . don't blame him, whatever happens. The drink . . . it's not been easy for him. He's going to his death . . ."

She stopped him with a gentle hand over his mouth, and felt the dampness of blood as it trickled between her fingers. "Shush. Just rest. We'll get out of this somehow."

She twisted then, as the demon showed her his back, and she remembered her dagger. She pulled it, cocked it back over her shoulder, preparing to throw it as she'd been taught, but a hand of iron caught her about the wrist, and Toothpick gargled in warning.

The swamp witch threw her back upon the stone flooring, and the knife clattered away.

Kory's eyes glittered, and she bent to pick up the torch. "Lie still or I'll settle with you before the demon has a chance to!"

Sharlin bit her lip and did as she was told.

Dar had caught a glimpse of the witch moving out of the shadows, but a bare glimpse it was. The hairs on the back of his neck prickled. Where were the hazers? As the demon maneuvered him, was Nabor waiting to plunge a sword through his back? Valorek only had to have him alive . . . if barely.

He looked, despite himself, to the shadowed streets

beyond the fire, searching for other forms lurking there. Mnak saw his gaze waver, and jumped.

With a grunt, Dar collapsed to the bluestone flooring, the demon snapping in his face, and they wrestled. Talons dug into his arm as Mnak beat his sword hand to the floor, smashing the blade from his grip.

"Dar!" Sharlin screamed. She dove for her dagger, knocking Kory from her feet, and the two women wrestled as Mnak straddled his quarry and wrapped his thick hands about Dar's throat.

Dar heaved, throwing the demon to one side. His fists pounded the creature, as Mnak shook him, snapping his neck back. Dar brought his knee up sharply into the beast's loins, and as Mnak roared, dragged himself toward the sword.

The beast jumped on him. Dar slammed face first onto the stone, but his hands wrapped around the hilt of his weapon, still warm from his handhold on it. He swung it toward his back. The blade whistled and sank deeply into the demon's flank, sucking into it like a slab of meat. Coughing, Dar pulled himself from under the limp being's form and staggered to his feet.

One of the women screamed sharply, once, and it was cut short. He lurched toward them, crying, "Sharlin!"

"I'm all right!" Then, "Dar!"

He turned as the demon crashed into him, knocking him head over heels, bouncing him into a column, and the pain roared through him, blacking out sight and sound as he gasped for air.

Sharlin pulled herself from under the swamp witch's body as the dwarf called out, "Get up, bucko! Get up or ye're done for!"

She saw the silver gleam under Toothpick's broken form and scrabbled for it. "The stinger gun! Give me the stinger!"

Toothpick fished it out, and his flinty eyes opened wide as he recognized the silver quarrel. He batted away her hands. "Let me, gurlie. I've had a bit o' practice with 'em."

She pulled him to his feet, white beard hanging damply

to his chest, his left arm dangling uselessly, and he raised the stinger.

Dar struggled to his feet. He parried a blow with his sword, but he looked dazed, as though not sure where Mnak even stood. The demon growled confidently and closed on him as Toothpick raised the stinger and fired.

Mnak twirled as the bolt pierced his hide, and he roared and gnashed his teeth, silver fire erupting from the wound. He fell to his knees, buckling over.

He crashed at Dar's feet, and the swordsman leaned on his blade like a cane, standing over him, as the demon thrashed into his death.

Mnak snarled. "Now you're done for. My master comes after you himself!" He lashed out, talons curled, and cut Dar's legs out from under him, toppling him onto his own form as he died, in a cold, cold world.

Sharlin choked as Toothpick crumpled in her arms, the stinger falling from his hand. The dwarf blinked up at her.

"Take care o' the bucko, princess. And Thurgood, if ye can. . . ." The damp beard ceased to wag, and he shuddered out his last breath.

Sharlin gently released his dead body. She looked at the demon and Dar, and weaved toward them. She pulled Dar off the beast and cradled him in her arms as she sank to the floor and bolstered her back against a column. "Oh gods, oh gods," she muttered. She cradled Dar and rocked him and tried to stanch the tide of blood that soaked out over her clothes.

That was how Thurgood found her in the morning. He pried Dar from her arms, saying, "He may make it yet." Her eyes were too dry to cry any longer.

The wizard's face had been bruised, and one eye was nearly screwed shut. He cringed when he saw Toothpick's dead body, but he laid Dar gently on the bluestone floor and began to apply his hands to the wounds, deftly cleaning and sewing them, clucking as he bent himself to helping the living.

Chapter 15

The first time Valorek came for him, no one in the village was quite sure who the man was or why he wanted Dar. As people will who've grown up under a tyrant's rule, they were close-lipped when he began searching house to house with his two lieutenants.

It was just after milking time, and the herd had been turned back into the pasture, and Darvan stood framed by the door of the milking shed when three strangers dismounted and walked across the yard. He moved an arm protectively over the shoulders of his wife and looked at the wiry man in black leathers who wore his short-cropped beard like a growth staining his jawline and his hair trimmed to a fuzzy pelt. The man removed his helm and tucked it under one arm. One soldier knew the other soldier in the way he moved, and he even had his guess about who the lord was, but he said nothing, and urged Gerta toward his back.

"May I help you, milord? What do you need from me?"

No one noticed the boy coming from the pastures, where he had played springing and leaping with the young gunters, riding their spiny frames when they couldn't buck him off. In the shadows of the hay shed, he stood and watched the visitors talking to his father.

Darvan sensed him, but they didn't. His father had always had a sixth sense about Dar. Instinctively, Dar knew that this was one of those times when he was better off remaining hidden in the shadows. He recognized the

185

men from yesterday. He lay down and crept forward on his elbows, stomach pressed to the cool grass, and listened to the strangers talking to his parents.

"I'm looking for a boy," the lord said. He hooked his thumbs in his belt, rattling his scabbard slightly. "A boy with brown eyes."

His mother gasped, and hid the noise with a tiny sneeze after that. Face pale, she curtsied, saying, "I'm sorry, milord. The dust and the hay . . ." Wrapping her hands in her apron, she clutched the material to her chest fearfully.

The lord seemed unmindful of her lapse. He held his hand, palm down, so high off the ground, saying, "The boy would be about this high. Eight or nine years, I think. He's well-boned for all his youth."

"What has he done?"

"Nothing," the lord answered, as one of his lieutenants spat to one side. "I saw him fighting in the street. The other boys treat him like a warrior king"—this with a soft, ironic laugh.

Dar felt a cold hand clutch at his insides. The lord was looking for him—and his father knew it, and that's why Darvan stood firm in his milking shed, patiently asking questions about what boy and why the man in black leather wanted him. Two or three others had brown eyes, but all were farmer stock—not one of them could hold a wooden sword to him. He got to one knee.

Darvan laughed, a big booming sound that filled the yard much as it did their small cottage in the evenings. The reassuring noise thawed Dar a little. "That description could fit any of the boys, milord, depending on who had the stoutest stick! And there are a few about here with dark eyes."

The lord rubbed his scalp and sighed. The two lieutenants tensed, and Dar knew that the lord had reached the limit of his patience with his parents. "If you should see such a boy, or know of him, I'll be staying at the inn. Send word to me . . . you'll be well rewarded. Ask for Valorek."

Gerta pressed the heels of her hands to her mouth. She trembled in the wake of her husband.

In the shadows, her mother's fear frightened him even more. Now he knew that this man in the courtyard was the evil Valorek, the man his father had been sent as a soldier to destroy, the sorcerer king who remained undefeated, the man who had conquered his mother's kingdom when she was very young. At those words, and his mother's gasp, Dar knew he had to run. And run. And run.

He took to his heels, bolting from the shaded barn, leaping fences and ditches, running across the fields. Shouts followed after, and at the back of his mind he heard his father bellowing at the king to leave a simple farmboy alone.

When night fell, Dar had run far from the familiar boundaries of his village and staggered into a trench by the side of one of the roads. Sweat plastered his hair as he tumbled into a heap, wondering if he could ever go home again . . . wondering why the black king wanted him. He wondered what he had done . . . what he could do.

He lay in the ditch panting like a frightened softfoot until his heart slowed to a normal beat, and he curled up to sleep.

A boot toe thumped his ribcage, and a blinding yellow light pierced his eyelids. "Get up!"

He stared, unable to see more than black outlines beyond the light, and he blinked at the voices.

"He's got brown eyes," one said.

"Yes, milord, he's got brown eyes. And if I stood him on his feet, he would be about so tall."

"He's filthy and he stinks," a third grated.

A guard grabbed Dar and jerked him to his feet, his fist crumpled tightly in the collar of the rough homespun shirt. Dar kicked at the man, striking him in his shins, and twisted away, his shirt ripping free, and he sprinted off through the night.

He was tackled, slammed into the ground by the heavy impact of the guard's body, and he lay gasping for breath.

His eyes lost their vision and his ears roared until he was deafened. The two other men loped up, bringing the glaring yellow lantern with them.

He lay tucked on the ground, unable to breath, his lungs and throat convulsing.

He heard a voice . . . but it wasn't a man's voice, it was a woman's. He seemed to hear her saying, "Do you think he's going to make it?"

An old man answered her, fatigue and age in every syllable of his mild tones. "He will, princess, if he's got the heart to do it. I've done all I can, and the lyrith has helped all it will."

The roaring faded from his ears, and he was yanked to his feet once more. The man with the brilliant yellow lantern lowered it, and he saw a face. A face with cruel cheekbones, and flat eyes, the eyes of an animal, and the man smiled.

He said, "I'm going to teach you everything I know."

Before Dar could protest or plead that he hadn't done anything, the man swung, the back of his hand smashing into Dar's face so hard that his teeth rattled, and the pain shocked him to the back of his head as it snapped back on his neck. Dar fainted dead away.

Afterward, he could never remember the year that followed. He didn't remember anything except stumbling onto his parents' doorstep and falling to his knees before they could yank the rude wooden door open, and he was so happy he could have kissed the ground. His mother and father spilled out over him, and took him in their arms and carried him inside. Darvan cared for him when Gerta could not, and when they questioned him about the time Valorek had had him, they wiped the cold sweat from his brow and held his hand until his gasping returned to normal, and then his father said, "It's like battle fever. When you have it, you soar through the field, and the blood, the death, it's as if nothing can touch you . . . and afterward, the memory is gone, a black stain sinks into your mind, and you don't have to worry about remembering it later—it's just not there."

He patted Dar's hand, and though both of Darvan's great, huge, battle-nicked paws cradled his, Dar remembered looking, and thinking, my hands will soon be as big as his.

Those great paws of hands held him safe for two more years. Then when he was nearing thirteen, and growing, a strapping lad, Valorek rode into the dairy yard, and though Darvan fought, they caught Aarondar, wrapped him in chains and shackles, threw him to the floorboards of a wooden cart, and took him away again.

Dar looked slantwise through the cracks of the cart at his mother kneeling over his father, dabbing at his head with her apron, weeping.

Valorek's captain, Barnerd, grunted and sank onto the driver's seat. "Man has a thick skull. He'll be all right." His statement was directed to Valorek, who didn't give a damn, but Dar knew he was meant to overhear it. He lay back on the wooden flooring, his eyes squeezed tight, fighting for breath, and he knew he was back in the hands of the enemy. He began to remember, and this time, there was no one to hold his hand and reassure him.

"Suck in your gut and pick up the blade. This isn't scribing, boy! I'll work you into the dirt or I'll cut you down!"

Dar stood, head down, rib cage heaving. Barnerd stood before him, covered in leather armor from toes to neck, while all Dar had was boots and trousers. His exposed chest was livid with welts and bruises from the wooden swords they used, and his own lay in the dust at his toes, where he'd dropped it, too weary to continue.

Barnerd waved the practice weapon, aiming at his knuckles, when a sharp voice cut the air.

"Don't mark him any more, Barnerd!"

The captain moved aside to make room for his king.

Dar didn't raise his head, for he didn't wish to look at

Valorek, but he knew Valorek looked at him the way he always did, with those flat, dark eyes that devoured him, drank him in, made him feel as though he were a morsel on a plate before the dark king.

He jumped as cool fingertips grazed the welts along his flank.

"Don't forget to rub him down when you're done. I'll send oils to your room, captain."

Despite himself, Dar looked into Valorek's eyes. The king smiled then. Dar shuddered, and the man turned on his heel and left him on the practice field. Passing Barnerd, Valorek said quietly, "A beautiful boy, is he not? And intelligent. All that I could ever want or hope to be. See he stays that way!"

"Yes, sire!" Barnerd snapped to, saluting with his blade, though it was wooden, and did not move until Valorek left the field and they were alone. Then the captain looked at him, and his lip curled. "Rested enough? Pick up your sword!"

A gentle voice pierced his weariness. He seemed to have heard the voice before. "He's resting now, Thurgood. But his eyes . . . they move constantly, as though he's dreaming. . . ."

Was it a dream? Dar swallowed convulsively, his throat dry and tight with dust and exertion. Would he live long enough to wake up?

He learned much in the two years that followed . . . much that even Valorek did not know, for reasons Dar knew not. Tutors were brought, trembling and timid, through the night on dragon wings. He often heard the dragonlord as he swung low over the fortress towers and landed in the massive courtyard, and Valorek would croon to the creature, and give him cream. When they spoke, the words carried a spell so that Dar's eyes closed and his ears grew deaf no matter how hard he tried to listen.

As he reached a man's height, it was almost as though he were two people . . . as though Valorek leaned over his shoulder, whispering into his ear slimy insidious thoughts that penetrated his own. It was then that he learned how to slay the Valorek inside of him even more vigorously than any opponent Barnerd sent against him on the practice field.

And he bided his time, pacing himself, waiting for the day when they thought him no further trouble, and beyond, and heard Valorek's whispered tones one night to a dragonlord, and this time no spell put him to sleep, for he was Valorek, too.

"This imprinting is nearly finished."

A deep sound. A low rumbling, musky and hot. A voice that carried power in it answering, "Then, my lord Valorek, you have one last imprinting to do after this next ritual, and you will become the boy . . . with the boy's lifespan for yourself, and when that begins to fade, you will know how to take another Face, and another, and another."

"And the magic?"

"By all means. You sacrificed much for your sorcery. It will be implanted with the last ritual, Valorek, never fear. It can't be done until then, or the boy will have as much power as you, and you could never take him over." The dragonlord's voice lowered even more, until it was like the fog that seeped out of the stony ground. "Heart and soul, he will be yours when this next is done to him, and then you can let him grow a little more, and train him a little more, and the third ritual will begin."

"Thank you, Nightwing," Valorek answered, and his voice husked with gratitude.

The dragonlord laughed. "The third time pays for all," he said, and launched, with a rustle of wings and wind, and was gone in the night.

Dar lay awake in the cold warren of the soldiers' barracks, and ached, and wondered how he could live if Valorek possessed him.

"What did you do to him?"

"Never mind about that," Valorek rasped. "Throw

another bucket of water on him. He's in shock! Go down
to the village and get that old woman, the one they use for
a midwife, and bring her back. And hurry for your life,
captain, for this is one fight you don't want to lose!"

At the back of his mind, where he lay curled, Dar heard
the men arguing about him. It was as though he no longer
had a body of his own, for he floated above the room, and
saw his form sprawled on a bed below, naked, rent,
savaged, with Valorek standing over him, as Barnerd gave
a salute and ran from the room. The dark king was
wrapped in a linen sheeting, his arms and shoulders bare,
as he paced, back and forth, back and forth, his hands
balled into a fist. From above Dar saw for the first time the
seamed welts that snaked down his pale white skin,
rakings across his back.

Valorek bent over the body Dar had once known as his
own. The king's voice lowered in malice and desperation.
"Breathe! Don't die on me now, boy! Fight! Too many
drugs. I gave you too many drugs. Breathe, dammit!" He
flipped Dar's naked body over and beat on his chest
angrily. "Breathe!"

Then he staggered back and clutched his own chest—
the movement Dar had seen before, though not often, and
Barnerd usually shielded him quickly whenever it happened. This time, though, Valorek grabbed his neck and
massaged himself as though in intense pain, and he
doubled over then, clutching at Dar's bare leg as he
himself slid to the floor.

"Live, dammit," he whispered to the boy's body. "I
haven't the time to start over again!"

Barnerd ran in with the bucket of water and tossed it,
and the cold wash of liquid shocked Dar in his floating
oblivion, and he once more felt his body, and sobbed, and
knew that he would live.

Days after that, Barnerd took him hawking, and when
the captain looked the other way, Dar slipped him a
dagger in the throat and left Valorek's kingdom. He ran
his horse into the ground going back to his own village of
Milik, and when the beast sank under him, pitching him to
the ground face first with a gasping breath, and crimson

ran from its nostrils, and its pink tongue pushed out of its mouth and swelled black, Dar drew his foot back first to kick it, angry that the beast had failed him.

Then, with a sob of his own, for the Valorek beast that raged in him, he sank beside the horse and took the silken head in his lap and petted the creature and told it what a brave mount it had been, and while the horse quieted and struggled toward death, he quietly slit its throat to let it die in peace.

He ran, walked, and crawled the rest of the way home.

A mist curled about the vales of the farming community as he found it, and made his way to the dairy farm, on the far outskirts of Milik, thinking that although it had grown a little, it looked much the same, and his thankfulness choked his throat.

Barefoot, his shirt rags about his shoulders, his trousers torn at the knees, he staggered into the yard and saw in gray morning light the ruins of his home.

Fire ate at the last beams of the cottage. The gunters ran in the far pastures, still bawling with fear as ashes and cinders drifted on the air. The breath caught in Dar's throat.

"Bastards!" he cried and lurched to the step of the leveled cottage. Valorek's men had fired it!

"Mother! Dad!" Whirling, he gave voice to a shout that was barely more than a whisper, his own wind broken like that of the horse he'd run to ground, but the sound carried, a little.

He went to his knees where stones marked the front door, actually, where his mother had used stones to mark a flower and herb garden. The ashes were still hot as he reached out, trembling, to touch them.

A great flat rock that used to be his, for he'd found it one day when very young and lugged it all the way home, though his mother favored small round rocks for her borders, nudged his knee. He touched it, and the soot rubbed off on his fingers.

Blinking rapidly, for hot salt tears clouded his vision, he looked down and saw that runes were carved into the rock's flat surface. His father's crude writing:

"Be free."

Dar's breath caught in his throat. Valorek hadn't fired the place, though undoubtedly he and his men had been there first. No, Darvan knew the value of a hostage, and had taken the only way out he could to set Aarondar free . . . free of being found again for certain.

Dar dropped the rock. He got to his feet and made his way through the house.

In his mother's bed, small bits of bone and teeth and metal still remained, unconsumed by flames. By the looks of it, they had died together, holding each other.

By the time the tears had dried to sticky runs on his face, Dar had found the old breastplate in the milking shed, and his father's best clothes, a small pouch with two gold coins, and a larger pouch, empty, for general purposes. Boots, tight, but still wearable. A nicked war ax, not much good, but better than a quarterstaff where he was going.

He took the pouch to the ruins of his home, and there he filled it to bulging with the ashes of his parents' remains. Tying the pouch to his belt, he licked his lips. Then he left his childhood, and began to run.

Cool water laved his brow, and he twitched, and began with great effort to open his eyes.

Dark-blue eyes met his own, then widened in surprise, and Sharlin looked down, bruises of fatigue staining her pale face under her eyes, and she reached out.

He took her hand and cradled it to his cheek.

"I'm back," he said, and found it to be a great effort, as though he'd come from very far away.

"Thank the gods," she murmured, and smiled.

When Dar woke again, he found himself riding on a litter being dragged behind Brand, the horse led by Sharlin as Cloud paced the chestnut. She brought the horses to a stop, for which he breathed a grateful sigh, being jolted in every limb by the conveyance.

The cream-colored mule stumbled into his line of vision, and Thurgood wavered in its saddle.

"Awake again, lad? Good," the wizard slurred.

Dar blinked, weak as he was, and thought, Drunk as a lord. He struggled to sit up, and found in amazement that his wounds had nearly closed and healed, though soreness followed every movement.

"Can you ride?" Sharlin asked anxiously, as she handed him a waterskin.

"I think . . . I think so."

"Good." Thurgood waved at a bug as it danced in front of him, and nearly fell off his mule.

"Where—where's Toothpick?"

Sharlin's expression closed as she helped him stand. "Don't you remember?"

"I—no, not much."

"He's dead. Mnak got him."

"And you got Kory . . . yes . . . I remember that much. The demon? Did Thurgood send him back again?"

"No. At least, I don't think so. He seemed to die, but I'm not sure. Toothpick used the stinger on him."

Dar fumbled along beside her and made it to Brand's side. A crude leather saddle rested on the chestnut's back. "Where'd you find this?"

"In the temple. We found a lot of things, including an inner sanctum that was sealed. Even Thurgood couldn't break it open. We used the lyrith on you . . . I think that's why you're healing so fast."

"And just in time, too," Thurgood said. "We're nearly to the island's end. Today's ride should bring us to the brink."

Dar found it took all of his strength, and Sharlin's, to clamber into the saddle, but he made it. She had to lengthen the stirrups, for when he leaned over to do it, he nearly pitched headfirst onto the ground.

"Dar!" She sat him back up. "Let me take care of this. You're not fit yet."

He watched her head bend over the task, and the sun glinted off her amber hair, and he remembered other things, too, and he smiled quietly.

"What are you looking at?"

He broadened his smile at her. "I was just thinking."

"About what? Oh. . . ." And she turned very pink as she skirted Brand's head and came to the other leg to do the second stirrup. She said nothing more, just mounted Cloud and gathered up her reins.

He gained strength throughout the day, and that night Thurgood, his breath strong enough to stop a dragon in its tracks, rubbed lyrith paste into his wounds, and he suggested Sharlin brew a tea from it, and he drank that, and as he drifted back to sleep, he could feel the healing spread throughout his body.

Dar stood in the stirrups and pointed at the cliff that plunged to a narrow beach, leading straight into light-blue waters. Fog hung all about them, and even the horses stood dank and misted by the veils.

"That's the end."

Thurgood shook his head. He let go of the map half in his hands, and it curled back into itself. His eyes, though very bloodshot, were halfway clear this morning. "You're right, Dar. Glymarach does end here. There's no doubting that's the sea . . . it's not illusion."

"Then we've found nothing!"

"No. There's no sign that Jet came this way, or where he went, either," the man said, and gave a sigh that rattled into a cough. He rubbed his sagging profile wearily. "All this way for nothing."

Sharlin snapped the reins on Cloud's rump and kneed the horse forward, even with Dar and the wizard. She snatched the map out of his hands. "It isn't all! It can't be!"

Dar eased his shoulders carefully, still a little bruised. He made a note to gather as much lyrith as he could find when they passed the city again. "We tried, Sharlin. Now our best chance of getting off Glymarach is to return to the boat Kory and the hazers used, before the hazers get back. Otherwise, we're marooned here."

She looked at him. "I'm marooned here, anyway—no matter where I am. Or have you forgotten that?"

He had, until now. Their gazes locked. "Sharlin, I—"

"I've only got one chance now, and that's to reach the graveyard." She kicked the gray savagely. "If I have to swim until I drown, I'm finding the rest of the island!"

With a surprised whinny, Cloud plunged ahead on the path, scrambling to gain his balance. She drove him over the cliff's edge, down the slanting sands to the beach.

The fog blocked all else from view as Dar and the wizard followed her down to the white-and-pink sands, though his last sighting had told him that the rest of the terrain was heavily mountained, and this was the only beach. It pointed into the waters like a spearhead.

Hands shaking, the girl unrolled the map. Then she looked up at the water, and smiled.

She turned and said triumphantly, "Remember the words on the map that made no sense—'Walk a day upon the water'? Well, here goes nothing." She swung her leg over Cloud's back, dismounting, and began to lead the stallion into the ocean.

"Sharlin!" Dar cried in alarm. He kicked his chestnut after her, and the tiny pack donkeys that remained brayed and scrambled to keep up. Thurgood swayed, and kicked his mule finally, not to be left behind.

A curtain of fog dropped between him and the girl, and she disappeared, striding into the ocean, its waves breaking about her.

A gasp echoed back to them. "It's cold! But it's not getting any deeper!"

"Get out of there," he called back.

"No!"

Brand balked at an invisible wall. Dar kicked and whipped him, and though the chestnut attempted to breach the fog, he could not. Then, in desperation, the swordsman slid down and walked after Sharlin.

The fog gave way. He found himself, after the first numbing shock of cold water, up to his chest in the sea, the water stretching bright blue around him, the fair sunlight glinting off the caps. The water was so clear he could look down and see his falroth boots gleaming back at him. Sharlin stopped, waved, and turned back.

He twisted and yelled back to the wizard, "It's no good riding, Thurgood. Get down and walk it—maybe it'll sober you up, while you're at it." Clucking encouragement, he led Brand after him, and the donkeys swam, the water surging about their beige necks. Sharlin waited for him to catch up.

"Why didn't we just sail down here?" he grumbled, as he did so. The water began to feel warmer now, but it filled his boots and dampened every part of him, and now and then a brightly colored fish darted past, much to Brand's snorting amazement.

"This part of Glymarach is hidden," she answered. "You said so yourself—nothing exists. And if we had sailed, we'd probably have wrecked on shoals or something, and gone down."

"We did shipwreck," he pointed out.

"Yes, but not out there. I think if we had, we wouldn't have made it." Sharlin pointed across the sparkling waters, and he saw then what she pointed at.

Gray-and-black bodies cut the deep water, swimming parallel with them. One of the sea beasts leaped from the water, twisting, and crashed down. He caught a glimpse of bright eyes, and rows of flashing teeth. Not a sea serpent or even a seagoing dragon, but big enough to swallow a man or horse whole, and pacing them.

"I think that's what we saw washing up on the beach that day," Sharlin said.

Dar nodded. He looked down. "These waters are too shallow for them to come in and get us."

The gray-and-black beasts, fins sticking up on their backs like proud sails, swerved and came a little nearer, closing enough so that Dar could have hit them, if he'd had a stone to throw.

A question remained in his mind, however, as to whether the situation would stay the same.

"Get behind me," he ordered. "Single-file from here on out."

The morning light slanted to midday, and then toward sunset, as they slogged through the water. Dar slipped once, and when he fell to the side the bottom literally went out from under him, and only Brand's reins kept him from being washed away. He hauled himself back to his feet.

"It's like a bridge," he said, when the other two caught up. "I nearly fell off."

A fin came close, and he caught sight of the eye watching him, and the beast swerved off again. He shuddered in spite of himself.

They tired. The water pushed at them like a heavy weight. Their boots chafed at their raw feet. One of the tiny donkeys gave a bray and drifted away, too spent to swim any longer.

Dar grasped for its lead, and it tore from his fingers. Jaws opened as one of the beasts came up and chomped, cutting off the little creature in midsection.

Sharlin cried softly. Crimson spurted in the azure waters, and the donkey disappeared in a flash when a second creature hit at it, and foam sprayed upward.

Dar said, "Come on. We've got to keep going." He reeled in the lead of the second donkey and held it in his arms, the water helping to float it as he carried it.

Thurgood snared the pack of the first as it floated past. For once, the wizard was silent.

Sharlin took the lead again. The sun glinted low on the horizon in front of them, its light wavering. She squinted, shading her eyes with her hand.

"It's as though something obstructs it. But I don't see anything."

Abruptly she halted in the water. Panic tinged her voice. "Dar—Dar, the bottom's gone. I can see it, a step or two in front of me, then nothing!"

"We'll have to turn back."

"No." Dar disagreed with Thurgood. "We've come too far." He let the pack donkey down and straightened, flexing his shoulders. He ached in every limb. "This is why we brought you, wizard," he added harshly, jolting Thurgood to his sensibilities.

Thurgood rubbed his brow in a circular motion. The sea

dragged at his robes, and even the cuffs of his sleeves hung from his too thin arms. "Ay," he said finally, in a faint echo of Toothpick's mountain-dwarf accent. "Indeed, this is why you brought me." He frowned and stared at the horizon. Then, faintly, "Illusion masks Glymarach. Don't trust your senses. Do what you know is right." His eyes focused, and he stared at Dar in amusement. "Plunge ahead, swordsman, if you're brave enough!"

The sea killers cut a wake near them, too near them, and one yawned. The low sun flashed off its sharp teeth.

Sharlin took his arm. "Dar, you can't."

"Something blocks the sun. I say it's a low ridge of mountains between us and it . . . land in front of us. You two stay here."

Eyeing the fins that paced him, he passed Sharlin. A stride or two of white sand, then the bottom sloped off. Nothing but dark-blue water. A stride or two and they would be in water so deep they'd drown.

If the killers didn't get them first.

With a deep breath, he strode forward. Sharlin gasped. The water pushed back at him, and then, when his senses told him there was no purchase under him, he stepped onto solid rock—rock, not sand. And he climbed out of the sea and stood on a beach, a beach that hadn't been visible to him before. He turned, and viewed nothing but an expanse of blue water.

"Sharlin! Thurgood!"

Water splashed and thrashed, and then Sharlin climbed out of nothingness in front of him, pulling both horses after her. She dropped the reins and hugged him tightly.

"We made it!"

Chapter 16

The wizard's mule climbed out of the sea behind him, and the donkey scampered onto the beach and shook itself like a dog. Thurgood fixed a wan smile on them.

Sharlin broke away guiltily, but before she could say a word, the man toppled from the saddle and hit the sand with a thump.

Dar went to Thurgood's side, his disgust over the wizard's drunkenness fading, for something else ailed the graying man. Sweat ran down his brow, and his hands shook as he reached for Dar.

"Too weak. My life is linked to my powers, and I'm too weak. . . ."

Dar looked over his shoulder to Sharlin. She rummaged through the packs quickly and held up a sprig of lyrith.

"One of the last," she said, "except for my stock. Build a fire and I'll make him a tea."

"No," protested Thurgood weakly. "Let me go. Let me follow Toothpick."

Dar let him slip gently onto the beach, but answered, "Not yet. You're going to have to hang on a little longer." And he left to gather driftwood for fire.

Once brewed and sipped gingerly by Thurgood, the lyrith worked quickly. In moments, the wizard straightened. Health flushed his pale cheeks. His mild blue eyes gained some of their old confidence, as though he continually knew more than they did about life.

Sharlin smiled triumphantly. She unrolled her map and laid it out in the sands. "Now we're close to the end."

Thurgood tapped the skin. "No . . . we've only just begun to face the real dangers. Glymarach will be baited and trapped every step of the way. Now it begins."

The last of the sun disappeared behind a ridge of low green hills, and the only light on the beach was that from the fire. It outlined Sharlin's face as she rocked back on her heels, considering Thurgood's words. Dar noticed a strain, an unhappiness that hadn't been there before, and knew she thought of her people . . . gone to dust, conquered hundreds of years ago, her quest defeated even before she reached its end.

She set her jaw. Without another word, she lay back on the sands and curled into sleep. Dar stretched out a hand to pull her nearly dry cloak over her, and hesitated, for the way she lay told him that she wished to be alone. Instead, he got up and gave each of the animals a small handful of fresh water in his half-helm, hobbled them for the night, then banked the fire and settled down himself.

Thurgood blinked. "No dinner?" he murmured. Then he shrugged and leaned back himself, after pillowing his head on his packs. Bottles and vials clinked as he rearranged the leather bags more comfortably, then settled down.

The neighing and jostling of the horses, mule, and donkey woke them all in the morning, as the very first rays of the sun came up. Even from where he lay, Dar could hear the rumblings of the mounts' stomachs. They looked toward him, ears pricked and eager, muzzles sniffing.

He stood up and looked himself at the horizon of green hills. "Water and grazing," he told the other two. They got up, Thurgood stiffly and Sharlin trembling with the cold of the early morning. "They went without yesterday, and it's been a long hard trail for them."

"Agreed," said Sharlin. "One day, more or less, won't make a difference. Let's get to a river and then I'll make us a meal of whatever I can find. The seawater got into almost everything, though."

She helped him tighten the girths and ready the horses. The tiny donkey flattened his ears at having to carry two packs instead of one, for he inherited that of his eaten companion, but both packs were relatively light, since supplies were running low. Sharlin smiled at Dar and handed him the donkey's lead.

"Maybe fresh fish," she said.

"Sounds good. I haven't been fishing in a long time." The roar of the surf pounded at his ears, and he thought longingly of the tranquillity of a small river, and a grassy bank to pillow his shoulders while he tried to outwit the river denizens.

They mounted and left their bonfire behind, banked to glowing embers, to burn itself out on the beach.

The green hills grew steep, and the sound of rushing water drew all of them upward, the horses with wide nostrils eagerly smelling the scent of fresh water, trotting forward eagerly. Dar ducked swinging branches and called back warnings for the others as Brand charged into the forest.

They plunged to a halt on the banks of the river, swift water gray-blue with foam as it descended from rocks above. Pale-silver light seeped through the deep green of the pines, the scent of their broken needles filling the air where his passage had bent and bruised them. Beyond the waters lay pastures and lush grasses, and a game trail. Dar blinked, thinking he saw a movement, a round face staring out at him from the other side, but other than two blackbirds they'd startled at their emergence, nothing moved in the forest. Not even a softfoot.

He considered the river and pointed. "I think we can ford it. It looks to be cold . . . the horses might balk at first, but keep after them. On the other side we can pitch camp for the day."

Sharlin gathered up her reins tightly. She said nothing, but he thought he saw fear in her eyes as she kicked Cloud down to the water. It surprised him—he had gotten used to thinking of her as afraid of nothing. Not even Mnak had startled her very much. But she hadn't been the same since reading the histories written in the temples of Lyrith. Nor could he blame her.

Tightening his knees, he moved Brand after her. She let out a sharp cry when the gray plunged into the water and it sprayed up around her. A second later, Dar felt the same sensation, and for a moment, fear gripped at him too. Too swift. They'd made a fatal mistake.

"Keep going!" he yelled at her. "Keep going to the other side!"

The horses fought to keep their heads above the rapid current, and Sharlin wrapped her hands tightly in the gray's black mane, struggling to keep her balance in the saddle.

The blue turned to silver, and the water's roaring filled his ears. Brand struggled, but the river carried him downstream despite his legs cutting against the current.

Thurgood cursed and whipped his mule, and the donkey spun past all of them, its lead whipping taut in Dar's hands.

Then Brand seemed to find the river bottom under his hooves, and he caught himself and began to buck against the water, pulling himself toward the riverbank.

Sharlin screamed. Cloud rolled out from under her. The river swept her from the saddle, and she held on to the stirrup for dear life. The gray stallion disappeared, then bobbed back up to the surface, tangled in weeds.

Brand snorted, stumbled, and came up fighting. Dark vines wrapped about his forelegs, and the more he fought, the tighter he wrapped himself.

Nets! Fishing nets, laid against the rapids, now tangled them to their deaths. Dar pulled his sword and leaned forward. Sharlin gasped and cried, her arms nearly pulled out of her sockets as the river threatened to tear her away from Cloud's side.

"Hold on," he shouted. "I'm cutting you loose!"

"No! No! Don't cut our nets! We'll pull you ashore!"

Dar wiped his forehead of mist and spray, astonished to see men on the riverbank, bending their backs and eagerly pulling the nets from the waters. They shouted, "Heave to! Heave to!"

Cloud emerged from the river, legs tucked under him, and lay on his side on the sloping bank, too tangled to get up. He began to kick almost immediately as Sharlin staggered up. She pointed, ordering, "Get him out before he breaks a leg. Here . . . this strand this way and this one that. . . ." After a moment's hesitation, two of the fishermen followed her wishes.

Brand fairly leaped from the river, the netting dropping from about his legs. Dar reeled in the donkey, which, though shuddering with cold and half drowned, had not tangled. Thurgood followed on the mule behind him. He had gotten himself tangled as well, and sat muttering darkly, shrugging out from under the fishing nets.

Fishermen swarmed about them like mosquitoes, plucking and lifting the webbing away, and soon the party stood free. Cloud got to his feet, shook himself out, and snorted, as though complaining.

One of the men in brown laughed and rubbed the horse's forehead. "Sorry, big fellow," he said, in a light, lilting voice. "We didn't mean to catch you."

Dar kept his sword out, but felt uneasy. The other fishermen quickly laid out their nets to dry, and the leader turned to him.

"My apologies, stranger. We're netting for eels . . . the rivers will soon be full of them, and we wanted to be ready. The eeling festival starts with tonight's moon."

"Eels?" Sharlin gave a shudder of her own as she tried to wring her hair out in the sunlight.

He flashed a grin, an open, innocent smile. "Yes! Smoked, dried, fresh-broiled over a greenwood fire . . . wonderful stuff. Wait until you try it! And my wife uses the teeth for needles, and the powdered skulls make medicines. Come with us, please, and take supper with us. Then tonight you can feast with us. Call me Loar, and accept our hospitality. Strangers are rare in our lands, and if the truth be known, there are dangers here you should be warned of—dangers far worse than our misplaced nets!"

A shout rang out from behind him. Four men struggled to pull a last net from the river, only this one was full of sleek, wet bodies and gnashing teeth, greens and browns and blacks. It was bulging with eels.

Loar gave a delighted laugh and joined his companions. Once the net was beached, they used hooked sticks to grasp the biting serpentine fish and drop them into baskets produced so quickly from the shrubberies that Sharlin laughed and said, "I think they're grown in there."

When the eel net was emptied, Loar turned and bowed to them once more. He shouldered a basket of squirming eels, many as thick and long as his own arm, their teeth clacking as they thrashed about. "Follow me, if you would." He swung off down the game trail, his villagers following.

Dar, Sharlin, and Thurgood stared at one another. Then Dar shrugged and set out in the wake of the fishermen.

Smoked eel was tough and rubbery and carried only a faint suggestion of the flavor of the rich broiled meat, Dar decided as he licked his fingers and finished the last of his dinner. Sharlin sat with the women, already finished with her meal, and now making use of slim needles to repair their clothing. She flashed him a quick look, a half-smile, and bent back to her business. He caught a glimpse of her, what it would be like to be around her in a house and home, with children around her feet, their children . . . and a chill ran up the back of his neck, raising hairs, as though he'd suddenly seen into the future. Had he? Or had he only wished he had?

Not that Sharlin would ever be confined to a house to do the darning, he decided. He was too used to having Sharlin at his side, helping him struggle with their destinies.

He got to his feet and stretched. Loar wiped a greasy smear from his chin and looked up.

"Is everything all right?"

"I ate too much," Dar told the fisherman. "We thank you for your hospitality."

"It's nothing. It's the bounty of the river. Every year, about this time, the eels come down, migrating to the sea. We have plenty to see us through until the next running, and that's enough to ask." Loar cleaned his fingers on his trousers as he stood. A thick, bushy brown eyebrow went up. "Now it's time for other matters, eh?"

The fisherfolk all looked much alike, thick brown hair, some curly, most thick and wavy. The men wore beards and tied their matted hair back with leather thongs, and the women knotted theirs into buns. Children ran back and forth, most undressed except for simple shifts. Their eyes were a light, smoky green. Dar looked at them, wondering if they had come from the people who built Lyrith, and couldn't find it in himself to think they ever could have. No, these were a simple, happy people.

Thurgood joined the two of them. He held up a foaming mug. "This is uncommonly good."

Another wide, childlike smile from Loar. "Thank you, old man. It makes our nights a little shorter." He sat down on his knees under the shade of a broad tree and pulled up a stump as a table. Other fishermen watched them curiously, but didn't join. They went back to eating and drinking, and someone brought out a set of reed pipes, and they began to make music as well.

Loar leaned upon his elbows on the stump, peering at the two men. "Only once in my lifetime," he said, "has a stranger come to our villages. We have old laws pertaining to visitors and strangers, that they are to be honored and assisted, from beyond my father's father's time. Where are you going?"

Thurgood looked at Dar, cleared his throat, and said, "We seek gems in the high mountains."

The fisherman twisted around and looked at the towering peaks that framed the smaller mountains. He nodded. "As the others. Well, we can take you partway on your journey, by flatboat, and leave you. Otherwise you will risk crossing the plains where the striders roam, and although the great beasts are few enough now, I still wouldn't want to meet one." Loar grinned.

"Striders?" Dar moved uneasily.

"A few. They don't come into the mountains . . . too big and stupid. They feed off the grazers on the plains. Here . . ." And Loar got up, strode over to the fire, got a blackened stick, and came back to sketch on the stump. "Our mountains are like a bowl, and in the basin are the plains. We'll boat past them to here," and he made a crude sign. "Then you cross through this pass into the high plains, and to the only pass that will take you into the mountains where the gems lie." He stopped and frowned. "I don't like your going there, my new friends. Very few come out. Evil spirits lie in the mountains."

Dar murmured, "Tell me about it," for the man had sketched out the last leg of the journey to the dragons' graveyard. "What do you call this region?"

"I'm told the mountains are hollow, like another great bowl. The Pits, we call them, though no one I know has ever been." He shrugged. "What need do we have for pretty rocks? The gods give us everything, right here."

Thurgood cleared his throat before asking, "But you can get us clear of the striders, correct?"

"Oh, yes." Loar looked away uneasily. Then he said, "I'm told that the high plains are dangerous in themselves. Fires . . . spirits . . . I don't understand."

Thurgood raised his hand and said soothingly, "You have helped enough, Loar. You've fulfilled your laws, and your ancestors will be pleased."

"What about Nabor and the hazers?" Dar said.

The wizard looked at him. "I doubt they will make it across the water, unless they watched us begin the trail."

"But if they did? Loar, there may be some others following us, desperate men, not nice. . . ."

The fisherman put his hands to his face, then said,

"Dar, my friend, I must treat all the same. It is part of my duty—"

"We understand." Thurgood got to his feet swiftly. "You do as you must, and don't worry. Simply realize that these men are not always honest and fair, and be on your guard. But carry out your laws as they were given to you." He caught Sharlin's glance and signaled to her.

Loar caught the wizard by the elbow. "Please . . . don't be angry with me."

"We couldn't be angry with you." Dar took the man's hand in his own and grasped it tightly. "We'll dance with you!" He added, for the piping had turned into a vigorous tune, and other fisherfolk danced and reeled about the fires, as late day neared evening. The horses were resting in a nearby glen, and there was little else to do. He bounded to Sharlin, caught her up by her slim waist, and spun her away.

Loar poled the flatboat up a placid stream that bore little relation to the waters that had nearly drowned them two days before. Dar watched the man, thinking that he knew little of the outside world, nor did he care that he knew little. His pleasure came from living in harmony with his island as he knew it. Living in the shadow of the dragongods, Loar had no god but nature.

Sharlin shared the flatboat with him, but she lay back on the packs, drowsing in the sun, a dreamy smile curving her lips. Another flatboat bore Thurgood and the donkey, and a third one held the mule and horses. Thurgood had persuaded Loar to give him a corked barrel of their homemade drink, a potent, foamy beverage that bore as little resemblance to beer as the rapids did to this river. The wizard sat, unaware that Dar watched him, and the swordsman knew without asking that the man was mourning again, wrapped in melancholy.

As they poled past the great plains, similar to the small tip of Glymarach where Lyrith had ruled, Dar kept a sharp watch for the striders, but saw none, and was a little disappointed. He'd heard so many tales of the great lizardlike beasts that he wouldn't have minded seeing one, from a distance. He moved restlessly, rocking the flatboat as he stood.

His shadow crossed the girl, and she opened her eyes, smiled, and closed them, thinking thoughts of her own. He swallowed as he remembered holding her in his arms, and abruptly pushed the thoughts away. Once they found the Pits, they had no future together, not unless he was able to rid himself of Valorek's hold once and for all.

Loar motioned to him. "Lie down, my friend Dar, and be patient. Rest while you can."

Taking the fisherman's advice, Dar stretched out in the sun and let the warmth heal the last of his hurts, though it couldn't penetrate his soul, where Valorek's scarring ulcerated and spread, like a black disease.

Chapter 17

Dar rubbed the muzzle of the chestnut stallion fondly. The horse lipped at him and stamped, impatient to be on the trail. The two days' rest had done them a world of good, and though his ribs still protruded more than Dar liked to see, a sleekness had returned to the horse, and he pricked his ears alertly.

Thurgood and Sharlin had already mounted and were waiting for him. The wind picked up a little, and the tall grasses of the plains began to rustle. They'd come far since leaving Loar at the river, where the fisherman had stammered his goodbyes and pressed gifts upon them before turning his flatboats around and poling back downriver. Now they crested the last ridges of the smaller hills and made ready to enter the plains, and the grasses shimmered before them like gold, ringed by dark, forbidding purple mountains that gathered clouds for a coming storm.

Dar wore his breastplate again and his half-helm, his leather wrist cuffs and his sword eased in its sheath, ready to be drawn. He mounted, and Sharlin glanced at him.

"All right?"

He nodded and drew the stallion's reins in, patting the steed companionably. They'd come a long way together. It didn't ease the knowledge that worse lay directly ahead.

He kneed Brand forward into the breast-high grass, thrusting green out of the soil and mellowing to gold at its feathered tips. Sharlin rubbed at her eyes and kicked Cloud after him. Suddenly Brand let out a loud squeal of pain and anguish and plunged out of the grasses. Cloud followed with a whinny and reared, striking at the air before twisting down. Sharlin clung to the saddle, her face pale. The two horses backed out of the field, their eyes rolling and white as though crazed.

He swung down quickly, for slits of crimson had appeared on Brand's legs. He ran his hand down, the horse shivering under his touch, and brought his palm away, sticky with blood.

The grass had cut him as neatly as any blade. Dar stretched his fingers toward the grass gingerly and then immediately brought his fingertips to his mouth in pain. He straightened.

"They'll be slashed to ribbons trying to cross."

"What'll we do?"

He opened his pack and began to rummage through it, searching for anything he could tear to strips, but most of his spare clothing was gone . . . his shirt cut off him at the temple and used for bandages, and his cloak long ago shredded.

Thurgood threw a basket at him, one of Loar's offerings. "Here, try this."

It was filled with eelskins, tanned and stretched, their scaled colors reflecting in the sun. Dar pulled one out. It was as tough as the falroth-hide boots he wore.

Sharlin read his pleased look and dismounted. The two of them worked quickly, wrapping the legs of all the mounts, then stepped back and surveyed their handiwork. The four animals stamped, a rainbow of colors flashing in the light, blacks, reds, greens, and bronzes. Thurgood's mule looked most garish, and even the wizard smiled as he leaned over to survey the wrappings.

"That should do it." Dar gave Sharlin a leg up on Cloud, then mounted his own stallion. He kneed Brand forward, the horse stamping, then mincing ahead in caution. After a stride or two, the stallion realized he wasn't going to be injured further and settled down to a steady gait.

"For a simple fisherman, Loar knows more than he's told us."

Thurgood considered Dar's comment and answered, "They've probably been exploring this far, for all the stories. But I doubt they've been farther."

The grass bent, leaving a wake as they traveled, and dust and pollen rose. Sharlin's eyes reddened and teared, and she sniffled once or twice.

Thurgood dealt with his hay fever in his own manner, Dar observed. The wizard steadily imbibed from a hard leather case and retreated to a more or less sullen silence. Dar had thought of confronting the man before, knowing that they all needed their wits about them, but the lull at the fishers' village had snapped Thurgood out of his doldrums temporarily, for the children flocked around the wizard, begging for small illusions. He'd even managed a display of colored lights and explosions for the farewell dinner that lit up the sky and awed his small friends. But now the burden of Toothpick's death seemed to weigh him down again . . . and the uncertainty of his own future. Sharlin had told Dar of Toothpick's last words, that the wizard rode to his own death, and knew it.

Which of us, Dar wondered, could ride to his own death and take it as calmly? He flicked Brand's reins and left the aged man to his thoughts, and his drink, and let it go.

The buildup of dark clouds shaded the sun, dotting the plains below in a black-and-gold pattern. The clouds fled quickly over them, lending only a little relief from the sunlight, but the wind cooled their brows when they rode into the shadow of the mountains.

Cloud stumbled to a halt at the edge of the plains, and Sharlin gave a cry. Dar dismounted and went to the horse's side, but Thurgood on his mule, with the pack donkey following, merely ambled past. Dar looked up in irritation, but the wizard only gave him a bemused smile and headed toward the yawning pass.

Sharlin tapped Dar on the shoulder with the toe of her dusty boot. The beautiful blue color had long since faded away, scuffed by wear and stained by seawater. "Let him go. He can't ride far."

Dar shrugged in response, turning his attention to her horse. "What's wrong?"

"I think he's picked up a stone."

Dar curled his hand around the stallion's foreleg and ran it down, answering, "Let's hope so. We can't afford to have him lamed." He leaned into the horse's shoulder, forcing Cloud to throw his weight to his other legs, and picked the hoof up. A pebble rested in the soft frog, and he pried it out, then carefully examined the soft interior of the hoof. He let the hoof down. "He should be okay."

The donkey burst into loud brays and bucked at the end of its lead, pulling Thurgood right off the mule, somersaulting onto the ground with an *ooof!*

Sharlin gasped. "The ground's moving!"

Dar pivoted and saw the dark shadow creeping upon the ground, where the plains grass had given way to sparse green and the rocky dirt of the mountains' foothills. Thurgood sat in a daze, as a patch of darkness moved right toward him . . . not a shadow of cloud or stone, but a patch that made a sucking, squishing noise as it moved.

"Get up!" Dar yelled at the wizard, who sat in a stupor, head nodding, and beamed around him.

A shrub went up in flames when the patch reached it. The patch consumed it, then moved downward from the pass. Sparks floated into the air at random, then fizzled out.

The donkey panicked and jerked at its lead, and Thurgood's arm, like a puppet attached to a string, jerked with it. Dar remounted and drew his sword. The patch, emerging from the mouth of the pass, spread and thinned. Everything living burst into flames as it was touched, leaving behind only blackened ashes.

"What is it?"

"I don't know, but Thurgood's going to be in the middle of it!" Dar kicked Brand toward the wizard, shouting, "Get up, you old sot! Get up!"

Thurgood frowned, but staggered to his feet, weaving about. The wave of darkness drew close, and tiny flames could be seen issuing from it.

"They're worms," Sharlin cried as she joined Dar. "And they're on fire!"

"Not on fire," Dar corrected, reaching down and

grabbing Thurgood by the shoulders. "They're breathing it!"

The worms rippled toward them, each a handspan long, and from their slits of mouths came the tiniest of flames, but there were thousands of them. It was like facing an unstoppable wildfire. Thurgood, his face creased in panic, danced at the end of Dar's grasp and finally made it onto the saddle of his mule.

The donkey brayed, gave a last jerk, and freed itself, dashing to the edge of the pass. It bolted through the fireworms, squealing as the worms answered with a gust of flame, then it was through the mountain path and galloping across the stone, frayed end of rope trailing after it.

Sharlin reined Cloud to the side and yelled, "Follow me!"

Dar slapped the mule into movement, and Thurgood gulped and wrapped his hands frantically in the animal's scanty mane.

The wave of fireworms thinned at the sides, where it had fanned out coming out of the pass, and there Cloud jumped, sailing through the air. The stallion landed at the far side of the patch. He nickered as the worms scalded him, then he was through the wave. Sharlin fought him to a halt.

"It's your only chance," she called back. The wind sang about her, picking up to a frenzy.

As the first of the fireworms hit the plains grass, brushfire roared up in answer. Flame as tall as he was now licked at Dar's back, and, in answer, he whipped Brand forward.

The chestnut stallion flattened and leaped over the patch. He landed with a repellent squashing sound, and bucked and squealed as sparks played over his leg wrappings. Thurgood's mule followed, plunging through the mass to join them.

Behind them, the plains caught fire, and a dark stain moved upon it and followed, invulnerable to the flames.

Sharlin made a tiny sound in her throat. Then she said, "If we'd been caught in that . . ."

They stared at the wall of wildfire roaring away from

them. Dar turned his horse and reined him down the pass. "I suggest we hurry. Something equally unpleasant may be moving down the pass."

The horses danced nervously upon the scorched earth, and here and there a lone worm breathed a fingerling of fire at them from cracks in the rock, but the main mass had passed. A blackened carcass of softfoot, caught by the fireworms, was covered with their bodies; they fed, picking scorched and blackened flesh off white-and-pink bone, and Sharlin ducked her face until they had ridden past.

Finally, she looked up. "What will happen to them?"

Dar thought about it, then said, "They'll hit the river. Probably drown there . . . and the river will stop the fire, unless it rains first." Dar looked accusingly at Thurgood. "If you hadn't had your nose caught in your flask, you might have sensed the worms."

They glared at each other, the wizard with his sagging expression, and the swordsman with a mark of soot over his temple.

"I wasn't that drunk," Thurgood responded. "As if I could predict the mountain would sprout fire-breathing worms."

"There were signs to be read . . . charred tree trunks, the few we passed. You could have had the wards set up, so we'd be prepared no matter what happened."

Thurgood took a deep breath. "I have no strength for wards," he answered.

"Then what good are you to us?"

"I don't know. Since you're such a great thinker, why don't you ponder us a way out of this?" Thurgood shrugged into his frayed robes, kicked the mule into a trot, and left them behind.

"Dar," said Sharlin gently.

"I know, I know. He's an old man . . . I shouldn't bother him."

"It's not that—it's just that he's changed so much since Toothpick died. Can't you see him wrestling with that . . . as if he were wrestling death itself?"

Dar looked at her, instead of glaring at the retreating back of the wizard. He measured his words, but said them anyway. "We're all wrestling with death." He kicked Brand into a lope and followed the wizard.

They made camp in the pass. It was as though the stone itself had indeed sprouted the fireworms, for as they climbed, the green foliage returned, and it became obvious the fireworms hadn't come this far. Instead, stunted pine trees cracked the rock and thrust themselves out, drinking in the water that seeped out of the granite. Clouds of green grass crowded the run-off, and these delectable patches were nibbled by Brand and Cloud and the mule and donkey.

Withdrawn, Thurgood said not a word while they chewed tough smoked eel and ate sweet berries given them by the fisherfolk, but stared resentfully at his companions, pulled his tattered robe about his shoulders, and lay back on his packs to sleep, his flask gripped tightly in his hands.

Dar followed Sharlin when she left the camp to stretch and cup a handful of water from the rock, and to look at the brilliant stars overhead, for the clouds had swept by.

He put his hands upon her shoulders to turn her around and draw her close, but she shrugged out from under his touch.

"Don't."

"He's gone . . . he'll never hear us. I just want to hold you for a moment, to feel you. . . ."

She pulled away sharply, and even in the darkness, he could see the blaze flare up in her eyes. He stopped, bewildered.

"I asked you not to."

Dar tilted his head a little, thoroughly confused. "I thought we . . . I thought there was something . . . what happened at the temple . . ."

The girl looked away, no longer willing to meet his eyes. "There was, then. Not now, Dar. Not ever again."

Anger flared through him, tightened his throat, made the veins stand out on his arms. "What do you mean?"

Sharlin ran her hand through her hair, fanning it from the right side of her face, and its heavy fragrance stabbed at him. "You're running from your past as fast as you can, afraid it'll catch up with you, and I—I'm running toward mine, scared to death I won't be able to catch up. In a day or two, we'll be finished. I have . . . I have something to do, and I can't think about you. I can't let you stand between me and the reason I came to this place." She swallowed and looked up at the sky, her voice caught in her throat. "I can't think about me or what I want for myself any longer."

Dar watched her in stunned silence, her words making no sense to him. He turned on his heel then and left her without answer. He threw himself down by the fire. With a dried branch, he stoked it in anger.

Thurgood spoke wearily from his resting place. "Let her go, Aarondar."

"What would you know about it? Go back to your sorrows and your flask, old man."

The wizard sat up. He smiled sadly at no one, and watched the flames as though he could drown in them. "Sorrowed, yes, and old, yes . . . but I'd have to be blind not to know what has happened between you and Sharlin. She won't tell you all of her secrets, but I have guessed some, and in a few days, I'll know if I have guessed the rest."

Dar looked then. "You knew what she would read at the temple, didn't you?" he accused.

"I guessed that, yes. I knew she was descended from the House of Dhamon, though I didn't know how that could be . . . the house lineage ended long ago. The tiny birthmark on her throat is peculiar to the Dhamons, once great rulers. When she nursed you at Lyrith and told me what had happened, I wasn't surprised, though I was awed. This Rodeka's powers must be awesome, to have thrown someone across land and time. Awesome," he muttered and fell for a moment into his thoughts.

"Then tell me how to take her home."

"Home?" Thurgood laughed softly, ironically. "Across seas, a map will guide you. Across time? Only death crosses time. And as for yourself . . . you have a destiny of your own to meet." Thurgood lifted up a lean finger.

"You hope that Kory gave you the key to your freedom, don't you? Sharlin told me that also. Stay away from her, swordsman. You can only hurt her."

"What do you know about it?"

"I know that the body of Mnak disappeared from the temple before we could tell if he had indeed died. I know that he summoned his master. You have other demons of your own to face, and nothing that you're going to go through will help Sharlin! Leave her alone, I say! When this is done, we all have our separate ways to go."

In spite of himself, Dar's hand curled about the hilt of his sword.

Sharlin approached the fire, her fists clenched. "Will you two stop arguing about me as though—as though I were a choice bone? Your voices are echoing all over this mountain. What do either of you know of what I want . . . or what faces me?"

Thurgood's face hardened, and he said, in a quiet, menacing voice, "I know more than you think . . . and if you attempt to do what I believe you will, you'll have me to face, princess. I have but one goal left now—to reach the graveyard and destroy my enemy."

"I have no intention of standing between you and your dragon."

"Oh, no? We'll see. We'll see." And Thurgood got to his feet and lurched away in the darkness, on a mission of his own, as the two of them stared after.

"What's he talking about?"

"Nothing," answered Sharlin a little too quickly, but her face was shadowed in despair.

"And is he right?" Dar pursued. "Will we each go our own way?"

Sharlin's look of desperation turned to him, and he saw a glimmering tear well in her eye. "We have no choice," she whispered, and pressed her hands to her lips before fleeing from the light of the campfire.

Dar sat by himself thinking. Suddenly he knew he was alone in his quest to free himself from Valorek, and wondered if the freedom would be worth it. He sat there for a long time and let the fire burn out.

Chapter 18

The dawn came up, slivers of light beaming through the high mountain peaks, the air crisp in the shadows that lingered behind. The wind spoke of winter, even to these far southern lands, and the end of what had seemed to be endless summer, and a faraway breath of rain.

Dar noticed nothing as he savagely pulled the girth tight on his horse, after first kneeing out a lungful of air, an old habit Brand indulged in when he was feeling his oats. The first time the horse had done it, Dar had girthed his expansion and thought the saddle on tight, only to find it slipping as he swung aboard and the horse exhaled. Today he would have none of it; as Brand gasped, he strapped the girth tight.

Sharlin had not met his look over a scant breakfast that morning, and neither of them spoke to Thurgood either, though when the wizard toddled over to put his tack on his mule, it was obvious Thurgood had already had a snoot-ful.

Dar swung aboard and gathered his reins before the other two had finished. He put his heels to Brand, trotting off in the direction of the last pass.

"Dar—" Sharlin started to call, but the wizard interrupted her.

"Let him go."

"What did you say to him last night?"

Bleary blue eyes considered her. "I thought you heard our voices all over the mountain."

"Most of it."

Thurgood's mouth twitched. "I said nothing more to him than you did. Perhaps our friend feels it's time for us to break up the company, since we're close enough to our destination."

She shivered in the crisp air, for she couldn't shake the feeling she was being watched. She looked up, to the tall, jagged spires above them, and saw nothing. With a hop, she got her boot toe in the stirrup and swung aboard Cloud. His black-tipped ears flicked forward and back. "And what about you?" she challenged. "Have we no more to do with each other?"

"On the contrary, princess, now I must stay closer to you than ever." Thurgood's thin smile stretched and pulled at his face, even the paralyzed jaw. The smile never reached his eyes, however, and they stayed as cold as the autumn wind.

Jet hugged the mountain's crag, shivering as the keen wind rattled through his spines and the jagged hole in one sail, and he breathed with difficulty. Below, in the Pits, he would sleep in the warm sand, and perhaps spawn, and perhaps die—but he would rise again. That he had ensured for himself, and now he waited for the one he'd called to appear. Curled in his paw slept the demon Mnak, ragged, close unto his own death, but still as full of spite and the purpose of his mission as he had been the day Valorek called him out of the nether regions. The dragon had found the demon, and their desires, for the time being, crossed.

To have lived so long, only to die! Jet's talons cut into the granite, and the rock powdered, then resisted him, and the claws ached dully in their sockets. He sensed, more than saw and heard, movement in the passes below, as the three who dared rode closer and closer to the dragon and into the snare of illusion set in times more ancient than he could guess for anyone who breached the pass.

He moved his head, scratching his jaw on a boulder. When the three had ridden into the web and were caught, they would answer to him, black dragon full of venom and malicious power.

They caught up with Dar sooner than expected. The pass ended abruptly in a dark, yawning mouth into a mountain, and he sat on a rock, wrapping a dry branch with grasses and an eelskin, fashioning a torch.

Sharlin started to ride past, but Cloud slowed at the blackness ahead, and Dar moved quickly to block her.

"We'll need torches."

"Oh," she answered. "Is it 'we' again?"

His teeth clenched, then relaxed. "I rode ahead to scout the pass. There's something up there . . . I can feel it."

She forgot her spite. "I feel it, too. Have you seen anything?"

"No." He finished wrapping the torch and handed it to her, then started a second. "But if it's a dragon, they say they can see for leagues. And it could be perched up there anywhere, blending with the rock."

"Jet?"

"Maybe." He pointed toward the tunnel. "I can't see light from the other side . . . and I won't go in there blind."

Thurgood giggled. "We're already blind."

Dar ignored the wizard. He finished his torch, then took his flint and iron out and sparked it carefully into flames. Then he fired Sharlin's torch. "Stay behind me."

She closed her mouth on a retort and instead did as he bid. The darkness of the cavern swallowed up the torch-light when they entered, reducing the light to a smoldering orange flame that guttered unsteadily, and they all felt the oppressiveness of the air around them.

Pebbles clicked and rolled from the horses' hooves, and Sharlin trembled. There was no echo! Nothing, as though everything she knew and believed in were swallowed up. She held the torch up higher, and felt a cold touch lick her arm, and the flame went out.

She screamed. Dar reined Brand around and jostled

her, holding the torches together until the second one flared again. They looked at each other.

She swallowed. "I'm all right. The wind . . . just startled me."

"There's no wind, Sharlin," Dar answered, with a puzzled look, before turning back and taking the lead again.

She pressed her lips tightly together, knowing that he thought her a bundle of nerves, but she couldn't deny what she felt closing in around her. Evil . . . dark, sly, malicious, something invisible was crowding her ever more tightly. She looked to the side, though the torch shed no light that way, and a pair of slanted green eyes blinked at her, flank-high. She swallowed and ignored them. They disappeared, blotted out.

Dust. She tried to swallow and could not, her throat dry and closed. If she had to scream again, she couldn't. Dust . . . like the bones of her parents and family, gone to dust. She had no right to be alive when they were dead so long ago few even remembered their names! She had no right to think of life and living and loving . . . none at all! Her hand curled tightly about the reins, and her fingernails cut into her palms, drawing blood, but she did not notice it.

Lies, she told herself. The darkness is lying to me. I know it! For a moment, she could breathe easily, and then the cavern closed about her again. Ahead of her, the figure of Dar could barely be seen, his torch shining an aura about his half-helm, his brown hair waving down his neck from under it. Dar! If she could just reach Dar . . .

And hope stopped, as the evil swirled about her, pressing in on her, making it impossible to both think and breathe. Don't think, it told her. Don't think. He is wrapped up in his own destiny, which is to die at the hands of a sorcerer king. He has no time for you. He has nothing to offer you.

Not true! Sharlin gasped, forcing her mind to function even as she struggled to keep air in her lungs. She closed her eyes a moment.

When she opened them, torchlight illuminated a figure striding along beside her, and she stifled a cry of gladness, for the broad-shouldered, slim-waisted man turned and smiled . . . her father, Balforth, King of Dhamon, his light-colored locks brushing his shoulders from under a pale-gray coronet of iron, a single blue stone gracing it.

"Father!" she said softly, and leaned out of the saddle to reach him. The figure stopped in his tracks and smiled, then turned to ashes before she could touch him.

Dust! Gone to earth and death without her.

Tears stained her cheeks before she knew she cried, and her hand trembled. She clenched the torch tightly and stretched her right arm up. "Dar!" The darkness ate her voice, but she gathered all her strength and shouted again, "Dar!"

The figure riding ahead of her did not flinch or waver, intent upon his own purposes.

Did he also ride with the dead?

Sharlin turned in the saddle, reaching out the torchlight toward the wizard, limning a face with eyes squeezed shut as though in torture, as Thurgood gasped for breath and held on tightly with both hands.

Dragon lies.

"No!" she muttered to herself. "I won't let you turn me back. I won't believe they're dust until I see them. I will raise Turiana if it's the last thing I do, and when Turiana lives again, I will ask her to take me back!"

At the sound, or thought, of the golden dragon's name, the darkness eased its hold on her a bit. She breathed easier. Not all dragons are evil, she told herself. Magic is what you make of it. Power is wielded by the user, and the user is molded to it. Turiana. Turiana.

The torchlight grew brighter. Now she could see the gray floor of the cavern as Cloud traversed it. Ahead, perhaps, she could even see the light flowering from the tunnel's end, drawing them onward.

Dar gave a yell and kicked Brand as he drew his sword and plunged at the flower of brightness. He threw his torch to one side, where it broke apart on the stone when it hit, and the cavern echoed with Brand's pounding hooves.

Dar charged headfirst into the brightness and disappeared. The last Sharlin saw of him was as he bent over Brand's neck, and the horse curled his legs and leaped, their bodies silhouetted against the disk, and then they were gone, swallowed up.

She reined Cloud to a halt, and Thurgood bumped into her. His eyelids flew open.

"What is it?"

"We've lost Dar."

Dar woke, and rolled, his head and rib cage pounding. The last thing he remembered was Brand arcing through the sky. . . .

A voice broke into his pain. "You grew up well."

He sat upright in fear, his heart pounding, and looked into a face he knew well, too well. Valorek stood and smiled, and crossed his arms

The wide-mouthed cave opened onto a mountainside, and outside on the rocks he saw a black dragon curled, apparently asleep. Inside, in the shadows at Valorek's back, red eyes flared into being as Mnak snarled. The demon couldn't be alive, yet there he stood, hunched, heat rolling off his scaled hide.

The sorcerer king moved, his black leathers creaking, and he appraised Dar.

"How . . . am I . . ." Dar stopped, moistened his lips. He remembered only charging Brand at a line of goblin soldiers, as their dark blood lapped at his boots, and before that, entering a tunnel . . . with Sharlin and Thurgood. His mind quickened as he remembered. What was, couldn't possibly be. Illusions . . . snared with illusions.

He reached for his sword. "You don't frighten me anymore. I know what you are. Lies. . . ." His sheath was empty.

Valorek laughed, familiarly cruel. "Not lies, not I. No,

Dar. I was summoned here to deal with you. You remember living with me." The man leaned forward and traced a finger down his captive's jawline. "I know you used to listen to the dragon when he came to me. You know where my powers come from." He straightened and pointed at the great beast curved outside the cave. "Meet Nightwing, my dragonlord, source of all my well-being . . . a bit ragged right now, assuredly, but soon to be fit again. Some call him Jet. He gives me you, and I will give him resurrection. Mnak here will guard me long enough to ensure that the third imprint is done, and then you are no more . . . you'll be mine completely, as you are nearly mine now. Say goodbye, Dar." The king leaned over him, cupped his face in his hands, and gave him a lingering kiss, as Mnak straightened and lumbered over, the stink of death hanging on him.

Dar sank back, and darkness swarmed about him.

"Do something."

Thurgood returned Sharlin's accusing look and shrugged sadly. "What can I do? I can't see where he's gone. He could have fallen into a pit for all I know." He clutched his flask to his chest. "Let him go, Sharlin. It's just you and I, as I always thought it would be."

"You're an old fool!"

For a moment, the wizard held himself tall. "And you're a young one. Are you any better?"

"At least I believe he can be helped." She picked up Dar's fallen sword and gripped it tightly. The bright flower had disappeared, and only the torch which burned toward its end gave light. Soon they would be without even that. She stood. Cloud tugged at the reins and appeared eager to move forward. Did the horse see what she did not? Or . . . did she see what never existed?

"For Dhamon! Dhamon forever!" Sharlin cried, and she suddenly kicked the stallion and plunged him after Dar, his dropped sword clutched in one hand and her silver dagger in the other. Thurgood stammered, "Wait for me!"

She burst through a curtain of vile darkness, gasping and shuddering for breath, and the cavern widened into air and sunlight.

A man stood over Dar's body where it was spread-eagled over a boulder, and the huge form of the black dragon lumbered over both of them, spreading his aura like a star of darkness.

The man straightened, a candle in one hand and a dagger in the other. "No! Not yet!" he cried and pointed. "Stop them!"

Mnak sprang out of nowhere, grabbing Sharlin and dragging her from the saddle. After a paralyzing moment, when all seemed to freeze in midair as the demon's baleful eyes pinned her own, she swung, not with her right hand, which held the sword, but with her left, and the silver dagger cleaved the beast's throat. He fell to the ground, pulling her with him.

Thurgood staggered to a halt, gargling in fear. The dragon reared, one eye a gaping wound healed over in a spidery white web of tissue, a jagged hole in his breast.

"Wizard!" the beast roared, and laughed, and the sound made the mountains shake. He stretched his wings and flapped, raising the dust in a whirlwind. "Do you cling to me yet?"

The man went to his knees, trembling, caught by surprise, his hands shaking as he covered his face.

Sharlin pulled herself off the stinking carrion of the demon's body. It dissolved into a pool of steaming sludge. "Dar," she cried. "Wake up!"

Valorek smashed the candle to the ground, drew his sword, and faced her.

He lunged at her, and she parried the cut, but felt the jar of his blow all the way to her teeth, which rattled in their sockets. Too strong . . . she'd never be able to hold him off! A curious insanity blazed in the man's flat, dark eyes . . . this man who snarled at her.

"He's mine!"

She stepped back, trembling, her leg brushing the rock, and the icy coldness of Dar's hand touched the back of her calf, exposed in the gap between boot and skirt. The touch burned into her skin, and she jumped.

Valorek came at her *en pointe*.

She put her chin up, thinking of the pallans, who'd helped her when she needed help, and Dar, who treated her as though she might break, and her family's battle to save its kingdom, lost long ago. "He's not yours yet," she challenged, and her voice lowered.

Underlying her words, she heard Thurgood sobbing with fear, and the deep-throated chuckle of the dragon as he snaked his head down, jaws wide. Valorek lunged, and the swords met, metal ringing. He twisted, and her hand lost its grip, the blade flying away, and she stood without a weapon. The dragon hissed as he struck at the wizard.

Only her silver dagger remained, pooled in the sludge of the demon. Sharlin jumped for it, rolled on the ground, cocked it, and threw it down the gullet of the black dragon, as his forked tongue lolled out and fangs glistened. Valorek stood in disbelief.

Nightwing screamed. Pain shrilled forth in his cry, and Valorek went to his knees, covering his ears in agony. Thurgood toppled over, and the dragon rose, curling his talons around Valorek and lifting him, and launched himself, keening in agony. She got to her feet as the black dragon winged away, the whirlwind following him, and then the mountains went deadly silent.

Thurgood moaned. Sharlin helped the aging man stagger to his feet, mindful of the goo that covered her, and the stink of the liquor on his breath.

"A fine pair we are," she muttered, as she helped him limp to the rock altar where Dar lay.

"I wasn't ready," Thurgood moaned. "Tomorrow. I meant to meet him tomorrow. . . ."

"To hell with tomorrow," Sharlin snapped. "Wake Dar up. I can't seem to reach him."

"No." Thurgood shook his head. "I can't anymore. It's beyond me. The dragon is reeling me in . . . the threads are near breaking. . . ."

"Tell me something you don't know, tell me something you haven't lived with for most of your life! Why did you go on living? Why didn't you slit your throat in a tub of warm water and give it up? You'd have saved Toothpick and me a lot of trouble. Why quit now?" Sharlin ducked from under him, making him stand on his own two feet. When the wizard looked at her, face dissolving in a blur of self-pity, she opened her hand and swung.

The slap cracked through the mountain air, and a bright-red spot bloomed on Thurgood's cheek. She shook with anger and fear. "Wake him up, I said!"

The man straightened. After a long moment, he put his hand to his face and held it, but his gaze met hers, and then he nodded. "As usual, princess, you have the winning argument. Tomorrow is soon enough to die." He turned to Dar's limp form and began to chant, hands held out palm down.

The sun hung low in the sky, and Thurgood's voice had pared to a bare, hoarse whisper, before Dar stirred, and when he came awake, it was like a drowning man, flailing and grasping at Sharlin, pulling himself out of the trance as if to pull himself out of the water, or pull his rescuer in with him.

She grabbed him back and braced herself. His hands bruised her arms deeply, and then his brown eyes focused, and the life came back into them.

"Sharlin!" he whispered as though he couldn't believe what he saw. Then he thrust her arms away and snarled, "Don't touch me!"

Chapter 19

They got ready to finish what they had started. They camped on the rim of the mountain pass, and each looked at the other, features drawn, eyes deep in their faces, for the journey was ended, except for the morning. The rim of the ancient mountain, once a burning peak, was still warm. Mud pools bubbled and gurgled, and they skirted an endless pool, like a jeweled eye reflecting back the sky, except that Thurgood looked into it and said, "There's no bottom." Sharlin had to take him by the elbow and pull him back.

Winged clouds darkened the sky in fleeting moments while they tethered the horses and mule and donkey. Each time, one of them looked up quickly—but it was impossible to tell if they spied creatures or rain. They made a point of camping where rock spires bowed over them like doorways and nothing could strike from above.

Dar would not speak to either of them. He took his water and his eel stew, and curled up, back to the rocks, his pack and recovered sword tucked under his legs.

"Like thieves," Sharlin whispered to Thurgood. "He eyes us as though we were thieves!"

The wizard patted her shaking arm as she banked the fire for the evening. "He's had a tremendous shock. You mustn't blame him for anything he says or does tonight. Tomorrow will bring us back the Dar you love."

It didn't make the haunted look in Dar's eyes any easier to see, and soon Sharlin rolled into her pallan cloak, laid

her head down on her sleeping bags, where the lyrith
within crushed a little and gave out its gentle fragrance,
and slept with her back to the suspicion emanating from
Dar.

Thurgood finished his last draught of the fisherfolk's
potent drink. He drained his cup and then looked into it
by the ebbing light of the fire to make sure he had not
overlooked a drop. Tonight, at least, he should sleep well.
He slumped back onto his pack and snored his way into
drunken slumber.

Dar spooned up the last of his meal, the deep breathing
of the other two telling him they slept. He put his bowl to
one side and drew his knees up, laying his sword over it.
Then, with a stone, he endeavored to renew the cutting
edge, while the Shield and the Little Warrior came out to
see what he did.

His hands shook as he worked. He was no longer totally
himself; and his heart beat first as Dar, then Valorek, then
Dar, then Valorek again. The other's presence boiled
through his veins like a poison, and he couldn't shake it
off. He stopped, his hands resting on the sword, and
looked at Sharlin.

Valorek stiffened like a stallion in heat, and Dar tipped
his head back to the cool rock and shut his eyes tightly,
willing the feelings away. But he couldn't keep the vision
from his memory when he closed his eyes . . . the vision
of Sharlin naked as she lay in his arms, and now Valorek
wanted to stroke her, take her, ravage her savagely.

Trembling, Dar opened his eyes and laid the sword
aside. He took his pack and moved into the shadows, as
far away as he could, near the horses as they stamped, and
lay down to sleep there, the cords on his neck straining as
he fought to keep from screaming her name, for she
couldn't help him, and if she, gods save him, touched him
now, he would rape her.

The wizard slept uneasily, his arms folded over his
chest, and his hands flapped slightly as he fought with
himself, in dreams so deep that no numbing potion could

reach them. In the morning he would die, and, knowing that, he now relived parts of his life whether he wished to or not.

"Talent small or large," a bent old man, with short-cropped fine white hair, said to him, frowning at him. "Large or small, mind you, Thurgood—pay attention!"— emphasized with a switch over the knuckles. "Each has its own destiny."

But Thurgood's mind wasn't on the instruction. He'd spent most of the last season's nights out on a high ridge, sleeping under the stars, and when the Shield arose, waking to search for a shadow, however fleeting, to cross its silvery expanse. And last night, finally, he'd seen that winged shadow—a dragonlord, making his way across the outlands. He'd known the dragon instantly, and the beast called to him, the way the wind called to the sea.

As Bril glared at him, Thurgood jumped to his feet, rubbing his smarting hand, and grinned down. "I'm off," he said.

"Off? Off where?"

The young man grabbed his pack and his satchel of books, swung them over his sloping shoulders—muscles were never part of his physique—and smiled down at the cast-off instructor. "I'm in search of the dragon."

Bril hobbled from the cottage after him, calling out irritably, "Dragon? What dragon? Don't fool with the gods, Thurgood—they'd as soon eat you as talk with you."

But Thurgood laughed as he skipped down the village pathway and disappeared, in hot pursuit of his destiny.

He found his dragon a few years later, a sleek black male, curled in the bowels of a mountain, where dragons liked to go, and he paused, daunted for a moment, as the blackness reflected off the beast's scales. He had never reckoned on a black dragon, for they were gods of evil, misfortune, and spite; and malice oozed from this creature with every sleeping breath. He backed off a little, but the beast had heard him and opened a glowing orb, and Thurgood was caught.

He reflected, years later, that Jet would have eaten him

on the spot, if superstitious farmers had not already fed him the fatted calf, as it were. And, as it was, Jet had never met a man who wanted to curry power from him, and so the two amused each other for several more years, Thurgood trying to mold good out of evil and Jet watching him attempt it.

Jet summoned him one day. Thurgood grabbed a scroll and hustled with it to the part of the cave where the dragon kept primary residence. A great flat rock rose in the center of it, where the wizard often spread out scrolls and read to the dragon, who liked to rest his chin on it and crack bones. They were both young then, Thurgood thought in his dreams, and he turned restlessly to one side, his weakened side.

"Another dialogue?" Thurgood beamed, then spread his robes and sat down. He thought he was making progress.

The dragon smiled, his forked tongue slithering between his great ivory teeth. "No, little worm," Jet rumbled. "Now it is time for me to teach you!" And his mind clamped down on Thurgood like a trap, and the wizard crumpled to the cave flooring, his senses overwhelmed by the evil snaking through them, and when the dragon released him, it was a decade after that, and Thurgood found blood on his hands and learned then that he had become an evil sorcerer, a scourge on the face of the earth, and he cried.

He staggered out of the mountain's bowels into the setting sun, all his knowledge, good and evil, at his disposal, as the dragon prepared to take off from a precipice, and they did battle then. He wasn't up to it—Jet had known of the weakening in his mind and heart before he released him—and as they fought, lightning crashed and the earth shook, and great stabs of pain crippled him, and he bent over, going to one knee.

With a whoosh, the dragon dropped on him, talons raking his hand as he held it up to point a killing spell at the beast, and blood fountained from the flesh of his arm.

"Die!" the dragon hissed, and pressed on his fragile

mind again, and fiery pain blossomed inside him, and he spoke one last word before crumpling to the ground.

That word drove Jet away from those mountains. It didn't kill him, as it could have, but it drove him away, and the dragon fled, thinking the man doomed to die its puny, mortal death.

Thurgood sat, his weakened arm over his knee, and, left hand shaking, attempted to stitch himself up. He cried and moaned silently, stopping to pinch the white flesh together in an effort to stem the tide of blood, growing more and more light-headed.

Thus it was that he didn't think he saw what he saw when an apple-cheeked dwarf boy looked at him, lantern hanging from his hand, eyes wide at the sight of the destroyed mountain, trampled ground, and the wizard's own bloodstained robes.

"I tol' 'em there was a rumbling," the lad said. "Are ye all right?"

"No, I—I—" Thurgood fought to contain his shaking. The cold threatened to do him in.

"Ye've fought th' dragon," the mountain dwarf continued in his rich brogue. "A heroic sorcerer! An' he's cut ye bad. Let me help you."

The boy bent over his arm, pulled the last few stitches in, and wrapped the wound securely, but Thurgood had fainted long before he was done, and the dwarf sat with him all the night, his lantern a golden orb of caring shining into the dark, and that was when Thurgood knew that he had power enough to keep himself living.

The boy mountain dwarf wouldn't leave him in the morning.

Thurgood drank the steaming hot brew the lad fixed him. Dwarves lived two hundred years or more, he knew, far beyond the span of ordinary men. "What do they call you?"

"Toothpick, master," and the lad bowed with a grin.

"I'm not your master," the wizard protested. "I'm hardly old enough to be your father."

"Nay, sir, ye're right there . . . but there comes a time

when ever' man must choose his master, and I choosed ye. That's why I climbed this mountain to find ye." He scratched his bushy head of hair and grinned. "I can't hardly go back now, can I?"

And so he didn't. He never went back, not even when he died, two hundred and forty-seven years later, an old man even by dwarves' standards. In his sleep, Thurgood hugged himself and mourned anew.

Sharlin tossed in her slumber. She relived the night she lay on her stomach, listening to the low voice of her father, mother, and their counselor talking below, unaware she overheard from the stairs.

"How did she break the lines?"

A shrug from Henry. "There's no knowing, my lord, but I'll vow she did it the way she always does . . . goblin warriors, and berserkers, in addition to her own troops. She carries both death and despair as her banners."

Lauren gasped and reached for her husband's arm. "They'll be here, next."

The king nodded. "You'll have to leave, go south. Take Sharlin and Erban with you."

"I won't leave you."

"There's no choice, dear Lauren." He raised his hand to stroke her face. "The three of you are the House of Dhamon if I fall."

"And what will you do?"

King Balforth looked at his queen before turning his attention back to his counselor. "I'll get ready for the siege. They'll be a long time breaking our back . . . Dhamon's never been conquered before. We might be able to withstand her."

"Bah! Rodeka's made a pact with the dragongods. She's got sorcery on her side. Sire, you're a brilliant commander, but you've got to fight fire with fire!"

"And where do you suggest I find the power? The dragons hold it tightly within their claws. None escapes but they give it out—and there are few enough dragons that bear us goodwill. Turiana was the last who openly opposed black magic. There are no golden dragons now, Henry. We'll have to stand the way we are, men and mortal."

Their voices rose angrily, and at her back, in the children's wing, Sharlin heard the fitful cry of Erban as he stirred, waking. She lifted herself from the warm stones of the staircase and crept into his room, where he rubbed sleepy eyes until he spied her in the moonlit room, and he smiled.

"Sharlin!"

She cradled him the way her mother did, and rubbed his fair curls. All in the family were fair, fair as ripened wheat, while she alone had darkened, taken on the hair color of burnished gold. From her grandfather, they told her. As she rocked Erban, she watched the moonlight slant in through the high rock window. Gold, she thought. Only a golden dragon could save all of them.

The griffins had long memories. Gabriel, who talked to her when she rode him hunting or reconnoitering, often told her stories of Turiana. It was said that dragons never really died . . . that their skin and bones faded, but the dragonlords kept their souls and magic intact, and that if the right sorcery was worked and the gods were pleased, the dragons could rise again. If only Turiana . . .

It was then she tucked Erban back under his covers and kissed him lightly and whispered in his ear, "When Mommy comes in the morning to get you, tell her I've gone for help. Tell her I've gone for the golden dragon."

She dressed quickly then, in her riding leathers, to enlist Gabriel's aid in her endeavor.

When Sharlin woke, it was with the same feeling as when Gabriel plummeted to Rangard, bearing all her hopes with him. She gasped for breath.

In his dreams, Dar wrestled. He knew what he fought for, and who he fought with, and knew that he did more than dream . . . he walked through his own mind, and if he lost, he would not wake as Aarondar in the morning, but as Valorek, and neither Sharlin nor Thurgood would be safe from him.

Without the power, perhaps, but not without the darkness of soul and the lust for the pain and hurting of others . . . that would be the Valorek he projected, and he knew he would seek the king out wherever Nightwing had taken him—to the Pits, probably. Dar clenched his fists. He groaned, deep in his throat, and thrashed and tried to grip his elusive enemy.

"Grew up well, didn't you, boy?" the dark king mocked him.

They faced each other on the practice field Dar had come to despise. He flinched, surprised that he was there, and met Valorek's derisive gaze. "I grew up better than you," he said, dropping into a crouch.

Both were naked, except for loincloths, and oil glistened on their muscles. Valorek relaxed and dropped into a similar pose, and flexed his arms. "I wouldn't brag about it. You had a mother and father, didn't you? More than I . . . but then, you don't have anything left of them but ashes, either."

"They gave me more than ashes," Dar returned, but his bitterness dried his mouth, and he shook his head. The hot sun beat down, and his brow was sweaty, and rivulets of salty water dribbled down his face. He was bruised, and the back of his shoulders dusty, and he knew, somehow, that Valorek had already taken him down once.

"They gave you nothing, not even yourself," Valorek spat. The king rushed him then, bowling him off his feet, and they rolled in the dust. His nails tore into Dar's biceps, and he gasped but refused to cry out, for pain made the king stronger.

He arched his back, flipped the king off, rolled out from under him, and got to his feet. Before Valorek could gain his, Dar kicked, lifting the man up. His body weight slammed him onto the ground on his back, and Dar jumped, flattening him.

He fought to pin Valorek, but the other was too well oiled, and too strong, and they grappled.

"I'm winning, Dar," Valorek husked, between clenched teeth, as the sinews on his neck and shoulders stood out, his face straining.

"No," Dar gasped back. "I'm going to put you down and keep you there!" He dug his fingers in and pushed.

"I'm winning," the king whispered, "or you wouldn't even have to wrestle me!"

"No! No!"

Sharlin lay gasping, her heart pounding in her chest, until she realized that the fall was one from sleep, and not from the heights on a mortally wounded griffin. As her senses regained balance, she heard the moans and gasps of Dar, who thrashed on his blankets.

She got up on her elbow. Thurgood had warned her to leave him alone, and after that first frightening moment when Dar had awakened and recoiled from her, she didn't have to be warned twice. Whatever the dark king had done, the swordsman was like a man possessed.

But she couldn't stand to see him like that. She got to her knees and slipped a bud of lyrith out of her pouch. The moonlight showed her that there was only a small store of herbs left, perhaps not even enough after all they'd been through. She clutched the lyrith in the palm of her hand as Dar's muffled cries carried to her. Then she took a deep breath.

Walking softly, so as not to awaken him, she gained his side. He quieted a moment, forehead running with sweat, his eyes tight and his jaws clamped solidly. Sharlin crushed the lyrith tightly in her hand, rubbed her palms together until the flower was a powder, and sprinkled it over him from head to toe.

"For whatever good it does," she whispered. "For whatever strength or hope it gives you, my love."

Then she stole back to her own blankets and pulled them up over her head as she lay down in them, and prayed that they both could find rest before the night was over.

Thurgood crawled on his hands and knees in the morning, aches and pains in every joint, like an old man, he told himself. Then he smiled in spite of himself. He was an old man—nearly two hundred and seventy-seven years old. He'd far outlived any of his enemies, with the exception of Nightwing and the town boss of Murch's Flats. Thurgood grunted and forced himself to stretch upward to the sun, and blinked, for the sun was nearly at eye level, so high on the rim had they camped. He hobbled to his packs and foraged for another draught, couldn't find one, cursed and searched for his discarded flask on the ground. It was uncorked, and he remembered then having drained it just before sleep.

"Looking for a hair of the dog, old man?"

Thurgood whirled and saw Dar sitting cross-legged against a rock. He worked on oiling his swordblade, methodically wiping the metal with an old cloth. The wizard felt his cheeks sting heatedly.

The swordsman stood up. He had repaired the breastplate cut away from him by Valorek and stood there in full battle dress, and despite the youth of his tanned face, he looked hardened. "I threw your bottles away," he said. "You drained your flask, but I didn't think that was good enough. You'll need your wits about you today, my friend."

"Friend?" Thurgood gathered his dignity about him much as he did his worn robes. "With friends like you, I have little need of enemies. You're feeling better this morning, I take it?"

Dar strode across the dirt-packed clearing. He wrapped his fist in the wizard's collar and lifted him until he stood on tiptoe. "No time for small talk or niceties, Thurgood. You're to stay with the girl and protect her."

"And—and what about you?"

An expression, almost like a light, flickered through the warm brown eyes, and Thurgood shivered.

"I have business of my own today," Dar said, "and I won't be there when she needs me. Perhaps later."

Thurgood choked, and Dar lowered him to the flat of his boots. The wizard met his gaze, however, and his own voice was cold and flat as he answered, "The girl will have to take care of herself, then, for I, too, have business of my own." He pulled out of his handhold, and Dar let him go, clenching his hand tightly about the guard of his sword.

The night's dreams had settled nothing, and he had waked this morning still tortured by Valorek's taunting laugh . . . but now, he was more afraid of himself than he was of Valorek. He couldn't trust himself, and because of that, would not ride down into the graveyard by Sharlin's side. Valorek was somewhere in the Pits, guarded by Nightwing, and if a dragon's claw didn't work as the swamp witch had prophesied, then he would go after the dark king, and finish the man off . . . or die trying. He would do whatever he had to to be free!

Thurgood's voice broke into his thoughts. "Whatever you intend to do, you'd better hurry," the wizard called. He stood over Sharlin's sleeping form, wrapped in the pallan cloak. He toed it open. Saddlebags and brush gave it shape, but no one slept there.

"She's already gone."

Chapter 20

Sharlin paused on the rocky pathway. The wind moaned around the crags and spires and tore at her hair, whipping it across her face. She combed it down, fighting with the wayward strands much as she fought with herself.

The pouch containing the prayer scroll and the herbs and spices was the only thing fastened to her belt. In her left hand she carried a dagger she had scrounged from Thurgood's packs . . . probably one of Toothpick's spares, for she knew the wizard carried no weapons other than a sharp tongue. She shivered, missing the precious pallan cloak she'd left behind to decoy the men until she was far on her way, on foot, for the rocky precipice to the Pits could be traveled no other way.

She'd left behind all the new things she'd picked up in this adventure . . . Cloud, the old wizard, Dar. She wore her old riding boots, pinching now at the toes . . . could she have grown? She left behind all but the self-doubt that gnawed at her now, that slowed her steady footfalls on the edge of the rim. How could she possibly hope to save a people long conquered, long dead?

Because it has to be me, she thought. Because I didn't let Thurgood read the rest of the histories, or go in myself to look at it, to see if my name is written. Because even if they were defeated, the House of Dhamon could possibly have risen and fought back. I know my father and my mother, and Erban. They didn't just give up!

Yet she couldn't shake the despair she'd felt at the temple of Lyrith, or that blossomed anew during the cavern crossing. Dragon lies, she thought and wavered again. Dragon lies!

Clouds shadowed the morning. Sharlin looked up, then threw herself against the ground, panting in fear, afraid to scream, as a green-winged dragon sailed over her, eyes glittering and sail spread to catch the very wind that chilled her.

Had it seen her? Sharlin pressed into the shadows, cursing herself for her stupidity. The peddler had talked of dragons winging the skies above the graveyard . . . live dragons, sentries, and dragons hatching their broods. She kept herself still until certain that the young winged dragon had gone, then she got to her feet.

Swoooosh! It darted at her from behind, talons extended, jaws agape. She scrambled away from its grasp, but the claws knuckled into her, knocking her off the path.

With a scream she couldn't hold any longer, she dug her nails into the dirt, frantically grabbing at a stunted bush. It pulled to the length of its scrawny roots, then held, as her feet kicked into thin air.

Sharlin looked down. It was a long, swift fall, to jagged rocks below. She threw back her head. "Dar!" she screamed with all of her might, the sounding tearing at her throat. "Dar!"

It echoed down the canyons and on the wind, and at the sound of it, the green dragon soared back. It veered off as she clung precariously, unable to swing down without snagging its wings. With a loud hissing, it flew off, and she guessed it was to raise the alarm. The brush gave a little more. She feared to move, to dig her toes in, afraid the shift in weight would pull it out altogether.

Pebbles and dust fell from the lip of the path, and Dar looked down. "Hold on a little longer," he ordered her, and began to unstrap his belt.

His forearm, lean and hard, stretched down to her, holding the belt at length. "Grab on."

But Sharlin had already clawed at it and wrapped her hands in it, and with a grunt, he pulled her back to the safety of the ledge.

She threw her arms about him, and he stood unmoving, until she dropped her embrace and stepped back, face hot with uncertainty.

"Be glad you weren't too far ahead of me," he said, but he spoke flatly, and his forehead creased in irritation.

"I didn't want to hamper you. I thought it best to go on by myself."

His reply was interrupted as Thurgood came around the bend, his robes rustling, and Sharlin gasped in surprise.

He wore resplendent crimson robes, not a brilliant satiny red, but a deep red, like blood that has freshened from a cut, deep and thick. He eyed her clearly, and gave a half-smile. "I was saving this for something important . . . something majestic in my life. It's likely to happen today, if it's ever going to happen." He held out his arm. "Shall we?"

"The sentry—it spotted me."

The wizard nodded and closed his eyes, murmured a few words. "It won't see us now. I have a few illusions of my own left. We have to stay together now—the magic works to separate us."

With an irritated sound, Dar followed after them. The path they traveled was narrow and thin, worn by who knew what, cut so deeply into the rock that its sides hid any view, as though they journeyed in a deep trench. They spiraled down, and turned, and then paused, on a final ledge above the canyon.

The wind took the gasps from all three throats.

The gods themselves had carved this place from the throat of a burning mountain. Deep, deep into the canyon stretched a river, and a pooled lake, and beyond that the mountains turned upside down in reflection, their jagged peaks throwing purple shadows onto the rose floor of the

Pits. They stretched across for leagues, so deep and wide they were, and spires rose like columns to the sky, a dusty rose color, repeating the shades of the canyon floors and sides.

And they looked out on bleached bones, skeletons intact, that littered the canyon floor and various niches, and even a lofty ledge here and there. Hundreds of dragons must have come here to die . . . and as Sharlin took a deep breath, she thought of the peddler's description of this place.

Even as she thought, a winged shape screamed and rose from the depths of the canyon, a brown dragon with creamy underthroat and stomach. It gained the sky with tremendous wingstrokes, higher, higher, higher, until it rose above them, and higher yet, and its shrill whistles drowned out all noise and thought.

It held a moment. It pinned itself to the sky and the sun and the clouds, wings unfurled. Then, with a fiery burst of flame, it plunged to the earth and crashed, and the fire hid its carcass from view.

Sharlin found herself clenching her fists and biting her lip. Thurgood breathed, "It knew its time," and Dar said nothing at all.

A stillness followed, and then a humming that grew in strength. It was the green dragon, and Sharlin pointed it out, atop a carven spire, where it pointed its muzzle to the skies and mourned for the dead dragon, a song that held the three humans entranced, and when it ended, the green dragon spread its wings and left the canyon, sailing far into the sky and away.

The graveyard was silent. Sharlin leaned forward to look, and she whispered, "Where are all the dragons? Chappie said there were dozens, dying, flying, resting on their hoards."

Dar leaned on his sword, for though he had rebuckled his belt, he kept his sword in his hand, ready now for anything. "They're gone, Sharlin. All that is left is bones." He laughed bitterly. "No wonder the gods rarely hear us. They're not gods at all."

"No," answered Thurgood, as he moved away from them and began to limp down the incline. "I could have told you that."

They gained the canyon floor perhaps an hour later. The morning sun had risen a little higher and slanted down into the Pits, and the sand answered with a warmth of its own that Sharlin felt through the battered soles of her boots. The deathly stillness of the canyon did little to still her nerves, for she hadn't forgotten that Nightwing had come this way and could spring from any bend or niche in the immense gorge. Dar raised his sword point and walked cautiously beside her, balanced toward the balls of his feet, ready for trouble.

The stench of decaying flesh rippled across them, and as they entered the vast canyon, the black bulk of Nightwing blocked their path, surrounded by a ring of skeletons of no lesser size, though ages dead.

Thurgood staggered to a halt. "Dead," he gasped, and his eyes widened and skin grayed. "He's dead!" He lurched back, jolting Sharlin, and grasped for her. "How can he be dead and I still living?"

"Your power was greater," Sharlin said, awed by the vast carcass, not having realized until faced with the creature in death just how great he was.

Dar circled the dead beast, and came back. "No sign of Valorek."

"If he ever was," said Thurgood, as he regained his composure.

"What do you mean?"

"Illusion. Dragon magic. They're the true sorcerers of Rangard, without question. Perhaps what you faced was merely a shadow of your imagination. Let's get the treasures you came for and get out."

Dar's hand went to his throat, traced the purple bruise of Valorek's hand upon his flesh. "No," he denied. "That wasn't illusion."

Sharlin walked around the decaying creature and toward a long-dead remnant. Great cracks were in the basin, and from a few of those cracks came hot air, damp with steam. She leaped down and halted beside the bleached bones of an ancient dragon. Small, leathery objects rested inside the rib cage, and she toed one.

It was warm and soft, and as she moved it, the object, the size of her foot, split open, and she jumped back with a yell. A worm crawled out, and a fingerling of flame licked at her.

A fireworm . . . and from the remains of a dragon. And she backed away from the leathery eggs. Hatchlings! Of course, she was stupid not to have seen it . . . dragon hatchlings.

The fireworm crawled down into a crevice and disappeared.

The sight threw despair even deeper into her heart. Here was the rebirth Gabriel had talked about. The dragons came here, knowing they were being called to die, and spawned, and laid their clutches, and died. And even centuries later, from the shelter of their bones, the hatchlings crawled out. She looked at the nest. There must be hundreds of eggs. How many would hatch? And of those, how many would survive the trek across the plains, and drowning at the river, to become . . . what? She sensed she stood at the edge of the mysteries of the dragongods, and she had no heart for it.

Even if she could find Turiana's skeleton, she doubted she could raise her now, knowing that it was all a myth, a twisted understanding of the dragon's nature.

Dar moved beside her, and bent, and picked up a great ivory claw from the ground. He grasped it tightly in his hands, waiting.

Nothing happened. The Valorek beast that raged in his mind did not subside . . . he had the dragon's claw, and it severed nothing! Dar threw the claw to the ground and bent over, in pain, gasping for breath, knowing that he couldn't reach out to Sharlin for comfort or help . . . knowing he wasn't himself any longer.

"She lied," he forced out, between heaves of air. "The witch lied!"

"Dar—"

He sensed Sharlin reaching out for him and batted her hand away. "I don't need your pity!" he snarled, and then closed his eyes in agony, as he/Valorek drove her away.

Thurgood caught up with her and toed the ivory claw. "A white dragon," he mused. "Rare indeed."

"White? How do you know?"

"The color of the claw, of course. Nightwing's are as onyx as he himself."

Hope sprang into Sharlin. Then Turiana's would be gold . . . and how many golden dragons were spoken of in legend? She spun away from the skeleton and grabbed Dar's arm.

"Help me find a golden claw."

"What?" He looked at her, dazed.

"A golden claw. The dragon I'm looking for was golden."

Thurgood hurried after them, with his curious, limping gait, gathering pink dust on his magnificent robes. "Sharlin, what are you doing?"

She raced from one skeleton to another. Lightened by sun, aged by wind and rain, the claws yet retained a faint semblance of their appearance in lifetime. Brown here, black, green, a deep burgundy, brown again, green again. She ran until her sides ached, and she sent flocks of birds whirring into the sky, heedless of the danger of the Pits as she raced, and Dar followed her, and Thurgood gasped after them.

"Gold!" Sharlin halted and swallowed for breath, then knelt reverently. Golden claws lay stretched on the ground. The great white skeleton that curled in front of her was one of the largest she had seen. No leathery egg casings were here. Gold coins littered the ground under the bones, and shields, and she even thought she spied a crown. This dragon had kept a hoard. Hand trembling, Sharlin reached for a coin and polished it on her sleeve, then held it glittering in the sun.

"In the year of the reign of Dhamon, 437," she read. The last words caught in her throat, and she clutched the coin tightly until her knuckles turned white. Her father had reigned in Dhamon in 679! This could be Turiana . . . it could be! She had no choice.

Sharlin jerked her pouch free, dumped the spices on the ground, and made a nest of them, then pulled the twine from the scroll.

Thurgood shadowed her, and he said quietly, "What do you think you're doing?"

She pulled out flint and iron and struck it, patiently trying to coax a spark to life in the nest of herbs and spices and precious lyrith. She looked up at the wizard and frowned, for he stood in the light, and it blinded her momentarily. "I'm going to raise Turiana."

He folded his arms solemnly. "Then it comes to this, after all, when I hoped it wouldn't. Princess, I came on this journey to destroy the Pits, to destroy Nightwing if I could, and to ensure that no others followed him."

"Turiana was a good sorcerer!"

"One of the few. She, above all, would understand the sacrifice of a few, so that the many could be destroyed." He spread his hands palm down over her head, and began to chant.

Sharlin froze. Her muscles stiffened, except for the corner of one eye that ticked. She grated out haltingly, "Dar . . . help me. . . ."

Thurgood stopped long enough to point at him. "Stay out of this. What she does could resurrect them all . . . the skies full of dragons, even Nightwing himself again. She works a magic she can't control. Think, man—do you wish to kneel to gods that crawl from an egg like a snake?"

"I kneel to no one," Dar flared, then took hold of himself, for it had been Valorek who had answered.

Sharlin lifted her chin, torturously, to look at him, and her dark-blue eyes glistened. It struck him like a knife to his heart. "Sharlin," he whispered. "Nightwing would bring back Valorek."

"Tur-i-ana," she whispered, in pain.

Thurgood faced him, one brow arched.

They tore him in two. Valorek/darkness/Sharlin/light,

hate, love, his head roared and his heart thumped. Dar stood motionless, then threw back his head and gave a mighty shout of agony and fear and launched himself at the wizard, knocking the man head over heels.

Sharlin unfroze and struck the flint, and a spark blazed. As Thurgood got to his knees, chanting in a singsong voice that raised the hair on the back of her neck, she unrolled the scroll and read the words scribed therein, words that Gabriel had dictated to her, in High Rangard, words such as were carved in the temple of Lyrith.

Thurgood jumped on her, and they twisted in the dust. Dar grabbed the wizard by the back of the neck, and she stumbled to her feet and with one final word threw the scroll into the blazing nest of herbs and lyrith.

The nest blazed up. It reached into the sky, a whirling column of sparks and smoke, with a noise of its own, a whistling, sparking noise that drowned out the wind, and they all staggered back.

From in front of them, the skeleton got to its feet. Silently, all over the valley, bones rolled together and clacked into semblance, and got to their feet. As the whirlwind spun and the scent of lyrith filled the air, Sharlin grabbed for Dar's hand. He didn't even notice her touch, as the beast in front of them gained substance, golden flesh over bone, and great amber orbs in deep, widespread sockets, and wine-red nostrils that curled, and claws of gold that flexed into the ground, and then the dragon spread her wings . . . wings so transparent they could see the sky through them, wings that grew solid and bated the air.

"Whooo?" the beast said, in a hollow voice, and looked down at them, craning her neck.

"I did," Sharlin gulped. "I called you, Turiana."

The sky filled with the thunder of beating wings as dragons took to the air, and the beasts screamed at one another. Thurgood raged, "Look what you've done! Look!"

The golden dragon raised her head, considering, and

spread her wings as though to shelter them, and took a deep breath, shuddering with it. "Life is good," Turiana said. "I thank you, fair child."

"I—I—" stammered Sharlin, and then, tongue-tied, halted altogether.

Dar ripped his hand from her and flung up his sword. "Look out!"

Hissing filled the air as a dark shadow plummeted over them, and Nightwing raged in the sky.

Turiana answered with a scalding hiss of her own, and reared. Their talons clashed, and Nightwing sailed past, turned, and readied himself for another pass.

The golden dragon launched herself. She met the onslaught of the black, and thunder crashed as the two great beings jousted with sorcery as well as fang and claw, and they curled about each other, talons ripping.

Sharlin fell to her knees. Scores of dragons circled the two battling ones, but kept their distance. Thurgood raised his hands and dropped them in confusion.

Turiana broke free. She trumpeted in mastery and flew out of reach of Nightwing, and sleek golden form led black through the sky, twisting, tumbling, striking, and recoiling.

She raced ahead of her assailant, undisputed queen of the skies over the canyon, and the scores of other dragons took perches on the rocks and watched. She sailed through them, her magnificent wings catching the glint of the sun and reflecting it back.

Nightwing dropped down from above. His vast wing-spread outmatched hers, and he fell like a stone, and their wings tangled.

"Turiana!" Sharlin pressed her hands to her mouth in fear, afraid to watch her only hope lost in mortal combat. Yet she couldn't look away.

The two plummeted, entwined, scratching and hissing. Then Turiana's body blushed a deep, deep rose, and she tore loose from the black dragon, but instead of fleeing or fighting, she curled in front of him, then wrapped herself about him before slipping coyly away.

She gained the skies again, and Nightwing followed. "What are they doing?"

"Mating," Dar answered slowly. "They're mating!"

And as Nightwing pursued this time, the furious hissing ceased, and instead the dragon whistled, as though to persuade the golden dragon to come back to him. She led him on, higher and higher. Sharlin shaded her eyes to watch the two of them twirl in the sun. He overcame her, and clutched her, and they entangled necks once more and dropped to the earth, this time in an embrace.

At the last possible second, both spread their wings and stopped the fall. Then Turiana broke loose and continued to fall, her sail not enough to stop her descent.

She boomed to ground not far from them, and lay there, spent, sides heaving.

Nightwing screamed in fury and dove at her from above, talons poised for the kill.

Dar moved then, for Nightwing skimmed the golden dragon and aimed at them. With a yell, he knocked Sharlin aside and took the first blow, cleaving with his sword at the beast, as fangs tore and talons grasped. Crimson spurted up in answer.

"Come and get me!" Dar shouted. He brandished his weapon, even as blood fountained from his flank, and staggered back to his feet.

Nightwing wheeled, hissing, and struck again, reeling the swordsman back. Dar swung the blade deeply. It bit an ebony claw away, and the beast roared in sudden pain.

Turiana struggled to her hind feet and batted at him as he wheeled her over, and Dar went to his knees, the ground about him wet with lifeblood. Thurgood blocked the dragon's third strike, throwing up his arms and shouting words, words of power that made the ground shake, but only deflected Nightwing.

When the black dragon rose for another attack, Turiana rose to meet him, hissing, her chest heaving, and flame issued, a deep-red flame. Nightwing responded in kind, and the two dragons launched to battle once more.

Their screams filled the air, but Sharlin had no stomach

for the battle. She gained Dar's side as he fell limply to the sand. His hand was cold when she caught it up.

Thurgood stared down, face pale. The vein in his right temple bulged and pulsed. He reached for her shoulders. "It's no good. He's dead."

She pressed her hands into the gaping wounds to stem the blood, but already the fountain was weak, for the heart pumped no longer. "Dar!" she screamed, and hot tears stung her cheeks. She lowered her face to his chest and cried, great heaving sobs that threatened to tear her apart.

Thurgood shouldered her away. "Stand aside," he ordered. When she didn't answer, he grabbed her and threw her to the ground, clear of the body. She lay there, defeated, and sobbed.

The wizard closed his eyes and his hands shook. He cried aloud words of sorcery that faded before Sharlin could hear or understand them. He clutched his head, as though in agonizing pain, and sank down to his knees before Dar's still form, and still he chanted, and the vein pulsed heavily, and his right arm dropped uselessly to his side, and when he stopped, he simply curled up and fell. His magnificent robes, the color of blood, merged into the sands.

Sharlin saw Dar's chest rise and heave suddenly, with a breath. She swallowed her sob and sat up, and clenched her fists in hope. The gaping wounds closed. The swordsman's right hand moved and twitched as though fighting yet to grasp his blade.

Thurgood groaned. Sharlin crawled to him. The sky above them darkened with the wheeling forms of the dragons, who yet fought and clawed at each other. A great splatter of dragon blood hit the ground and sizzled.

The wizard motioned for her to boost him up. She cradled his head in her arms, unable to move his limp form more.

He gasped.

"Lie still. You'll be all right . . . and Dar . . . you brought him back!"

"No," the wizard husked. "Dar back . . . but I'm going. Following Toothpick, you see."

She wiped his brow and found it clammy. "Thurgood, don't talk now."

"Must." The mild blue eyes fastened on her clearly. She'd seen him veil his expressions in secrecy, or irony, or drunkenness, but she'd never before seen the love she saw in them now. "If I had had a daughter . . ."

"Please."

"Listen. I lived for most of my life afraid of dying . . . afraid of losing my power. Now I am giving it up, for him. It's the best thing I've ever done. Let me . . . do it right."

"The dragons . . ."

"I should not have tried to stop you. Turiana can . . . rule them . . . if she survives. . . ." Thurgood's eyes rolled, and he muttered, "Light, pain, pain." He clutched her hand suddenly, hard enough to make her yelp, and then he was gone. The vein in his temple flattened to nothing.

Sharlin let his head droop gently to the bloodied sand. She crawled over to Dar, who gulped in air and convulsed, and she feared to touch him, remembering the last time sorcery had brought him back.

His eyes widened, and he struggled to sit up, reaching for his sword even as he did so.

"What happened? Did I get him?"

A dragon screeched, and he looked up. Black and gold tumbled through the air.

Then he put his hand to his head and felt his clothing . . . breastplate shredded, undershirt in ribbons, covered with blood. He looked at her and said in a low voice, "I died. Nightwing cut me open. I died, Sharlin!"

"I know." Still she feared to touch him, feared that the evil which possessed him and drove him would send her away again.

He grinned, and the expression lit his face, and he put his head back and roared with laughter. "I'm free!" He struggled to his knees and reached out for her, pulling her into a great bearhug of an embrace. "He's gone, Sharlin!"

She laughed too, and a sob caught it up, but she felt the happiness through her tears, for the man she hugged was the man she had fallen in love with.

The dragon's claw had cut him free.

Above, a keening cut the air, and they looked up as they helped each other to their feet, leaning on each other.

Turiana glided, wheeled, and trumpeted again, and as she struck at Nightwing, his body burst into flames, and he fell to the Pits. The black dragon tumbled from the sky, wings folded, blazing as he fell, and his evil voice at last was silent, until his body boomed into the canyon. The fire consumed the last of the vanquished dragon.

The golden dragon swung down to the sands. Her hide was laced with crimson, but she shook herself and bowed her neck triumphantly. She lowered her great head to eye the two of them.

Her forked tongue licked the air. Then she considered them again, before saying, "You took great risk. You said you came for me. What do you want of me?"

"Your aid, if you can give it."

The dragon licked a wound carefully before looking back at the two of them. "What is it you would have me do?"

"Cross seas and time, and carry me back to the House of Dhamon, and fight the dark magic of Rodeka."

The dragon paused. "Across time?"

Sharlin nodded, holding her breath. Her hand trembled in Dar's grasp.

"Ahead or back?"

Her hand grew cold in his fingers, and he tightened his grasp, as though aware he was going to lose her now, having just gained her and himself.

"Back. Several hundred years—I'm not sure how many."

"And how got you here?"

"The sorceress attacked me. Her powers threw me . . . I'm not sure how."

The dragon gave a dry cough, like a laugh, then rumbled, "Anything a human can do, I can do better."

She leaned down and extended a foreleg. "Climb aboard, daughter, and we will see what we can do."

Sharlin pulled out of Dar's hand so quickly that he had no chance to draw her back, and she ran to the dragon and climbed the foreleg, and settled on the graceful neck, across the withers, just ahead of the wings. Turiana kept the leg extended for Dar, then, after a hesitation from him, withdrew it.

Sharlin looked down from the beast and tightened her lips. "Goodbye. Don't forget your gold."

"I didn't come for gold!"

Turiana began to walk forward slowly, preparing to launch herself into the air.

Dar ran to keep up with her. "You once said I was running away from my past—"

"—just as I was running into mine! But now you don't have to run anymore! You're free!"

"Oh, hell!" He shook his head and panted. "Never! I have nothing if it's not with you," and he leaped, and gained the back of the dragon, holding on to one of her spines. Sharlin reached for him, and they embraced as the dragon took flight.

ABOUT THE AUTHOR

R. A. V. SALSITZ was born in Phoenix, Arizona, and raised mainly in Southern California, with time out for stints in Alaska, Oregon, and Colorado. Having a birthplace named for such a mythical and mystical beast has always pushed her toward SF and Fantasy.

Encouraged from an early age to write, she majored in journalism in high school and college. Although Rhondi has yet to drive a truck carrying nitro, work experience has been varied—from electronics to furniture to computer industries—until she settled down to work full time at a word processor.

Married, the author matches wits daily with a spouse and four lively children, of various ages, heights, and sexes. Hobbies and interests include traveling, tennis, horses, computers, and writing.

Although this is her first adult fantasy, it is the eighteenth published book to date.